CW00521976

DAY OF RECKONING

KEITH WAINMAN

Matador
9 Priory Business Park,
Wistow Road, Kibworth Beauchamp,
Leicestershire. LE8 0RX
Tel: 0116 279 2299
Email: books@troubador.co.uk
Web: www.troubador.co.uk/matador
Twitter: @matadorbooks

ISBN 978 1785892 448

British Library Cataloguing in Publication Data.
A catalogue record for this book is available from the British Library.

Printed and bound in the UK by TJ International, Padstow, Cornwall
Typeset in 11pt Aldine401 BT Roman by Troubador Publishing Ltd, Leicester, UK

Matador is an imprint of Troubador Publishing Ltd

To my family and Bill and Shirley.
Thanks for everything.

CHAPTER ONE

Present day.

It was early evening when Nathan Bush reached the top of the hill. It was the highest point on his 150-acre farm in Clun, Shropshire and he could look across to the Welsh border in the distance. It was the solitude and stillness that always drew him to this spot. It was the end of a very warm June day and up here, on the hill, the slight breeze gave a relief to the heat. He sat down on the grass, turned away from Wales and looked back down the slope that he had just climbed.

He had bought the farm in 2008. It wasn't anything special. He had no animals, which was unusual for this part of Shropshire. He just grew arable crops. It was isolated and any visitors were generally contractors who came to take away harvested crops or drop off fertiliser. Apart from that, he was very self-sufficient. Once every two weeks he would take a trip to the market town of Ludlow, which was just over fifteen miles away, to stock up anything he needed

He lay back and looked up into the blue sky. It had been a very strange journey that had brought him to this spot and tomorrow would be – what he had come to think of now as – the reason he had been born. He closed his eyes. He thought about the farm back in Montana he had grown up on. It had been so much bigger, but in some ways the same. It was just as isolated and remote. His mind turned to his family. He hadn't seen them for many years. He didn't even know if his mother and father were still alive or whether his brothers had children of their own.

***

Egypt. October 26th 1954.

It was late in the evening. Kamal Salah received a phone call telling him that the attempt on the life of Gamel Abdel Nasser, then the Prime Minister of Egypt, later to be the President, by a member of the Muslim brotherhood had failed. As a leading member of the Muslim brotherhood in Egypt, he knew that retribution from the army would not be long in coming. He phoned around some of the brotherhood members. There were confusing reports. Some said it would be alright to stay as there would be negotiations between the army and the brotherhood, and everything would be sorted out. It was only a hothead, they said. Others had the same opinion as Kamal, that the army and Nasser would use it as an excuse to dismantle the brotherhood organisation.

Once he was off the phone, he told his wife to pack enough clothes, food and water for a journey to the south of the country. His two sons, Mohamed and Anwar, fourteen and twelve respectively, were told that they were off to visit an uncle – so that they wouldn't be frightened about the sudden flight from home. Kamal put all the documents he needed in his bag and burnt any incriminating ones he couldn't take with him.

Kamal owned a number of shops in the Cairo area. He wasn't poor but he wasn't rich either. Even so, the shops allowed him to hold quite a bit of money and he had been able to save up some foreign currency, mainly American Dollars, which would be a blessing in the future.

They left Cairo just before nine that night and headed south towards Asyut. It was over 200 miles but he had an uncle there who owned an orange farm. They would stay with him until things had quietened down. On the journey Kamal had to take a number of detours due to police and army checkpoints, and they didn't arrive at his uncle's farm until seven the next morning.

It was obvious when Kamal spoke to his uncle about staying on the farm for a time that his uncle was not happy with the prospect. He knew Kamal had been an organiser for the brotherhood in Cairo and he had heard the broadcasts on the radio about thousands being arrested because of the assassination attempt on the Prime Minister. He had no wish to be caught up in anything like that. He told Kamal that his family could stay and rest, but that they would have to move on later in the day.

Kamal spent the morning catching up on the sleep he'd missed through his drive from Cairo, and in the afternoon he sat and listened to the radio with his uncle. The broadcaster appealed to all loyal Egyptians to tell the police or army if they knew the whereabouts of any revolutionaries. His uncle looked at him and said the workers on his farm would notice strangers at the house. Someone might say something. Kamal would have to leave as soon as it was dark.

His uncle told him that he would make a phone call to an old friend who worked in the coastal village Safaga. Kamal could either find somewhere to hide there, or hire a fishing boat to travel over to Saudi Arabia. It was still a good two days' journey to get there but Kamal knew he had no choice. The further he was from Cairo, the better his chances of avoiding arrest.

★★★

It was just before five in the afternoon when they resumed their journey, heading south again. His uncle had given him extra petrol in large fuel cans to ensure that they wouldn't have to stop off on the way to refuel. They followed the course of the Nile and headed for Qena, skirting the edges of the towns they came to and keeping a lookout for any checkpoints.

It wasn't until 03.00 when they reached the edge of Qena. Kamal was tired and decided to pull off the road to rest. He found a spot among some trees by the Nile and slept until 08.00. His wife sorted out some breakfast, while the children splashed around in the river for a while. He talked to his wife about his plans; he had decided to try and reach Saudi Arabia, and from there he would travel up to Jordan and make contact with some brotherhood members he knew in Amman.

The journey to Safaga was uneventful. Although he was worried that there was only one road from Qena to Safaga, they didn't come across a single checkpoint. When they finally arrived at the address of the man his uncle had mentioned, he explained that he wanted to get to Saudi Arabia. He told the man that his wife's brother was ill and they were travelling to see him. The man listened and said he would go and seek help, and in the meantime they could stay and rest at his house.

When he returned, he told Kamal he had talked to a fisherman who would take them over to Saudi. He gave Kamal the price the fisherman had demanded and though Kamal felt it was excessive, he didn't bother to haggle. Instead, he made some of the money back by selling his car to his uncle's friend. And so it was in the evening, with the sun just beginning to set, that they bordered the fishing boat and left Egypt. He didn't know it then, but it would be years before Kamal returned to the land of his birth.

★★★

Two months later, the family had fully settled into life in Amman. Kamal had, through brotherhood acquaintances, found work. It didn't pay much but with the money he had brought from Egypt, the family were relatively comfortable. His two sons were in good schools and were doing well. Kamal still followed the events in Egypt closely, though, and noted that lots of his friends had disappeared – either arrested or killed. Other Egyptians arriving in Jordan told him that the brotherhood organisation there had been decimated.

Kamal still worked tirelessly for the brotherhood, moving between Amman and Jerusalem. He helped to build up the organisation's network and made good contacts along the way. Over the years that followed, his sons continued to do well at school and moved on to university. Mohamed, the eldest, studied agriculture and Kamal got him a job on a farm owned by a brotherhood member.

The farm was alongside the Jordan River on the West bank. Although he was only twenty, Mohamed proved himself a good farmer and organiser. The owner came to rely on him and was more than happy when the wheat production on the farm went up due to the use of a new irrigation system that Mohamed had introduced. In fact, Mohamed was called upon by a lot of farmers along the Jordan valley, who wanted him to visit them and help to increase their crop production. Such an excellent reputation in the farming community for one so young gave his father great pride. Kamal's younger son, who he was just as proud of, studied medicine and was now in his last year at university.

Although he missed Egypt, he was happy that his family were doing so well. There was still trouble in the Middle East region, with Egypt and Israel clashing over land in the Gaza area and the Sinai, but Jordan was relatively peaceful. King

Hussein of Jordan had a pretty liberal attitude and life carried on without too much threat from the government.

***

It was 1960 when Kamal heard of an opportunity to move to Canada. It came from a member of the brotherhood who had relations living in Vancouver.

One evening, while having dinner with his family, he raised the subject. His two sons were excited at the prospect, as they knew the opportunities that could be had. Their mother, meanwhile, was more reticent. She was happy with their life in Amman and she had made some good friends. But after much talking over a number of weeks, it was eventually decided that they should ask for asylum in Canada due to Kamal's persecution for political reasons by the Egyptian Government.

It wasn't until early 1961 that they gained permission to move to Canada. On February 26th the family disembarked from the ship that had brought them to Toronto. Once they had been through all the immigration checks, the family set out on the journey to Vancouver, British Columbia, where Kamal had two addresses of Egyptians who would help the family get settled and established.

Although Kamal could speak some English, his wife could speak none. Their boys were both fluent, however, having learnt it at school and university, so they had no difficulties when they needed to ask for help or directions. They hadn't realised just how big Canada was, though, and it didn't hit home until they had travelled by train across the whole country.

***

It took the family a little while to settle. The Arab community wasn't that large in Vancouver at the time and Kamal's wife was unhappy for a number of months. However, she slowly made friends and settled down, while Kamal did what he always did: networked, made good contacts and prospered, having set up a small import business to bring Arab goods to Canada. His youngest son, Anwar, got a place at university to carry on with his medical studies, while Mohamed went to work for the British Columbian State Government in their agricultural department.

Mohamed was known as Mo to all of his work colleagues and the many friends he made. He proved himself to be a good worker and was seen to be very conscientious. It was just before the family's first Christmas in Canada that Mohamed was invited to the department's Christmas party. There, he struck up a conversation with an American called Hank Green, who had been liaising with the department over some cross border cooperation between America and Canada. Mohamed told Hank about his time farming in Jordan and how he wished to own a farm of his own one day. In return, Hank told him about farming in America and the many opportunities that could be had there. He said that he came from Montana, one of the biggest farming states in America, where there were always farms for sale. Hank added that if Mohamed ever decided to buy a farm in America, he would help him to get things sorted, including immigration clearance with the US Government.

***

The thought of owning his own farm grew in Mohamed's mind over the next couple of months, and moving to America sounded an exciting prospect.

At the beginning of March 1962, he approached his father

with the idea. He had little money of his own, so he would have to borrow all that he needed. His father listened to him and said that if that was what he wanted to do, he should find out the amount of money he would need and they would discuss all the details. Kamal did not tell his son, but he was immensely proud of his ambition to move to America. Kamal knew that any grandchildren he had would have opportunities he could never have dreamed of.

Mohamed spent all of his spare time getting figures together. He contacted Hank Green and discussed it. Hank, in turn, sent Mohamed details of all the farms that would suit his farming skills. In early April, Mohamed took a week off work, travelled to Helena – the state capital of Montana – and met up with Hank. He spent the next five days looking at farms that were for sale, and discussing with Hank about their potential and whether they would suit Mohamed.

When he returned to Canada, he had all the facts and figures to give to his father as well as pictures of the farm he wished to buy. His father questioned him because he doubted his figures. He could not believe that the amount of land Mohamed said the farm consisted of cost so little. Although it was still a lot of money, it was the amount of land that struck Kamal. It seemed vast. Mohamed assured him that it was all correct; all the farm machinery was included, which he and Hank had checked over, along with a house, barns and some livestock. The farm was about 100 miles from the town of Billings, alongside the Yellowstone River. His father questioned him a little more and asked him if it was truly what he wanted to do. Once Mohamed had assured him it was, Kamal said he would give him the money. Breaking the news to his mother was not easy, but she was assured that it wasn't too far to visit.

Things seemed to progress very quickly. Hank arranged all the legal papers for the purchase of the farm through contacts he had in the Montana State Government. He also arranged Kamal's visa and application to become an American citizen. It would take some time, Hank said, but it would all be fine once Kamal had showed he was a responsible citizen.

***

On the 15th July 1962, Mohamed opened the door to the farmhouse that was to become his home in America. He was twenty-two.

The first few months on the farm were hard. Mohamed had four workers who had stayed on when he had bought the farm from the previous owner, and it took time for them to get used to how he wanted to do things and for them to trust Mohamed. Gradually, everything settled down. He kept in touch with Hank Green, who had become a good friend and would make a visit every few weeks to help out with any problems with banks or government departments. He also helped Mohamed make connections with other farmers, farming supply companies and the big cereal companies that brought the harvested crops.

One shock to Mohamed was the violence of the storms that occurred. One hail storm, in particular, caused quite a bit of damage to the crops. It took weeks of work to save as much of the crop as they could. Then, when winter came, the farm pretty much closed down. There were general farm jobs to do but the land was covered by snow, and if not, was frozen.

As Christmas approached, Mohamed got ready to travel back to Vancouver to spend time with his family. He now knew that he could trust the farm workers to do all of the jobs that needed to be done while he was away. On the way to his parents, he planned to call in on Hank Green in Helena. He would stay for a couple of days and catch up on things.

He spent three days with Hank and his family, who treated him so nicely that he felt very much at home in America. On the last day of his stay, he accompanied Hank and his wife to dinner at their friend's house. There were about fifteen people present and Mohamed found himself seated between Hank's wife and a young woman with long, curly, red hair, who was introduced to him as Kathleen Bush. During dinner, he found himself spending a lot of time talking to Kathleen, who told him to call her Kate. Likewise, he said she should call him Mo. He told her about his family, their troubles and their travels in the Middle East, while she told him about her family, who lived in Seattle. She explained where Seattle was, as Mohamed had no idea of American geography yet. She had moved to Helena upon leaving university and had got a job with the Montana State Agricultural Department. Like Mohamed she had studied agriculture, so their conversation was easy. He talked about his hopes for his farm and what he would like to do in the future, and before Mohamed knew it the dinner was over and everyone started to leave. He shook Kathleen's hand as he left and said he had enjoyed talking with her. She replied that she hoped they would meet again.

★★★

When he arrived back in Vancouver, he spent the first two days assuring his mother that everything was going well and assuring his father that the farm was making money and had a long-term future. His brother chided him by saying that he was beginning to have an American accent. On the Friday, he accompanied his father and brother to the mosque, which was one of only two at the time in Vancouver. Mohamed hadn't been to a mosque for over a year. In truth he was not a religious person, though his brother was and followed after his father in that respect. After prayers, his father, who seemed to know everyone, introduced him to the majority of people there. Over the two weeks he was taken out to meet various Egyptians and other Arabs who had settled in Vancouver. It seemed that his father had built up quite a network of friends.

His brother was now working at the Vancouver General Hospital and he was enjoying it. His father's business was prospering and he told Mohamed that he intended to buy a new house in a better area of the city. His mother, meanwhile, hadn't changed at all. She still fussed and worried, and had friends that she spent the day gossiping or shopping with.

Just after New Year, Mohamed set off on the journey back to his farm. His father said that he would come down and visit him in the summer to see how well he was doing. On the way home, Mohamed again called in on Hank Green. He planned to spend a couple of days there, before finishing the journey back to the farm. Mohamed didn't know it, but Hank and his wife had observed how much time he had spent chatting to Kathleen Bush and had arranged a small dinner to which she was invited. Mohamed was more than happy when he found himself seated next to Kathleen at the dinner. Their conversation was just as easy as last time and at the end of the evening, Mohamed asked for her address so that he could write to her. He asked if she would like to come to the farm later in the year to see how things were working. She said that she would like that very much.

Like most things in Mohamed's life so far, things happened quickly. Kathleen visited the farm three times during spring and then, when she visited again in June, Mohamed asked her to marry him. She accepted and he phoned his parents with the news. They were visiting in July and would meet her then.

Everything seemed to go well. His parents got on well with Kathleen, and although she was not a Muslim, she was from a Catholic family and his parents gave him their blessing. There would be no big wedding; instead they would be married at a registry office at the state building in Helena. Kathleen's parents would travel up from Seattle and Mohamed's family from Vancouver. The wedding took place on September 19th 1963. Mohamed decided that he would take his wife's name, as he wanted his children to be accepted as normal Americans. After the marriage he became Mohamed Bush, known to everyone as Mo Bush.

Their married life settled down quickly. As Kathleen had studied agriculture, she was able to help around the farm and didn't feel out of place in such a rural and isolated environment. Within a couple of years, they had two sons: Marshall, who was born in December 1964, and Frank, who was born in August 1966.

Over the next ten years, they became a typical American family. The children travelled thirty miles to school each day, which was situated in the nearest town. The farm prospered and Mohamed added to his land through the purchase of a neighbouring farm. They now had more than 6,000 acres of land and twelve farm workers. Twice a year they would travel to see their families in Seattle and Vancouver, or their families would come to spend time on the farm in the summer. Mohamed's father especially liked to do that, as it meant that he could go walking with his grandchildren, who he doted on.

In 1976, Kathleen announced that she was expecting another baby. Mohamed was delighted but neither he nor Kathleen had planned on having any more children. When he phoned his family they were equally overjoyed, especially his mother who looked forward to having another grandchild. Nathan Bush was born in September.

The family went on much as before. Mohamed's two eldest boys were very much involved in the farm, to the point that they chose to stay and work there rather than go to university. The farm continued to grow still larger with the purchase of more land. It was now one of the biggest in the area.

As Nathan grew up, it became clear to him from about the age of fourteen that his brothers would be the ones that would take over the farm when their father died or decided he could not carry on. He had no ill feelings about it; he accepted it as being part of life.

His brothers were a lot older than him and always treated him like a little brother. He worked on the land and picked up all the knowledge he needed to pull his weight around the farm, but, in truth, he didn't think farming was his thing. He enjoyed hunting in the mountains at weekends, or during holidays with friends from school or other farms in the area. He was recognised as a crack shot and always brought his trophies back to the farm, which his mother was not keen on – so he kept them on the wall of his bedroom.

The other thing he enjoyed was being with his grandparents, from both sides of the family. He would travel to Seattle and spend time with his mother's parents. His grandfather would tell him stories of his time in the marines and fighting the Japanese in the Pacific. When he travelled to Canada to visit his father's parents, he would hear stories from the Middle East and his grandfather would take him to the mosque. Nathan could speak Arabic, as it was spoken between his father and his brothers – although their mother said it could not be spoken in the house – so he understood everything and took part in prayers. However, like his father, he wasn't very religious. He spent time in the Arab coffee shops with his grandfather, listening to the discussions about what was going on in Egypt, Jordan, Iraq and Israel, and who was to blame for the wars. The men seemed to blame America for everything that was wrong with the Middle East and, as an American, he found that strange.

★★★

It was 1992 and Nathan had just turned sixteen. His father asked him if he wanted to accompany his grandfather on a trip to the Middle East over the Christmas school holiday. His grandfather wanted to visit all his old friends and was now wealthy enough to make the trip. Nathan said he would love to. Apart from Canada and Seattle, he had never been anywhere else and had never flown on an aircraft.

His grandfather was treated like a hero when he met his old friends from the Muslim brotherhood. Nathan knew all about the brotherhood and the reason his grandfather had had to flee Egypt. He also discovered that his grandfather had been sending money back to help families who were going through hard times since he had lived in Canada. They hired a car and Nathan was taken to see the house that his grandparents had lived in when they had first fled Egypt with his father and uncle. Nathan couldn't believe how tiny it was. They then travelled to the border with Israel, where his grandfather pointed across the Jordan River to the west bank where Nathan's father had first worked on a farm. It was now owned and occupied by the Israelis. His grandfather told Nathan that the family who had owned it had fled into Jordan during the war in 1967 and had never been back. His grandfather took him down to visit Petra, which blew his mind. The colours of the city were truly amazing.

They left Jordan and flew to Egypt. His grandfather told him he was worried that the authorities might still want to arrest him, but nothing happened when they arrived. His grandfather's Canadian passport seemed to arouse no suspicion. Nathan found Cairo incredible. It seemed like a mad anthill. There were so many people; traffic seemed to go in all directions at the same time; the street of the markets were so narrow; and the noise – he had never known anything like it.

His grandfather was again received like a hero, as he had also sent money to Egypt to help the brotherhood, which was now a force in Egyptian society. They spent time talking with his grandfather's old friends and Nathan even met family members he didn't know he had. His grandfather took him to the pyramids and to Alexandria, and they sailed down the Nile with some of his grandfather's friends on a fishing boat. There he listened to discussions that could have taken place in the coffee houses of Vancouver. They seemed to discuss the exact same things here.

CHAPTER TWO

1994.

Having finished school and having done well in his exams, Nathan had the chance to go to university. However, he felt that he wanted to do something different. He still thought about the trip to the Middle East that he had taken a couple of years previously with his grandfather and felt that he wanted to see more of the world but didn't really know what to do. It was on a holiday to visit his mother's parents in Seattle that, after talking to his grandfather, the idea of joining the marines took root in his mind. On his return home, he raised the subject while sitting with his family over dinner one evening. It had a strange outcome, which he hadn't expected. His mother thought it was a great idea, but his father was against it. His two brothers just said that if that's what he wanted to do, he should do it. After much discussion and pressure from his mother, his father finally agreed to it.

★★★

Nathan never looked back. Once he passed the recruitment stage and the full marine training, he settled into military life easily. He got to fulfil his wish of seeing more of the world and made some good friends. Although he took part in a number of small operations, he had not yet fired his weapon against any enemy other than on training missions. All that was to change on September 11th 2001.

Following the 9/11 attacks, Nathan found himself part of the marine detachment that was sent to Uzbekistan, which bordered Afghanistan, in October. The men spent their time training and listening to the news of the bombing and special forces operations inside Afghanistan. On November 25th, Nathan, along with his fellow marines, set foot in Afghanistan with orders to seize Kandahar Airport. They were involved in sporadic fighting with either Taliban or Al Qaeda. For the first time, Nathan had bullets fired at him and he returned fire with the intention of killing someone. The marines took full control of the airport in December.

Over the coming months he went on operations in the Kandahar area, attacking Taliban-held towns and villages and driving them from the area. After their tour, his unit was rotated back to the United States and he got time off to visit his family. His grandfather in Seattle wanted to know everything about the action Nathan had been involved in and the truth about what had happened. When he got to Vancouver, however, his father's dad was a little more reserved. He was proud of Nathan, but he spent more time talking about where things might lead to if America did not leave Afghanistan to sort itself out, especially now that Al Qaeda had fled the country.

He spent the last part of his leave with his family on the farm. It was nice being at home. His brothers hadn't changed and still looked on him as their little brother; his mother fussed and his father talked about what he would do when he left the marines. Nathan had been a marine for over seven years by now, but he explained to his father that he had no intention of leaving and didn't know when that day might come.

★★★

Life in the marines carried on as normal, but everyone talked about the possibility of a war with Iraq. Throughout the whole of 2002 the rhetoric of the President indicated that he would attack if the Iraqi President didn't give up his weapons of mass destruction.

Around November, training started to pick up. As well as working with marine units, there were joint exercises with the army and drills with the air force. Everyone knew that something was coming – they just didn't know when or what it would be.

In January 2003, his company was moved to Kuwait. Training became more intense and everybody expected war, but time seemed to drag on. Every evening, he and his fellow marines would gather in front of the television at the base and see the politicians going over the same arguments. Daily live firing exercises were carried out, but all anyone wanted to do was to get on with things or be back at home. Then, in early March, they left their base and were moved closer to the Iraqi border with Kuwait.

Everyone was on edge. There were false alarms about when they were going to attack or get withdrawn back to base. It was in the early morning of March 20th that they finally attacked. His unit was part of the group tasked with taking Nasiriyah, a town that stood on a major road junction with bridges crossing the Euphrates River and a close proximity to Talil airfield. It had strategic importance. They entered the city on March 23rd. The fighting in Nasiriyah was much harder than in Afghanistan and it was the first time that Nathan saw some of his fellow marines get killed. Though their training had readied them for war, nothing could have prepared them for this battle. Sometimes it was house-to-house fighting and you could hear the enemy moving around less than five yards away. The battle went on all day and through the night.

As they pushed through the town the next day, they started to isolate the enemy into pockets. This meant that they could call in air support to break the resistance. By late in the evening of the 24th, most of the town was secured, along with the bridges and airfield. His unit rested and they watched what seemed like the whole of the United States Army pour through the town heading north towards Baghdad.

★★★

Present day.

Nathan opened his eyes. He didn't know how long he had been laying down. He sat up. The sun was getting lower, but it was still warm. He glanced at his watch; it was just before eight. He would walk back down to the farm to make sure everything had been readied for tomorrow.

Standing up, he turned and looked towards Wales. He would miss that view. After a minute, he started the walk down the hill. As he got nearer to the farm, he saw a 17.5-ton lorry parked between the largest barns on the farm and behind it an articulated lorry. Poking out of the barn was a thirty-two seat coach, next to another articulated lorry, and behind that was a Royal Mail van. As the land levelled off, he made his way to a gate that led to the farmhouse and barns, then passed through it and closed it behind him. He saw a man approaching from one of the barns and recognised him as Rashid Maliki.

"Nathan," he said, "I thought you were never coming down from the hill."

Nathan laughed. "We have too much to do," he said. "Although I did nearly fall asleep. How is everything looking?"

Rashid turned and fell into step with Nathan as they walked towards the farmhouse. "I've had all the vehicles' engines checked over," replied Rashid. "They're all running perfectly and each has been fully fuelled up. All we need to do is attach the wiring and we are ready to go."

Nathan put his arm around Rashid's shoulders. "Tomorrow, we will make history," he said.

Rashid was the one who laughed this time. "You are right, my brother," he said.

They entered the farmhouse and went into the kitchen, where two other men were seated at the kitchen table.

"You are just in time for some tea," said a large man with a Yorkshire accent, who was seated at the table. His name was Abdul Baari and he had a close-cropped beard.

The second seated man pulled out a chair for Nathan, who sat down. Rashid walked around the table and took the chair next to Abdul, who poured out four cups of tea.

"Did you check out the roads?" Nathan asked the second seated man, whose name was Samir Hamidou.

He answered with a clear French accent. "There are no new road works and the journey should be trouble-free provided that we don't run into any big accidents tomorrow."

Nathan picked up his tea and took a sip. "Have you told everyone we are getting together later?" he asked Abdul.

"Yes, no need to worry," he replied.

"We will watch the news at nine, then sit down and go over everything." Nathan said. "How does everyone seem?"

"They are excited," said Samir. "Some of them have been waiting for years to take this journey."

Everyone quietly drank their tea, thinking their own thoughts.

★★★

Iraq 2003.

When Nathan's unit moved out of Nasiriyah they went north, encountering some opposition but nothing major. They made their way up to the city of Fallujah to join other marine units there preparing for an attack on the city. There were a few small skirmishes with Iraqis, but it wasn't until the night of April 4th when the marines launched their attack that things got hot. If the fighting in Nasiriyah had been hard, it was nothing compared to this. As soon as the attack started, they met stiff resistance. It seemed that each battle Nathan found himself in was harder than the previous. He hoped it didn't always work out like that.

They were fighting for most of the night but only moved through two streets at the northern end of the city. Each house seemed to be defended or booby trapped. At one point, they were ambushed as they came to a junction. The front of Nathan's vehicle was hit by two RPG rockets. Everyone scrabbled from their vehicles to engage the enemy and rescue the wounded from the Humvee that had blown up. The fight lasted over two hours. Nathan had no idea how many of the enemy were killed, but two of the marines in the Humvee were dead. His unit took shelter in a shop and organised firing positions on the street where most of the enemy fire was coming from. The noise of explosions and the crack of bullets hitting a wall or whistling past their ears kept each man focused on what they were doing. Once they had beaten the ambush, the unit started to move forward again.

They continued to fight for a number of days and Nathan saw a few casualties on the marines' side. He caught fleeting glances of the enemy darting into or between buildings, but did not come face-to-face with one. Everyone was tired and dirty, and though they made progress into Fallujah, only about a quarter of the town was in their hands. Then, on April 9th, word came through that a ceasefire had been agreed. Nathan found his unit moved back from the front line to get some rest. He heard that there was still fighting in other parts of Fallujah – ceasefire or not. It wasn't until the beginning of May that the marines withdrew from the whole of Fallujah and left it to Iraqi troops that were loyal to the coalition forces to carry on the fight.

Nathan found himself in a base a few miles outside Fallujah for most of the summer. They were occasionally involved in the odd skirmish, but it was generally quiet and time was spent listening to news from the rest of Iraq or on what was happening in Fallujah itself. One thing he did find was that the fighting had two effects on the troops – or so it seemed to Nathan. To him, it made the marines more cautious and it nurtured a disdain for the Arabs. The latter annoyed Nathan due to his background and he found himself biting his tongue on a number of occasions. It wasn't just enlisted men he heard making comments, but officers as well.

It was November when word came through that they were returning to Fallujah and that the town was to be cleared of insurgents completely. Nathan didn't know it then, but an event during the battle was to change the path of his life.

★★★

The fighting had been going on for nine days so far. Progress had been slow and the battle had been hard. His unit were fighting their way through a market area of the town. One morning, his unit came under heavy fire from a house. They were pinned down for a while until they could get some heavier firepower up, such as tanks and armoured cars. Nathan and some of the unit edged along the street. One marine managed to throw a couple of grenades into the house and the firing stopped. They edged their way into the property and found three dead insurgents on the ground floor. Nathan and two other marines made their way slowly upstairs, checking each room carefully for booby traps. When they entered one room, they found a dead body and another injured man. Nathan knelt down next to the injured man and realised he was a young boy. He had a head wound and his arm was bleeding, both from shrapnel. The two other marines said they would carry on checking the upstairs rooms and left Nathan alone. Nathan took out his battlefield first aid kit and started to clean and bandage the wounds. The young boy looked at him with frightened eyes. Nathan spoke to him in Arabic and he saw shock in the young boy's face. He assured him that he wouldn't be harmed and to sit still while he tended to his wounds.

The boy told Nathan that he had only been in the house to bring food and water to his brother, pointing to the dead man by the window. He told Nathan that the bag by his feet had the food and water in. Nathan stopped tending to the wounds and looked at the bag. Was it a booby trap or was the boy telling the truth? He spoke to him again and looked at his face as he answered. The boy swore it was only food and water in the bag, nothing else. Nathan took a chance and lifted the flap of the bag. He saw two water bottles, some bread and a couple of pieces of cheese. He pulled the bag up beside the boy, who told Nathan he was thirteen.

Suddenly an officer and a marine came into the room. The officer said to tie the boy's hands, as he would need to be taken back for questioning. Nathan protested that the boy's injuries would cause him pain if he were tied up. The officer replied that all captives must be bound before being transported to headquarters for questioning. Nathan spoke to the boy, telling him what was going to happen. He took some hand ties from his belt and slipped them around the boy's hands, tightening them to make sure they wouldn't come off. The officer told him to rejoin his unit, who were moving to their next target. They would sort out the prisoner. Nathan stood and assured the boy that things would be okay and turned to leave. As he did, he picked up the AK47 rifle that was beside the dead body and took it with him. They had been told in training not to leave any weapons laying around that could be recovered and used again by the enemy.

His unit pushed on away from the house, but again came under heavy fire a street away. Their Commander said to fall back until they could bring up support, as they were close to being cut off. They made their way back to where they had been and set up a defensive line. After a couple of hours, there seemed to be a lull in the fighting and all the marines grabbed a drink and something to eat. Nathan saw he was only a couple of doors from the house where he had left the boy, so he decided to check that he had been taken away safely.

When he entered the house, the bodies of the insurgents were still lying on the ground floor. He made his way upstairs and entered the room. The man's body was still by the window but against the back wall was the body of the young boy. There were three bullet holes in his chest and his hands were untied. Nathan knelt down beside the boy. There was an AK47 rifle next to his body, and the bag with the water and bread was at his feet. He looked around and saw the tie that he had used to fasten the boy's hands lying in the dust. He picked it up. It had clearly been cut through with a knife. He heard boots coming up the stairs and turned to see the officer he had spoken to before, flanked by two marines.

The officer asked him what he was doing. Nathan said he had wanted to check on the boy and then asked the officer what had happened. The officer told him that the boy had got free and had gone for the gun, and was shot in self-defence. Nathan stood up and said that the boy had been securely tied and he had taken the only weapon out of the room with him when he had left. The officer said he must be mistaken as there was clearly an AK47 lying next to the body and he must not have tied the prisoner up properly. Nathan lost his temper and shouted at the officer. He said he knew that he had secured the boy carefully and that there had been no gun left in the room. He said he thought the boy had been murdered. The officer shouted that Nathan was being insubordinate and told him to stand to attention, which he did. The officer then asked to see the tie, which Nathan passed over. He said that Nathan couldn't know that this was the exact tie he had used, and that he was mistaken and should return to his unit. If he did, the officer would overlook his behaviour. Nathan saluted the officer and left the room, but instead of going back to his unit he went to find the commanding officer who was based in an Iraqi Government building about a mile from the front line.

He managed to get in and see him on the pretext that he had a message from his Unit Commander. When he told the commanding officer the story, he was told to go and wait outside the office while enquiries were made. Nathan sat outside the office for two hours until the officer who had come into the room of the house appeared, knocked on the office door and went in. After half an hour, the door opened and Nathan was called in.

He stood in front of the commanding officer's desk. The commanding officer said he had spoken to the officer and the two marines who had been in the house. He told Nathan that he must be mistaken and that he was lucky another marine had not been killed due to his oversight in not making sure the insurgent's hands were properly tied and all weapons had been taken from the house. Nathan was about to reply that the boy was not an insurgent, but the commanding officer said he had to be quiet and listen. He continued by saying that Nathan had deserted his post in coming to the command centre and leaving his fellow marines when a battle was still going on. The commanding officer said he could not overlook it and Nathan was going to be placed under arrest on a charge of desertion. Nathan was too stunned to say anything. Two other marines came into the office and held his arms, relieving him of all his weapons. The commanding officer said he would be taken back to the marine's base camp outside of Fallujah and charges would be brought against him.

A few hours later, Nathan found himself in a cell at the main base. He couldn't understand what was going on. He had not deserted anyone; he had just wanted to point out what had happened to the young boy. He lay back on the bunk, running through everything that had happened. He realised that someone had cut the tie and murdered the young boy in cold blood – there was no other explanation for it. The weapon had been placed in the room, as he knew he had taken the only one with him. If he hadn't gone back, it would never have been discovered. He remembered that he had told the young boy he would be safe and treated well. He closed his eyes but he couldn't sleep. He kept seeing the frightened eyes of the young boy and wondered what he had thought was happening when his murderer had come into the room.

★★★

It was two days before an officer came to see him in his cell. He asked Nathan to tell him what had happened and made notes as he did so. When he was finished, the officer said he would be back tomorrow after consulting with others.

The officer returned late in the afternoon of the next day and said that there was a choice of outcomes. First, the Commanders wanted to make an example of Nathan for deserting his post under fire, so one option would be to take a few years in the brig, followed by a dishonourable discharge at the end of his sentence. Nathan explained, again, that he had not done anything wrong. The officer stopped him, saying he would have a hard time proving his case as a number of men would give evidence to the contrary.

Nathan sat for a few minutes, thinking, while the officer remained quiet. When Nathan finally asked what he should do, the officer said that there was a way out. If Nathan dropped the complaint about the young boy, he thought he could persuade the authorities to abandon the charge of desertion. He added that Nathan would have to leave the marines, but he would be able to leave with an unblemished record. The officer would return tomorrow to hear his decision.

Nathan sat still in the cell for the rest of the day. He went over and over the choice in his mind. When night came, he still couldn't think clearly. He kept seeing the young boy looking at him.

★★★

He opened his eyes. He didn't remember going to sleep, but the sun was streaming in through the cell window. He got up and looked out – all he could see was a grey wall. He heard the odd voice but nothing he could understand. As he looked up at the clear blue sky, his mind continued to go over all that the officer had said. He turned at the sound of keys in the cell door. A marine came in carrying a tray, which he put on the end of the bunk. The marine quickly turned and left, pulling the door closed without saying a word.

Nathan sat down on the bunk. He looked at the food on the tray but didn't feel hungry. He took a sip of the coffee and made his decision.

CHAPTER THREE

Two weeks later, Nathan was on a bus headed up the Californian coast towards Seattle. He was now an ex-marine. It had only taken a day for him to be moved to Bagdad, then a plane journey back to the States and on to camp Pendleton. All the paperwork had been sorted out and he was now on his way home.

Nathan still bore the hurt of not being able to give the young boy justice and he felt resentment at the way he had been treated. After all, he had put his life on the line for his country on many occasions. He had never even got to say goodbye to any of the marines in his unit.

The journey to Seattle was long and he slept most of the way. He stayed a night at his grandparent's house, then travelled home to the farm. His mother and father were glad he was back, as they had both worried about him while he was in Iraq. He didn't tell them the circumstances of his leaving the marines, though. His two brothers treated him as they always did – like their little brother.

Nathan spent six months on the farm and did anything that was needed. He drove tractors, helped to fertilise the crops and fixed fences. He knew, however, that his two brothers had no real need for him to be around.

He decided that he would travel to Canada and see his grandparents in Vancouver. When he arrived, his grandmother fussed over him and wanted to feed him Arab dishes. She told him she had prayed each night for his safe return. His grandparents now lived in a large house, which was too big for the two of them. His grandmother filled it up with lots of her Arab friends and they would sit on the porch, drinking coffee and gossiping. His grandfather took him around the shops and the big warehouse he owned. He explained to Nathan that he had opened twenty-four branches across Canada. Nathan also visited his grandfather's friends, who he hadn't seen since he joining the marines. He also started to visit the mosque with his grandfather more regularly.

One evening after dinner, he and his grandfather were sitting outside on the porch. His grandmother had just brought them coffee and had gone back inside, when his grandfather said he had been to see a doctor as he hadn't been feeling well for a couple of months. The doctor had sent him to have some tests done. He had cancer. Nathan sat quietly and didn't know what to say. His grandfather told him he mustn't say anything to his grandmother. Nathan promised and asked if he would have to go into hospital for treatment, but his grandfather said he was too far gone. The doctor reckoned he had six months to live. Nathan looked at his grandfather and silent tears ran down his face. It couldn't be – his grandfather didn't look any different and seemed as fit as ever. His grandfather then told him that he wanted to go home and die in the land of his birth, and he wanted Nathan to be with him.

★★★

Cairo. August 2005.

The house they were staying in was in the Nasr city area of Cairo. It was not one of the tourist areas, but his grandfather was among many friends from the brotherhood here. The men ran hospitals and provided aid to the poor in the area.

The streets were tightly packed and overcrowded. Nathan

again got used to the constant noise and began to talk in a loud voice like everyone else after a while. He hardly spoke English and his Arabic became the norm. He watched as his grandfather held meetings with some of the top people in the brotherhood, making arrangements to help finance new clinics and schools so that the children of the poor could get a decent education and medical care. They would spend most evenings sitting on the roof terrace of the house, which faced towards the centre of Cairo, and various visitors would join them. They would sit and discuss the problems facing Egypt and the wider Arab world. Many of the visitors were scornful of Egypt's pact with Israel and the money it received from America, which they said went straight into the pockets of the President and the generals and did nothing to help the poor in Egypt.

It was on one of these evenings that a brotherhood member turned up with a Palestinian doctor, who had been working in a clinic run by the brotherhood. Nathan fell into conversation with him and learned that his family were from the West bank. Nathan told him of his father's work on some of the farms there. The doctor, in turn, told him about the dire conditions that the Palestinians had to endure in the refugee camps in Jordan and Lebanon, and which he said the rest of the world were ignoring. He was in Egypt to gain more experience before returning to Jordan. He couldn't go back to the West bank where his family lived as he was banned by the Israelis, for no better reason than he worked in the refugee camps that, they said, aided terrorists. Nathan had a long discussion with him about the ongoing war between the Palestinians and Israelis, and the doctor said it would not end until there was a Palestinian homeland. He felt, in his heart of hearts, that it would never happen because the Israelis didn't want it – though they paid lip service to the idea. He sighed and asked Nathan what a Palestinian was to do – fight, or sit and do nothing? He reminded Nathan that the Americans had got their own land by throwing out the British. He had no answer to that.

At the end of the evening, Nathan made his grandfather promise some financial support to the doctor, so that when he returned to Jordan he could buy medicines and other things that were needed. His grandfather would make the money available to him through the brotherhood offices in Jordan. The doctor said that he was going to travel back home soon and if Nathan was ever in Jordan he should visit him. He gave him an address and phone number.

The rest of the time in Egypt was spent driving round, visiting old family or going to sites that reminded his grandfather of his younger years. The thing that surprised Nathan was how his grandfather always said that things looked just the same as they had all those years ago. Nathan called his grandmother each evening and then his grandparents would talk to her for a while. His grandfather's illness was never mentioned.

★★★

In late January 2006, his grandfather started to become visibly ill. Within a week he was in hospital, and two days later he was dead. It happened so quickly that Nathan didn't have time to think about anything. He called his grandmother and his father with the news, and his father said he would go and spend time in Vancouver with his mother. Nathan arranged the funeral with the help of the brotherhood and was surprised when thousands of people turned up at the cemetery on the day. He shook hands with many people he did not know, but all blessed his grandfather's name.

Nathan remained in Egypt for weeks after the funeral, but was at a loss as to what he should do. He received a phone call one evening from his father, who said that he should return to America and spend time with the family, as well as visit his grandmother to tell her what had happened in Egypt.

In late February he flew back to Vancouver and stayed with his grandmother, telling her about the number of people who had paid their respects to his grandfather at the funeral. He had pictures of his grandfather sitting on the roof terrace and meeting people, which he gave to her. She didn't seem upset or annoyed with Nathan or her husband for not telling her about his illness. She told Nathan that she had married a man that she loved and respected, and who did everything for his family. She could ask no more than that.

In March, all the family got together at his grandparent's house – his mother, father and brothers, who were both now married and had brought their new wives – for the reading of his grandfather's will. It wasn't very long. There were bequeaths to his son, and arrangements for his grandmother and uncle. Nathan's two brothers were left large sums of money, but it was Nathan who was given the bulk of his grandfather's estate. The lawyer explained that his grandfather had sold all of his business interests and property in the few months before leaving for Egypt. The only house that was left now belonged to his grandmother. When the lawyer told Nathan the sum his grandfather had left him, he, along with the rest of the family, were staggered. They had no idea that he had amassed such wealth, as he had lived such a normal life.

Sixty-five million dollars. The words seemed to repeat themselves in Nathan's head. The lawyer also said he had a personal letter from his grandfather, which he handed over.

Over dinner that evening, the talk around the table was how canny their grandfather had been in business. They also asked Nathan what he was going to do now he was a wealthy man. His parents suggested that he buy a farm near the rest of the family, while his brothers just said he should give the money to them. Everyone laughed. The family stayed together for another couple of days before setting off back to Montana. Nathan promised he would come down and stay before he did any more travelling.

It was only after his family had gone and he was sitting on the porch of his grandparent's house drinking a coffee that Nathan finally took the letter the lawyer had given him from his pocket. He could hear his grandmother talking loudly on the phone inside to one of her friends. He tore the letter open and pulled a single sheet of A4-sized paper from it. He recognised his grandfather's writing straightaway and began to read. Nathan scanned the letter twice and folded it up, then put it back in the envelope and his pocket. He picked up his coffee, leaned back in his chair and thought about what he had just read. His grandfather knew him better than he could have ever imagined. The letter seemed to crystallise all that he had been thinking of doing, and now his grandfather had given him the funds to achieve those ideas.

He spent another week with his grandmother and visited the lawyer again, who read the will and transferred the money to a new account that Nathan had opened with a bank. He then travelled to the family farm and spent two weeks there, before flying to Jordan. He had no idea if he would ever return.

★★★

Present day.

The five of them sat watching the nine o'clock news. Aashif and Abdul made disparaging remarks as it showed the state

opening of Parliament by the Queen. Rashid drank
with his feet on the table. They listened to the com.
describing the Queen's speech and what the gove
hoped to do in the next year.

Nathan stood up and said he was going to see what Sohail
was up to. Samir stood and said he would come with him.
They left the farmhouse and made their way to one of the
big barns. Nathan pulled the door open and entered. It was
brightly lit inside. They saw Sohail kneeling with another man
and laid out before them were twenty-six large holdalls.

"How are things going?" Nathan asked.

Sohail turned and smiled. "We are ready," he said.
"Everything is primed and all the bags are prepared. I have
rechecked the wiring in the vehicles and all are working."

"Well done, brother," Nathan replied. "You are a magician."

Samir walked forward and knelt beside Sohail and the
other man. "Just go over the triggering system with me again,"
he said.

Nathan watched them for a moment, then continued his
walk around the barn, looking at the vans and lorries parked
up. He had become good friends with Samir and Sohail. Samir
was Marie Hamidou's brother, who he had met him after the
trouble in Syria.

He thought back. It had been a month before he and
Sohail had slipped across the border into Iraq. They had all
split up; Abdul, Aashif and Rashid had gone their way, and
Sohail and Nathan had gone by another route. Nathan had
used the numbers given to him by Tariq to get help in avoiding
the Syrian police and the Mukhabarat. When they had reached
a safe house in Iraq, Tariq had turned up with Samir, who had
travelled to the region to find out why his sister had been
killed. He quickly joined the insurgency to exact revenge on
those he felt responsible.

It was a month later when the other three had appeared and the group had formed a fighting unit. They spent their time attacking Iraqi and American bases and convoys. Sohail had turned out to be a top bomb maker and Tariq had called on his services many times, with some spectacular successes. Nathan found that he didn't consider himself American at all now, and one day, while the group were resting after a hectic two weeks of constant fire fights and bombings, a discussion started about what they could do that would really bring home to the West just how committed they were. Numerous ideas were put forward, with attacking America the main one. Tariq had pointed out that after 9/11 the chances of getting a big spectacular there were next to zero, and then Abdul had suggested Britain. The rest of the day was spent thinking of ideas of what they could do. A seed had been sown.

A few weeks later, Tariq had pulled Nathan aside and asked him to walk with him. Over the next hour he laid out what he thought was possible and how they could go about organising things. The only thing he stressed was that it must be done in complete secrecy, with the minimum number of people aware of the final plan. Tariq also said that it would take years of planning. Nathan listened and the more he heard, the more he thought it was ideal.

Tariq also said that Nathan's money, which was currently sitting in various banks under assumed names, would not show up on any radar as being attached to terrorist organisations. It could therefore be used to finance the operation.

Nathan had sat down with the others later that day. He stressed that only they would be aware of the whole operation and everyone had to be prepared to wait years while they got things organised. The group all thought it was the right way to do it, and from that day on stepped back from fighting and started to organise, what they called, the day of reckoning.

The first to head back to Britain were Abdul and Aashif. They used stolen passports to slip back into the country and moved to North London where they set up a haulage business. It quickly became successful by undercutting other businesses to win contracts, as it didn't need to make money and was financed through Nathan's bank accounts. Anyone who knew Abdul or Aashif thought they were brothers from the North of England and they blended in as hardworking Britains. They won business to deliver goods all across London and purchased a block of flats adjacent to their business where they and the other drivers lived.

Meanwhile, in Iraq, Tariq had spent his time looking for individuals who proved themselves to be loyal, fearless and, above all, discreet. Over the next two years, he approached a number of people and asked if they were interested in joining a special mission. Details were never mentioned, but no one ever said no. Once they had agreed, they were spirited out of the country and, using Nathan's money, were given a small business to run in countries across the Middle East and north Africa. Most looked after small tobacconists or grocers shops and submerged themselves into the local communities. They never brought any attention to themselves by getting mixed up in politics or expressing any views. They were, after all, just shopkeepers.

Samir, Rashid and Tariq had worked on setting up a smuggling operation to move explosives and firearms into Britain. Tariq had tons of army grade explosives and, with Rashid's family connections, was able to move it across the Middle East into Egypt and Libya, while Samir used his connections in the French underworld to set up a smuggling operation into Britain.

Samir had travelled back to France with an assumed name and had made contact with people he knew smuggled large quantities of drugs throughout Europe. Due to Samir's reputation, these people trusted him without hesitation. He had met with some of the top French criminals in a small bar just outside of Marseilles and said that part of his drug smuggling operation into Britain had been broken by the police, and that he wanted to use their organisation to continue his supplies. To show good will, he handed them a quarter of a million Euros as a sweetener. They were impressed and came to a deal in which they would use contacts they had in the Irish Republic, ex-IRA men, to smuggle the goods over to Britain. Samir agreed on a price for each delivery, and it was decided that the goods would be picked up from North African ports and delivered to a place specified by Samir. He left knowing that what would really be delivered were high explosives and firearms. All deliveries were made well away from the farm. Samir also ensured that there would be no way of tracing the scheme back to the group. If any of the deliveries were intercepted, the police might be able to catch the ex-IRA men or French gangsters, but no trail would lead back to them. In the years that followed, the group were able to smuggle over twenty-five tons of explosives and all the weapons they needed into the country.

Sohail was then dispatched to Germany, where he had set up an electrical import and export business. He built it up so that it made money and employed nine staff, specialising in supplying top end circuit boards and specialised wiring. One of his best export customers was a small British company, whose address just happened to be a small block of flats adjacent to a haulage firm in North London.

Nathan moved to Switzerland and, with a Canadian passport to hide his identity, had spent his time looking for a suitable base for the final part of the plan. He had finally settled on the farm in Shropshire after many months of searching and, using Swiss lawyers to hide behind, had made the purchase. He used his background to run the farm without too much trouble. Over a number of months, he slowly dismissed the local people who had been employed by the previous owners and no one noticed the foreign workers who started to appear – not that anyone would, as it was too isolated for people to see what was going on. The foreign workers were the fighters who had been running shops across the Middle East for years. They had received a phone call and been given instructions, and at the end of that day had shut up their shops and disappeared. They were smuggled into Britain a few weeks later. Some of them ended up at the haulage firm in North London and learned to drive HGV vehicles, but most ended up on the farm in Shropshire. And so, here they were.

Nathan walked back to Samir and the others. "Let's get everyone together," he said. "We need to brief the individuals and the teams on what is expected of them." Samir, Sohail and the other man stood up. "Samir, get the others from the house and meet us in the other barn." Samir nodded and left them. "Come, brothers, let's get everyone ready."

The other two joined him and they left the first barn in the direction of the second. Sohail lifted the catch on the door, pushed it open and they walked inside. Along both walls were lines of beds, each with a small set of draws and a wardrobe. Men were sitting, talking or just reading. There were twenty-six in total. Sohail called out and the noise of voices died down. Nathan heard the door of the barn open and Abdul and the others entered. They came and stood behind him.

"Brothers," Nathan began, "tomorrow is the day we have all been waiting for." There was a murmur around the barn. "We will strike at the heart of our enemies." There were cries of Allahu Akbar, but Nathan held up his hand. "Each of you will have a vital part to play in bringing about the destruction of our enemies and you will each be told what is expected of you tonight. We will be leaving early in the morning, so after you have been told what you will be doing, we will pray together and then sleep."

For the rest of the evening, Nathan and the others spoke to groups and individuals about what their part in the operation would be. Some were given detailed maps of where they were going and what they had to do there, while others were told of their part as members of small teams. All were told that whatever they heard on the news, they must stick to the timings of the operation and not deviate from the plan. If they were intercepted, they should not surrender. When everyone had been briefed, they all got together to pray.

★★★

Jordan. 2006.

Nathan had been in Jordan for two days. He had walked around the centre of Amman, taking in the sites and remembering the time he had been there with his grandfather. He found there was a thriving society and he didn't feel threatened or ill at ease on his wanderings. There were bars and nightclubs, and at its centre Amman felt every bit a western city. He phoned Jamal Moshen, the Palestinian doctor he had met in Egypt, and arranged to meet him to talk over any help he could give. Jamal said he would pick him up from the hotel and take him to the Baqa'a refugee camp so Nathan could appreciate the problems that had to be tackled. Nathan also made contact with the brotherhood and said he would call and meet them to give any aid in line with his grandfather's wishes.

It was on a Thursday morning that Nathan shook hands with Jamal as he climbed into a beaten-up old Ford that looked out of place among the Mercedes and Porsche cars parked in the hotel forecourt. As they drove, Jamal spoke of the daily problems of the refugees – of not having enough food, and the health and educational needs that were not being met. He explained that the UN had worked hard alongside some European governments to do their best and the Jordanians had worked hard to get water and electricity to the camps. However, the numbers made it difficult. Some families had been in the camps since 1967 and were still living in small pre-fabricated houses. Whole families sometimes shared just two rooms.

They left Amman driving north, with every window in the car open to let in a breeze, along with the dust, to try and stay cool. Their conversation was carried out through shouting over the noise of the engine and the wind. They had been driving for about twenty-five minutes when they crested a hill and Jamal pointed to his right. Nathan saw a patchwork of houses and tents that spread out across the landscape. It was another ten minutes of driving along pot-holed roads and dirt tracks between tightly packed houses before Jamal came to a halt outside a two-storey building. There was a queue of people stretching down the street, many with small children in their arms or standing around their legs. Nathan couldn't see the end of the queue, as it seemed to disappear around the corner. Jamal explained that this was one of the two hospitals in Baqa'a that served the 100,000 or so refugees. He said that he and other doctors made daily visits to smaller clinics dotted around the camp, but the sheer number of people made it nearly impossible to meet their needs.

They climbed out of the car and Jamal led Nathan into the small hospital. It was just as crowded inside but the people stood or sat with stoicism that Nathan admired. In the west, this overcrowding would cause riots. He followed Jamal up some stairs and into a small room, where a woman in a white doctor's coat was sitting at a table. Her dark hair was pulled back into a ponytail. She looked up and smiled at Jamal, who turned to Nathan and introduced her as Marie Hamidou from France. She was an attractive woman, Nathan thought, but her eyes showed the tiredness her smile tried to hide. Jamal and Nathan pulled out chairs and joined her at the table. She had a file in front of her and explained to Jamal that they were running painfully low on vital medicines. There had been an outbreak of dysentery and young children were very susceptible. She said that every bed in both hospitals would be full by the end of the day and she expected that there would be deaths soon unless they could obtain vital antibiotics.

Nathan turned to Jamal and said he had the funds at hand to get anything they needed. Jamal explained that there were not too many places that medicine could be found in plentiful supply, but he would make a few phone calls to see if he could find anyone who might know. Jamal got up and left the room. Nathan got talking to Marie, who he discovered had been in Jordan for over six months. She had been due to return to France a couple of months ago but had found that she couldn't leave. Nathan explained he wanted to help in any way he could. Jamal came into the room, looking excited. He had got news of the location of some antibiotics, but it meant a journey up to the Syrian border. Nathan said goodbye to Marie, adding that he hoped they would return soon with all the supplies she wanted.

He and Jamal left the hospital and drove back through the camp until they reached the main highway. Jamal turned back towards Amman, saying that they needed to pick up a van for the journey to the border and he had an Iraqi friend who could help. Twenty minutes later, Jamal stopped the car outside what looked like builders' yard. Nathan got out and joined him as he pushed open the gates. Inside, wooden planks and bricks were piled high, and bags of cement were stacked on pallets. Jamal called out and a man appeared at the office door. Nathan followed Jamal as he walked over to the man. They embraced and Jamal introduced the man as Rashid Maliki. He shook Nathan's hand and turned and led them into the office. It was much cooler inside and he offered them some orange juice, which they both accepted.

Jamal explained what they were trying to do, and asked if they could use one of Rashid's trucks as the car would not be big enough. It was in such a poor state of repair that it may not even make it to the Syrian border and back. Rashid agreed but said that he had heard there were some problems on the road north due to some cross border attacks by Palestinians. The Israelis were keeping a close watch on any traffic on the road north and had intercepted a number of vehicles. They were arresting anyone, regardless of what they were doing, and taking them back to Israel. It was further complicated by some Bedouin tribesman who were robbing travellers, so it was a dangerous time.

Jamal explained that they had no choice as the situation in the refugee camp meant they had to get their hands on the medicine. Rashid asked Jamal who the contact was and where they wanted to go exactly, and Jamal told him. Rashid smiled at the mention of the name and said that if they returned in an hour, he would get hold of a truck or van that they could use.

Jamal and Nathan left the yard, climbed into the car and headed back into Amman city centre. They stopped at the hotel so that Nathan could collect the money they needed. From there, Nathan got Jamal to drive him to a house not far from the hotel. Nathan knocked on the door, which was opened by a large man in white robes. On seeing Nathan, his face broke into a grin and he stood back to let them in. Nathan, followed by Jamal, entered the house. When the man closed the door behind them, he turned to Nathan and embraced him.

"You're looking well," he said.

Nathan introduced the man to Jamal as Mohammed Hossaini, an old friend of his grandfather and they shook hands. He led them through the house to a courtyard garden at the back. In a shaded area, a number of men were seated drinking coffee or fruit juice. They all rose when they saw Nathan and, one after the other, embraced him like a long-lost son. Nathan and Jamal sat down. Fruit juice was poured for them and Nathan answered questions about how he had been and what he had being doing lately. He explained his and Jamal's intentions and again heard warnings about the road to the north being dangerous. The rest of the visit was taken up with stories of his grandfather's escapades, with much laughter at some of them.

When it was time to go, he and Jamal stood up to leave. Mohammed said to call and see him anytime, as he was always welcome. Nathan thanked everyone for their kindness before and after his grandfather's death and said there was one more thing he had come to do. He put his hand into his jacket pocket and pulled out a folded cheque. Passing it to Mohammed, he said that he hoped it would help with any projects they had. Mohammed unfolded the cheque, looked at it, looked at Nathan, then back at the cheque. It was for one million dollars. He passed it to the man seated next to him, who looked and passed it on. Not much was said. Eventually, each man embraced Nathan and wished him luck. They said they hoped to sit and talk again soon.

Mohammed led Nathan and Jamal back through the house to the front door. As he opened it, Mohammed told Nathan that his grandfather would be proud of his work. He said to get in touch anytime he needed help and passed him a telephone number. The brotherhood had contacts all over the Middle East, he said.

Nathan and Jamal made their way back to the builders' yard, where they found Rashid standing next to a lorry. It was dark grey and there were plenty of dents and scrapes in the bodywork. Jamal asked if he was sure it would make it there and back. Rashid assured them that though the bodywork looked rough, the engine was perfect. Another man then appeared from the office. He looked like a younger version of Rashid but with a fuller beard. He was introduced as Uday, Rashid's younger brother. He would be driving them, Rashid said, as he wanted the lorry back in one piece. He also said that they would be stopping on the way as some friends also had business with the man they were going to see.

CHAPTER FOUR

It was just after 16.00 when they set off north. The sun went down quickly and they were soon travelling in complete darkness, passing the odd vehicle but not many. When they reached the turn for Jarash, Nathan closed his eyes and dozed off.

He was awoken with a jolt as the lorry came to a halt. He had no idea how long he had been sleeping but it was still black outside. He turned to see Uday looking at a map, with Jamal running a finger over it. Uday was explaining that they couldn't go a certain route as it would take them too close to the Israeli border and the crossing from Jordan into Syria would bring them into contact with the Syrian Army. Nathan asked what was happening, and Jamal replied that the shortest route would be to go to Irbid, then head north and cross the border, as they needed to get to a Syrian town called Hyat to meet their contact. Nathan said to let Uday make the decision, as they wanted to get there and back in one piece without any trouble. Uday folded the map up and resumed the journey, explaining that he had made the journey north into Syria and then onto Lebanon a number of times for his family. Nathan asked what for, and Uday just tapped his nose and smiled.

After another few hours of driving, they came into a small village. Jamal and Nathan had no idea where they were. Uday pulled the lorry into a small turning, parking behind a squat building with no lights. He turned the engine off and the silence was a shock after the constant noise of the drive.

Uday waited a moment, then wound down his window.

46

He called loudly towards the building. When a second a voice returned the call, Uday shouted again and Nathan saw a figure approach them out the darkness. Uday told Nathan and Jamal to stay still for a moment. As the figure got closer, Nathan saw that he was holding a rifle of some sort. He came to Uday's open window, exchanged a few words and Uday turned to them and said to get out and follow him to the house. All three men got out and followed the man. At the house, he opened the door, stood aside and they entered.

It wasn't a big room. There was a table against one wall with chairs around it, and a couple of sofas against the other walls. Two men were holding what Nathan recognised as Kalashnikov rifles and the door behind them was shut. One of the men, who was standing, greeted Uday, but said they hadn't been expecting him. Uday had a whispered conversation with the man, who nodded and smiled. He then introduced Jamal and Nathan, who were invited to sit down. One of the men left the room for a while and returned with coffee. The man who seemed to be in charge spent a long time questioning Nathan. He seemed distrustful because Nathan was American. He made no bones that he thought all Americans worked with the Israelis to kill Arabs.

Uday assured him that Nathan wasn't a spy. Nathan understood their distrust and realised how dangerous the situation was. He asked if he trusted the Muslim brotherhood. The man nodded. Nathan said he could make a phone call and check him out, passing over Mohammed Hossaini's number. The man took the number and left the room. Not much was said while he was gone. The three of them sipped their coffee quietly, while the other two men cradled their Kalashnikovs and watched them.

The leader came back into the room after ten minutes, sat down opposite Nathan, passed the paper back and held out his hand. Nathan shook his hand. The man said, "Welcome to Syria, brother," and smiled. After that, things were more relaxed. Nathan learnt that the three men were members of the Islamic front. He asked Nathan if he had been in the American Army in Iraq. Nathan said he had and the man laughed. "We may have been shooting at each other sometime in the past," he said.

Uday asked if getting to Hyat would be a problem. The man shrugged. He said that the problems would be the same as they always were, with corrupt Syrian soldiers wanting bribes to let them pass. However, he warned that trouble was brewing between the Israelis and Hezbollah. They had received word that a lot of Persians had been spotted moving around in southern Lebanon, helping Hezbollah get organised. The Israelis would have noticed also, so they would be on the lookout for any suspicious movements. Their spies were everywhere. Uday explained to Nathan that Persians meant Iranians. The man said he and his friends would go with them to Hyat as long as they could drop some supplies and bring a few things back. Uday smiled and held out his hand.

★★★

They resumed their journey in the morning after grabbing a bit of sleep. It was about 08.00. The three men had joined them, having loaded some boxes into the back of the lorry. Nathan was in the back with two of the men while the other travelled in the front with Uday and Jamal. The leader sat opposite Nathan and they chatted as the lorry bounced along the back roads towards Hyat. Nathan explained that he had no idea when the Americans would leave Iraq, but it would not be for a few years yet. The man replied that the Iraqi people were becoming more and more disappointed with how things had turned out and were looking to take control of their own destiny. They thought America was giving all the power to western puppets and it could only end badly. Nathan said he tended to agree with him but didn't see a quick end to things. The lorry slowed and the man leaned out to see why. It was army checkpoint.

As the lorry stopped, he jumped out of the back. Nathan could hear voices, then the man appeared again and climbed in. The lorry set off again.

"Twenty dollars that cost us," the man said. "They stop every vehicle and charge what they think they can get away with. If a family can't pay, they steal any of their possessions that might be worth something." He spat out of the back of the lorry.

For the rest of the journey, the man and Nathan continued their conversation about Middle Eastern politics. Nathan discovered that the man was an Iraqi called Tariq. He had been studying law in Baghdad when the allied invasion had happened. He had fled the capital like a lot of other Iraqis and returned to his hometown of Ramadi, where he had joined a group that ended up fighting the American invaders. Nathan agreed that they may well have been shooting at each other at one time then as he had been in Fallujah, which was not too far from Ramadi. Tariq laughed and said, "And now here we are, trying to do our best for people who can't fight their own battles."

The journey carried on for another hour. Nathan found Tariq good company, and he had a funny sense of humour that chimed with Nathan's own. They felt the lorry slow again and Tariq leaned out of the back. "We are nearly there," he called to Nathan, who got up and joined him looking out. There was a cluster of small houses. The town was on a small hill, one side of which looked like it had been given over to farming. The other side had houses dotted across it. They seemed to be on the main road as there were quite a few other lorries and cars making their way along it. The lorry suddenly swung off the main road onto a smaller one, went another 100 yards, turned off onto what was no more than a dirt track and stopped outside a two-storey warehouse. Tariq jumped down. He was followed by Nathan and the other man who had travelled in the back with them. They joined Jamal, Uday and the third man, who were standing at the front of the lorry.

Uday and Tariq left them and went through the gates of the warehouse. A few minutes later, the main shutters of the warehouse went up. Uday came back, started the lorry and drove it inside. They all followed and the shutters came down behind them. Nathan looked around the warehouse, which was filled with large and small cardboard boxes. He also saw sacks of rice that were marked with the United Nations logo. Tariq called him and Jamal to follow him and he took them through some doors to an office, where a small man with a beard was seated. A larger man was sat to his side, holding a Kalashnikov. Without too much small talk, he asked Jamal if he had the money that had been agreed. Jamal said they had but he wanted to check the medicine out first. The man agreed and told the seated man to take Jamal away to check the medicine.

After they had gone, the man spoke to Nathan. "So, you're American?" he asked. Nathan said he was, and man smiled. "You must be the only American who can travel round these parts without being shot." He laughed at his own joke.

"Nathan has good guarantors," said Tariq.

"So I have heard," the man said, and invited the two of them to sit. He talked to Tariq as though Nathan wasn't there. Nathan listened as they did a trade for explosives that Tariq had brought with him. They would be sent over the border to Lebanon and Tariq would ensure the man's fuel smuggling operation from Iraq could travel without hindrance from Mosul to the Syrian border. They shook hands. Nathan realised then that Tariq was far more important than he had let on. Mosul was hundreds of miles in the north of Iraq. If he gave his word that no interference would come to the smuggling operation, he must be a very senior man in the Iraqi insurgency to be able to make that happen.

Jamal came back into the office and smiled at Nathan. He said that everything was good. Nathan took the roll of American dollars from his pocket and passed them to the man, who started to count them. As he did so, he began singing the song "Rum and coca cola" and shouted loudly when he got to the words "Working for the Yankee dollar". Once he had finished, the money disappeared into a draw. They all stood up and went into the warehouse, where the boxes Tariq had brought with him were unloaded and the medicine was put onto the lorry. Uday started the engine and they all got back into the lorry. Nathan heard Tariq call to the man as they pulled away, "I expect to hear of a safe delivery in a few days. We don't want lots of burning petrol trucks lighting up the Iraqi skies!" The man waved.

Tariq sat down opposite Nathan as the lorry made its way out of the town. It stopped on the main road and the man in the back with them jumped out and disappeared down a side road. The lorry then carried on its journey.

"What do you make of him?" Tariq asked.

Nathan said he would not be someone that he would place too much trust in. Tariq agreed and said he would let Nathan into a secret. The man was a member of Saddam Hussein's Baath party and had been a colonel in the Iraq Army. There were no explosives in the boxes they had just left, only clay that had been coated with gunpowder to give it that smell.

His group were testing the man out. They had been watching his smuggling operation for months and had brought it to a halt. Some local politicians who were taking bribes had been executed and the trail had led to this man, who, they suspected, was working with the Americans and Jews and passing information on. He thought he could bribe them and carry on making his money, but they would know in a few hours if he were honest or not. Tariq said some of his group were in a house not far from the warehouse and would pay the man a visit if anything strange happened on their way back.

They had been travelling for an hour and the sun was beginning to set. The lorry slowed and then came to a halt. They heard the sound of bells and Tariq stuck his head out the back. He jumped down and waved Nathan to join him, which he did. They walked to the front of the lorry and found a farmer with about forty goats on the road. The lead goat was on a piece of rope that the farmer was holding and had a bell around its neck. He was standing by the window talking to Uday.

"What's up?" Tariq asked.

Uday pointed to the farmer. "Not good news," he said.

Tariq asked what the problem was and the farmer explained that there were some strangers in a car about half a mile up the road, just around the bend. He told them he had brought his goats down from the hill and came across them, but their accents were not local and they were armed. He had also seen radios in their car. Tariq asked if they were Syrian police or the army.

"No," said the farmer, then spat on the floor. "They're from the south."

Tariq thanked him and the farmer walked away, pulling the goat on the string. Its bell started ringing and all the other goats followed.

"Well," Nathan asked, "what does that mean?"

"When someone from here says 'from the south'," Tariq said, "he doesn't mean Jordanians. He's talking about Jews."

"What shall we do? Go back?" Nathan asked.

"It's getting dark. We can't go back and we can't wait until night to try and sneak past. They might have night vision goggles and would pick us off," Tariq said. "This is the only road and that's why they've chosen it. If it wasn't for the farmer, we might all be dead now."

"So what do you propose we do?" Nathan asked.

"Well, they have no idea we know about their presence, so we will attack them and try and get the lorry through," Tariq said.

Nathan was stunned at Tariq's idea but saw the sense in it. If there was no going back, the marines had taught him to hit hard first and keep hitting until your opponent gave up. Either that or run away. "You don't know how many are there," Nathan said.

"Well, we will find out when the shooting starts," Tariq said, smiling, "but they won't want to stay around too long. They are some way from home and they don't want the Syrians to catch them. They won't stay too long," Tariq repeated, before adding, "I hope," with a smile.

He then laid out what he had in mind. Nathan listened and said he could think of only one change. He was used to combat so would join Tariq and the other man in the attack, while Jamal and Uday would try and drive the lorry through the ambush. Tariq laughed as he said, "My reputation will be dirt fighting alongside a Yankee."

Nathan laughed with him.

The three men made their way up the side of the hill to the left of the road, leaving Uday and Jamal in the lorry. Tariq told them to keep their eyes open, as the Jews must have a lookout to spot the lorry. Uday was told to drive as fast as he could up the road once he heard the shooting start. Tariq hoped that they would be able to draw most of the gunfire towards them and away from the lorry, as the Jews, he hoped, would be surprised and would be more worried about being shot at than trying to stop the vehicle.

They reached the crest of the hill that led around the bend and inched along on their stomachs, trying to be as quiet as they could. Nathan had a Kalashnikov in his hands. He thought for a moment of the young boy in Fallujah who had been shot. It was a rifle like the one he was holding that had been placed next to his body. Tariq signalled for them to stop. Nathan raised his head and looked down the hill, inched back.

"The car is about 100 yards away," he said. "I have spotted their lookout, who is about fifty yards down on the left behind some rocks. I can't see the others but I would imagine that they are near the road."

He signalled to the other man to make his way further along the ridge. "Well, brother, are you ready?"

Nathan gave a strained smile. "Just say when."

Tariq watched for a moment as the other man moved along the ridge and then stopped. He waved to Nathan to move up. He brought the Kalashnikov to his shoulder and took aim at the lookout, then fired. For a second, Nathan was taken straight back to Iraq. The Kalashnikov had a distinctive sound that all American troops would recognise from combat in Iraq or Afghanistan. Nathan joined Tariq and began shooting down the hill towards the car. From the corner of his eye, he saw the Israeli who had been watching for the lorry trying to get cover as Tariq fired at him. Nathan heard the other man open fire from further along the ridge in the direction of the car. A couple of men appeared, who were armed. They stood for a moment in the road and returned the firing. Nathan heard the whine of bullets whistle overhead and the ricochet as bullets struck rocks. He turned his head towards the lookout and saw him scrambling and half falling as he went down the hill towards the car. The men in the road ducked under cover as he and the other man concentrated their fire on them.

Tariq moved around to Nathan's right and joined him in firing towards the car. He shouted to keep shooting at the car as he could hear the lorry. Nathan kept his aim on the car and saw the windscreen explode as bullets tore into it. He saw the lorry come speeding around the bend in the road about fifty yards from the car. One man stood up for a moment and appeared to fire on the lorry, but quickly ducked down again as he and Tariq both fired at him. The lorry passed the car in a cloud of dust thrown up by the wheels.

Even from a distance, Nathan could see bullets fired by the Israelis hit the lorry and the side window shattered. He hoped Jamal and Uday had been ducking. They carried on firing at the car for another twenty seconds until the lorry was some way down the road. Tariq then signalled for them to move back over the crest. Nathan followed him out of sight of the road and they moved along in the direction the lorry had gone. Nathan could still hear the other man's Kalashnikov firing the odd burst and the sound of gunfire being returned. They had gone about 100 yards when the other man came over the crest of the hill and joined them. He said the Jews had got into the car and driven off in the other direction. He smiled and said he thought that two of the men had been hit as they had had to be helped into the car. The man himself was bleeding from his forearm, but said it was only a graze. Tariq said to Nathan that he was now part of the insurgency – the Yankee insurgent. The three of them continued along the hill until they came to a turn in the road. As they looked down, they saw the lorry parked up. Tariq led them down the hill to it. The engine was still running and both doors were open.

When they reached the road, they saw Jamal kneeling next to Uday. He looked up and said Uday had been hit. Nathan and Tariq knelt down with Jamal. Uday's face looked white and drawn. They could see blood pouring from a wound in the side of his face and he had another in the right side of his chest. Jamal was trying to stem the blood from the head wound with his shirt. Tariq said they needed to get him into the back of the lorry as the Syrians would not be long in coming to see what all the shooting had been about. He and Jamal lifted Uday up and carried him to the back of the lorry. Nathan climbed into the back, took Uday's shoulders and helped pull him into the lorry. They laid him carefully down. Jamal jumped up and joined him. Nathan pulled his shirt off and gave it to Jamal to try to stem the bleeding further. Tariq said he would try to get them to a safe house where they could get help. He and the other man ran to the front of the lorry and they pulled away.

After travelling for an hour or so, it became dark outside, and the moans and cries of pain had got fewer from Uday. Jamal said he was in a bad way from the loss of blood. The floor of the truck was wet and slippery from it. The lorry slowed, then came to a halt a few seconds later. Tariq and the other man appeared at the back. Jamal and Nathan passed Uday to them, jumping down and following them as they carried him into a house. Uday was laid on a sofa. The man whose house it was spoke to Jamal.

Tariq took Nathan's arm and pulled him back out of the house to stand in the dark with the other man. Nathan asked where they were.

"We are just inside Jordan," Tariq said. "The man is a friend. He is a doctor like Jamal, so perhaps they can do something for Uday."

All three of them leant against the wall of the house. "He looked in a bad way," Nathan said.

"You are right, my brother," Tariq said. He suddenly stood up. "I must make a phone call." He disappeared back into the house. Nathan sat quietly outside with the other man, who still hadn't said anything to him since their journey had begun.

★★★

Nathan had been back in Amman for a week. Uday's funeral had taken place the evening they had brought his body back from the border. He spent time with Rashid, talking about Uday and how things had happened. Tariq had also stayed for the funeral but had then disappeared. Before he left, he told Rashid and Nathan that the man they had met in Syria had been dealt with. He also left Nathan with a couple of numbers he could call and leave messages if he ever needed to talk.

Nathan spent a lot of time at the refugee camp. The medicine they had brought back had prevented an epidemic and the children were all responding to their treatment. One afternoon, he was at Mohammed Hossaini's house talking and passing the time when a visitor called who joined them in the garden. He was from Lebanon and was an organiser there for the brotherhood. He had news of what was going on, telling them that most people thought there would be trouble between the Israelis and Hezbollah and that many families were already moving further north from the border with Israel. Israeli planes had already bombed some sites in southern Lebanon and Syrians had been warned not to allow any arms to cross their border or they would suffer attacks as well. The man said the Syrians had now sealed the border to try and avoid Israeli attacks, although they were telling the global press that they would not bow to Israeli demands.

Nathan said he had heard that a lot of Iranians had been seen in the area. The man nodded, saying they were working with the Syrians to supply arms to Hezbollah for two reasons. First, they wanted to create trouble for Israel – this was a long-term aim of the Iranians, who wanted to become the leaders of the armed struggle for a Palestinian homeland but also use Hezbollah to fight a proxy war with Israel – and secondly, they wanted to destabilise Lebanon and gain power over any decisions made there. It also had the added bonus of annoying Saudi Arabia, who liked to think of themselves as the power in the region due to their money and the arms they filtered through to various Palestinian groups and governments. All of the time that Nathan spent in conversation at the house was enlightening for him. Whenever he thought he had worked out what was happening in the region, something else popped up to change it.

He left the house in the late afternoon. He was meeting up with Jamal and Marie Hamidou for dinner at eight. He knew how much they sacrificed to help others, so he had booked a table at the hotel's restaurant to treat them. After he had showered and changed, he made his way downstairs to the bar and ordered himself a lemonade. It was strange but he hadn't had an alcoholic drink since he had left America. It seemed natural now not to ask for anything stronger. Taking his drink, he went and sat at a table where he would be able to see the front doors of the hotel and Jamal and Marie's arrival. The hotel seemed quite busy with people coming and going. He suddenly heard a voice ask if they could sit at his table, Nathan turned to see two men in suits and sunglasses, which he thought strange as it was now dark outside. He agreed as the seats weren't taken and stood up.

"Mr Bush." Nathan turned in his chair. One of the men in sunglasses was looking at him. "It is Mr Bush?" the man asked.

"Do I know you?" Nathan asked.

"My name is Mr Smith," the man replied.

He had an American accent. "I'm sorry," Nathan said. "I don't think I know you."

"We just wanted a word about the company you're keeping," the man said.

"What are you on about?" Nathan said. "Who are you?"

"We are just concerned American citizens," the man replied. "We are also worried about the money you are giving to certain groups and charities."

"I don't know who you are," Nathan replied, "but who I meet or give money to is none of your business. Now, can you leave me alone as I am expecting friends." Nathan turned away and started for the hotel door.

Nathan felt a hand on his arm and he turned back to look at the man. "Mr Bush, we are just giving you a friendly warning. It has come to our attention that you have been travelling to places where American citizens should not be going." The man let go of Nathan's arm. "Some of our friends in the area even say that you may have been involved in a terrorist attack." Nathan carried on staring at the man but saying nothing. "Now, I am sure they are mistaken but if the American government thought you were supplying terrorist groups with funds, we might have to freeze your bank accounts. We would take an even dimmer view if there was any truth in your involvement in terrorism."

"I take it you're from the American embassy?" Nathan asked. The man made no reply. "I don't take to being threatened."

The man smiled. "Mr Bush, please don't misunderstand me. I am making no threats, just passing on some observations. The last thing we would like to see is an American citizen getting himself into trouble." The man leaned forward and lowered his voice. "The Middle East is a dangerous place. You can never know who your friends are. It would be good for your health, we feel, if you returned home." The man leaned back in his chair.

Nathan said nothing, and the man and his companion stood up. "I hope you will take the advice of a friend," he said, turning and walking towards the hotel doors. Nathan watched them go, picked up his lemonade and took a drink. He was still lost in his thoughts when Jamal and Marie came through the doors. He waved and they came over.

Nathan didn't mention the two men over dinner, but instead talked about the refugee camp and the plans that Jamal and Marie had to improve the living conditions and the schooling of the children. Nathan promised them the funds for teachers to be brought in and for a couple of schoolhouses to be built. They also discussed how to improve the water supply to the camp. Nathan told them about the news he had heard from Lebanon and Jamal said he hoped the Palestinian camps there would not get drawn into any trouble, as the conditions were all ready far worse than the ones in Jordan.

When they said goodnight, Nathan went back to his room and lay down on the bed. He went over what the American had said to him in his mind. He knew it was a veiled threat. He also remembered Tariq telling him that the man they had met in Syria knew who he was, so either he was being watched for some reason or someone was passing on information about him.

The next day, Nathan got dressed and left the hotel. He stopped when he stepped onto the street and looked around. No one stood out, although he didn't know who he was looking for. He felt he was being a bit paranoid. He made his way towards the centre of Amman and was passing the King Abdullah mosque when he decided to go in. He spent about half an hour inside, praying and sitting and just thinking about things. When he came out, he carried on his walk to the city centre. He found a cafe and took a seat at a table outside. The waiter brought him a coffee. His surroundings were a million miles from the conditions in the refugee camp, and the people who passed by were dressed well and wealthy. Nathan felt depressed, but he remembered the times he had spent with his grandfather and the things he had promised to do. It made his mind up. He would do all he could to improve the lives of those he thought to be downtrodden. The choices he made would be his own and so would be the path he chose. Mr Smith could go to hell.

CHAPTER FIVE

I t was the middle of June and Nathan was sitting in the office of Rashid's builder's yard, reading the *Jordanian Times* newspaper, which was an English language daily. As he read the news from Iraq, which was the front page lead, he realised it was the same old story of confusion; insurgent attacks; American bombings of insurgent areas, causing civilian casualties; and Iranian infiltration of Shia Muslim areas, causing the Americans to demand Iraqi government action to stop it. Nathan thought what a mess it all was. The whole region was now being polarised and he could see no happy ending.

After meeting Mr Smith, Nathan decided to move out. He had confided to Rashid about the visit and Rashid had told him to come and live in his house. It wasn't grand and Nathan just had a room, but Rashid's family made him more than welcome. His wife and two young children stayed in the background and were hardly seen. Rashid said the local people, who were mainly Iraq exiles, would soon spot outsiders hanging around, but he warned Nathan that the Jordanian government had a very good spy network and distrusted anyone from Iraq after the bombings of the Amman hotels in November 2005. Nathan settled into a comfortable life, travelling everyday to work in the camp and helping with anything he could lend a hand to. Nathan had already helped to modernise one of the hospitals there and had plans to improve the second one, as well as open a few smaller doctor's clinics. He had also spent time with Mohammed Hossaini, who had helped him with the transfer of his money from the American banks to various Arab ones throughout the region.

His thoughts were stopped by a shout from outside. Someone was calling his name. He put the paper down and walked out into the yard. "It's nice of you to take the time to help load the lorries," Rashid said sarcastically, as he lifted a bag of cement onto a lorry.

"I was just reading the paper," Nathan said, walking over to lend a hand. Two lorries were parked in the yard and a number of men were loading them up. They were supplies to go to the refugee camp to finish two schoolhouses there.

"Get those wooden planks on board the other lorry," Rashid said. "Your reading can wait."

Nathan followed the instructions and the men spent the next hour loading up the lorries. When it was done, they all got aboard and set off for the camps. Nathan sat in the front of the first lorry with Rashid. It took roughly half an hour to reach the camp.

The next couple of hours were spent unloading and moving the supplies around. Jamal was there and seemed happier, explaining to Nathan that not only was the medical situation and the schooling improving, but the building work allowed them to employ men from within the camp. Jamal had also managed to secure more funding from the UN to match the money Nathan had already put into the project, therefore doubling the good being done. Jamal invited Nathan and Rashid to join him and Marie and a couple of UN workers in the camp to a get-together for Marie's birthday on Thursday.

In the afternoon, Nathan travelled back to the yard with Rashid. When they entered the office, both were surprised to see Tariq sitting with his feet up on the desk. He was reading the newspaper that Nathan had left behind that morning.

"It's nice to know my business is safe from thieves when I'm out," Rashid said with a smile.

Tariq stood up and embraced Rashid. "Any thief could see there's nothing much to steal here," he replied and turned to Nathan. "And how are you, my Yankee insurgent?" He embraced Nathan

"Tariq, my friend. How have you been and what brings you here?"

"Let's sit down. I will get some coffee first, then we can talk," Rashid said.

Once they all had a cup of coffee in front of them and were seated, Tariq started to tell them what he had been up to over the last month. He said that since the killing of Al-Zarqawi by the Americans last month, the insurgency had been looking for a new leader. However, as there were many competing organisations and no single person who was strong enough to bring them together, things were more confused than ever and the place was even more dangerous than before. All he knew was that it would get a lot worse before it got better. He told them he had managed to get into Baghdad, which was now a divided city, the centre of which was controlled in the main by the Americans and their allies. The outskirts were now either wholly Sunni or Shia, with the Iranians holding influence through the use of Shia militias in Shia areas. Tariq said there was a lot of resentment in Sunni areas because they felt that the Americans were turning a blind eye to what was happening in the Shia areas. They didn't want to upset Iran but were attacking Sunni areas without hesitation. They carried on talking for another hour about the troubles and how they were spilling over into the region as a whole.

"So, my friend, what are you doing here?" asked Rashid.

Smiling, Tariq said, "I have come to ask for a little favour."

"I knew you weren't here for a holiday," Rashid replied and all three laughed.

"I can't stay very long, as the Jordanians would love to get their hands on me and I don't underestimate their spy network," Tariq said. "No doubt they already know I'm in the country but not where exactly, so I want to be gone before they find out. Rashid, I know your family can move things across the borders of Jordan, Syria and Lebanon with, shall we say, not too much interference from customs inspections. I want to get some goods to friends in Lebanon."

"You give me more credit than is due," Rashid said.

Tariq was the one who laughed. "I don't think so," he said, "your family has more contacts than many governments. In fact, you have contacts in those governments, but be that as it may, myself and my friends would look on it as a great favour and if you needed anything we could help with in the future you would only have to ask."

"I don't have to do it for favours, my friend," Rashid said. "If you need my help, asking is all you have to do." He put his hand out and Tariq shook it. "So, what is it you want?"

"Some goods have come into our possession. Many more than we can use in Iraq," Tariq said. "We wish to send some to friends in Lebanon. We can move them about in Iraq without a problem, but getting them through Syria and Lebanon would attract unwanted attention. That's where you come in."

"I shall not ask what the goods are," Rashid said.

"Just consumer goods," Tariq replied.

Rashid laughed out loud. "Very good, my friend," he said. "How many vehicles will you need?"

"At least two trucks," Tariq said. "I will supply a few men to travel along in case of trouble, but I need to know that trouble will not be a problem."

"It can be done. When do you need them?" Rashid asked.

"In a weeks' time," Tariq replied. "We will have the goods ready to be picked up from Al Qa'im near the Syrian border, but from there it would be down to you."

"And where would you like these consumer goods delivered to?" Rashid asked.

"Ain-al-Hilweh."

"What is Ain-al-Hilweh?" Nathan asked.

Rashid turned to Nathan. "It is a big Palestinian refugee camp to the south of the city Sidon in Lebanon. It is like a little country. The Lebanese government has no say on what goes on there and every so often there are gun battles between the Palestinians and the government troops stationed outside." He turned back to Tariq. "You don't ask anything easy, my friend."

"Once you get to the camp, I can assure you of a warm welcome. My friends there will treat you like a king," Tariq said.

"The people outside might not be so welcoming," Rashid replied.

"That's where I hope your contacts might smooth the waters," Tariq said. "If what we think will happen happens soon, our brothers in the camp will need the goods for their protection."

"What is going to happen soon?" Nathan asked.

"There will be a war. Hezbollah are planning something and the Israelis are just itching for an excuse to attack Lebanon again. Our Palestinian brothers will find themselves in the middle," Tariq said. "We just want to give them a few things to even up the sides."

"Okay," Rashid said. "I will try and make the arrangements. I will have two trucks cross over to Iraq and meet you in Al Qa'im. The journey back will take a few of days, but I will work out a route that stays away from large populated areas. Getting into the camp will be the most dangerous, as the

Lebanese Army is not something my family has many friends in."

"But doesn't that make life more interesting? Just one other thing, brother. The Syrians are on edge since the attack on the American embassy at the beginning of the month," Tariq said, with a smile.

"Thank you for that. It's nice to know that we have nothing to worry about," Rashid replied.

Tariq only stayed another hour until it got dark, then disappeared into the night. Nathan talked to Rashid once he was gone and learnt more about Rashid's family connections, which spread right across the Middle East. His family had been smuggling goods across borders long before Rashid was born and had a network of people that earned most of their living from smuggling. He also learnt that Tariq was a man who wielded power throughout Iraq and Jordan and was on the American list of most-wanted insurgents.

★★★

For the next couple of days, Nathan travelled to the camp alone to do work. Rashid stayed behind to organise the lorries and the journey to Lebanon. He didn't use the phone, but sent extended family members messages to make sure his instructions were carried out discretely.

Early Thursday evening, Nathan and Rashid showered and changed their clothes after a hard day at the camp. They were getting ready to meet Jamal and Marie in central Amman to celebrate Marie's birthday. A number of the UN workers were also going to be there and the night would be their treat. Rashid had a taxi pick them up and drive them to central Amman. They got out of the taxi by the big roundabout on Al Koroum Street and walked down a small side street. Rashid seemed to know the back streets well and told Nathan about the fun and games he had got up to there in his childhood, after his family had settled in Jordan after leaving Iraq.

They came out into a small square with restaurants on all sides. Tables and chairs were taking up much of the pavement space and any traffic had to drive slowly to avoid knocking people over. They crossed the square and entered a Turkish restaurant. Inside, they quickly saw Jamal and Marie who were with six other people – some who Nathan recognised from the camp. Everyone was introduced and they all sat down to eat. The meal was good and the conversation was light-hearted.

Marie announced that she would be returning to France next month to further her medical knowledge and to take some exams to become a surgeon. She hoped to raise the plight of the Palestinian refugees while back in France and get more funding to help, but said she would return when her studies were over. The UN people were a nice group and they promised Jamal that they would arrange for another doctor to come in and help when Marie left. Nathan found himself talking to Marie for most of the evening. She told him her family was from Marseille, and her father and mother were Algerian. She had two brothers, but she was the only one who had gone to university, as her parents couldn't afford to pay for her brothers to go as well.

Nathan learnt that one brother owned a tobacconist near the port, which her father and mother helped out in. Her other brother, Samir, was a bit of a tearaway and had been in trouble with the police on quite a few occasions, but she was closest to him. She told Nathan that he was very intelligent and would have done well at school, but because of the family's lack of funds hadn't been able to fulfil his potential. However, he had no resentment towards her. In fact, he had sent her money when she was at university to make sure she didn't have to miss lectures or studying time because of having a job.

Towards the end of the evening, Nathan excused himself to go to the toilet. He asked a waiter for directions and was told to go upstairs and the door would be on the right. Nathan walked up the stairs, which were next to a large glass window. From there, it was possible to see the whole square. When he came out of the bathroom, he had to wait at the top of the stairs for a couple who were coming up. As he waited, he looked out of the window. The square was full of people sitting and eating, or standing around and chatting. His eye was suddenly caught by a large black car that inched its way through the crowd and stopped by one of the side streets. He watched as a man got out and he instantly recognised him as being Mr Smith.

Nathan was stunned for a moment, but continued to watch as Smith made his way to a side street and stop next to another car. He leant down to talk to whoever was in the car, then returned to his own and drove slowly through the crowd. The couple got to the top of the stairs and Nathan quickly descended them. He took his seat next to Marie, but caught Rashid's eye and whispered to him about what he had just seen. Rashid replied that they should drive home via some back streets, where it would be hard to be followed.

When the bill had been paid, the crowd all got up together and went outside. The UN people were going to make their way back to their hotel, which was not too far away, and said their goodnights. Nathan, Rashid, Jamal and Marie planned to walk back to the main road and get a taxi from there. Nathan discreetly pointed towards the street where the car was still parked and Rashid led the group in the opposite direction. Jamal said they were going the wrong way, but Rashid said he knew a shortcut and everyone followed him.

Nathan walked beside Marie and looked over his shoulder. He saw the car had pulled out of the side street and was heading in their direction. He called to Rashid, who looked back and turned down a small side street. He shouted, "Run!" Marie and Jamal were stunned for a moment, but Nathan grabbed her arm and she joined the others in racing down the street. Jamal asked what was happening. The squeal of tyres behind them made him turn his head. The car was racing towards them. He ran faster.

Rashid was ahead and turned into another small street, quickly followed by the others. The street was less crowded and the lighting was poor so some areas were in complete darkness. However, it lit up as the car turned the corner and the headlights picked out the four runners.

The driver must have misjudged the corner, though, because they soon heard a crash and the scraping of metal. Nathan looked over his shoulder to see that the car had smashed into the wall. He then saw two men get out of the car and raise their arms. He heard the distinctive sound of gunfire and shouted for everyone to get down. Rashid and Jamal threw themselves to the ground and he grabbed Marie's arm, pulling her towards a doorway. He heard a few more shots and then the sound of the car engine being gunned. Then, silence.

It was Rashid who spoke first. "Is everyone alright?" he asked as he stood up.

Nathan realised he had a terrible pain in his foot and looked down. He saw blood. "I think I've been shot in the foot," he called. Rashid appeared at the doorway with Jamal behind him.

"Marie, are you all right?" Jamal asked. Marie was lying beside Nathan, but made no reply. Rashid knelt down and picked her up from the doorway. He turned her over and in the dim light all three of them could see that the front of her dress was covered in blood. She wasn't breathing.

Jamal and Rashid lifted her up and carried her through the street. Nathan hobbled along behind, wincing in pain with every step he took. They stopped at a shop, where Rashid used the phone while Nathan and Jamal held Marie's body. When Rashid returned, he said that someone would be with them in ten minutes. All three stood in silence, waiting.

The rest of the evening was a bit a daze for Nathan. He was taken to a hospital by Rashid and Jamal, who disappeared once they got him there. He was seen by doctors, who told him that he had lost two toes on his left foot. The police came in to interview him but he never mentioned Mr Smith. They left a guard outside the room and he was soon asleep thanks to the shock and the drugs taking effect.

★★★

He felt better the next morning, although he was still in a lot of pain. Doctors and nurses came in and out to check on him. He was able to watch some news on the television in the room, which reported a terrorist attack on westerners on a night out in central Amman. It said that one had been killed and another injured.

Later that morning, Mohammed Hossaini turned up with another couple of men that Nathan recognised from evenings spent at his house. The doctors and nurses seemed to melt away and the police guard also disappeared, leaving them alone with Nathan. Mohammed explained that Rashid had phoned him and explained what had happened. He told Nathan that the French embassy had taken Marie's body and was returning it to France for burial.

He asked Nathan to run through the events of that evening

and once Nathan had, Mohammed said Amman was too dangerous a place for him to remain. It was clear that people thought Nathan should be killed and they appeared not to care how it happened.

Nathan said he was happy in Jordan, though, and didn't want to leave as he was helping in the refugee camps and felt settled. Mohammed said whoever tried, would try again.

They had been talking for about twenty minutes when the door to the room opened. The police guard came in. He looked a little sheepish and lowered his head as Mohammed asked what he wanted. The guard said nothing but stood aside as a tall blond man entered, followed by a uniformed police officer. They all came to Nathan's bedside. The blond man introduced himself; he was a counsel from the American embassy. He asked Nathan if he was being well looked after and if he needed anything. Nathan said he was fine.

The counsel said that they would be arranging for him to be repatriated back to America as soon as the doctors gave him the all-clear to travel. In the meantime, Colonel Momani – he indicated the officer next to him – was investigating the terrorist attack and needed to ask some questions.

When the colonel spoke, Nathan was slightly taken aback because he seemed to have an impeccable British accent. He asked if Nathan's friends could leave them while they talked, but Nathan said he was happy for them to stay. The colonel's eyes turned to look at Mohammed and the other two men, and Nathan saw recognition.

He turned back to Nathan and asked about the events of last night. He wanted to know who was there, so Nathan went over what had happened and who had been at the dinner. The only person he didn't mention was Rashid.

Colonel Momani asked if Nathan was able to describe any of the attackers. Nathan explained that it had been dark and that they had been running. He realised as soon as he said it that he had made a mistake. The colonel asked why they had been running. Nathan thought quickly but could only answer that the car had seemed to be driving at them. He knew the colonel didn't believe it.

The colonel thanked him and said he would be back again to go over things. He said that Nathan should do all he could to try and remember as much as possible as they wanted to catch the terrorists quickly. The American counsel then said that Nathan should phone the embassy if he needed anything and gave him a card. He would make sure that Nathan's family were informed that he was well and would be coming home as soon as he could. With that, they turned and left the room. The police officer went out after them, shutting the door.

Nathan turned to Mohammed, who was smiling. "What are you smiling about?" Nathan asked.

"You must be considered important to have the famous Colonel Momani pay you a visit," Mohammed said.

"You know him?" Nathan said. "I thought I saw some recognition when he looked at you."

"Oh, I know the colonel and he knows me," Mohammed said. "He has family connections that run all the way to the king. He heads up the Jordanian anti-terrorist force."

"He has a British accent. Is he British or his family British?" Nathan asked.

"No," Mohammed said. "Like most officers in the Jordanian Army, the king included, a lot of their training is carried out by the British from a young age. The officers go off to Sandhurst military college in Britain for their officer training and the accent comes with it."

"I would have thought that with all the troubles in the Middle East, we Americans would have been training them," Nathan said.

Mohammed and the two other men laughed. "You Americans! Not everyone jumps to your wishes," Mohammed said. "It might seem that the colonel is working with you, but let me tell you, anything that has gone on here or happened last night will be on the desk of the British secret service in London. They have long connections with the Jordanians. In fact, it will be the British letting the Americans know what is going on – and that's if they want to tell them."

"You don't think the British were involved with the shooting, do you?" Nathan asked.

"I don't think so," Mohammed said. "From what you've told us, it has to do with the Americans and them not being happy with you. Either that, or it was a cover to kill someone else in your group. Maybe the Jews were involved. The young girl was unfortunate in being in the wrong place, but right now we have to get you out of this hospital if you don't wish to return to America. The colonel and the American diplomat will be back and you will find yourself taken, whether you like it or not, to the airport and onto a plane."

"I don't want to go back," Nathan said.

"But you can't remain in Jordan," Mohammed replied. "Not now the colonel has you in his sights. I will make a few arrangements, but we have to act quickly. The colonel will have his people watching me very closely. Someone will come and see you later. I will give them something to prove that I have sent them, and then you will do everything they tell you." Nathan nodded. "We will go and make some arrangements." All three stood, wished Nathan well and left.

Nathan lay back, thought about the events and poor Marie. He wondered what had happened to Rashid and Jamal. Had the colonel been to see them, too?

★★★

It was just after one in the afternoon. Nathan was dozing when the door opened and a man in a doctor's coat came into the room. He walked over to the side of the bed and handed Nathan a photograph. It was of his grandfather standing with a number of men who Nathan recognised as brotherhood members. Written on the photograph were the words: "a million dollars buys lots of food".

Nathan asked the man what he should do. The man raised a finger to his lips, went to the door and opened it. He went outside for a moment and returned with a wheelchair. The man helped Nathan from the bed and into the wheelchair, pushing him from the room. Nathan noticed the police guard was nowhere to be seen and no other staff appeared to be around.

They went down the corridor, turned a corner and went through another set of doors. The man never spoke to Nathan. They eventually came out of the hospital through what seemed to be the laundry. Outside was an ambulance with another man beside it. The man ran around and opened the back doors. Between them, they helped Nathan from the wheelchair into the back. When he was lying on the bed, they got out, shut the doors and the engine started. Nathan felt the ambulance move off.

He wasn't sure how long the journey took or where they were, but the ambulance finally came to a stop. The back doors were opened by the same two men, who helped him out. Nathan looked around; they appeared to be inside a warehouse. With an arm around each of the men's shoulders, he was carried to an office. They then passed through the door and then another, which led to some steps. They carefully helped him descend the steps and went along a passage. They then turned a corner and opened a door to what looked like a storage room. One man left Nathan and went to the shelves along one wall. He appeared to reach up and pull something. The shelves came away, revealing another passage.

The man took a torch from his jacket and turned it on. Then, he and the other man carried Nathan through the passage. They stopped for a moment and one of the men pulled on a cord. The shelves closed behind them, so that the only light came from the torch.

Nathan thought they carried him a couple of hundred yards, but he couldn't be sure. A door came out of the darkness and one of the men knocked on it. They stood for a few seconds, then Nathan heard some bolts being moved and the door opened. Light flooded the tunnel and Nathan's eyes took time to adjust as he was carried into a room and was helped into a chair. He rubbed his eyes and focused. The two men who had got him from the hospital were standing in front of him and were soon joined by a third. It was he who spoke first.

"Sorry for all the cloak and dagger stuff," he said. His voice was British, with an accent Nathan didn't recognise. " I understand you have had Colonel Momani wanting to spend time with you."

"Yes, I've met him," Nathan said.

"Well, let's hope we can help you avoid meeting him again," the man said. He turned to the other two, said something and they went back through the passage door. The man bolted it behind them and then pulled a wardrobe across, hiding the door.

"How are you feeling?" he asked Nathan.

"I've been better," Nathan replied.

The man reached into his pocket, took out a small container, opened it and gave Nathan two tablets from it. "I was given these for you," said the man. "They're painkillers." He handed the tablets over. Nathan swallowed them. "Now you can rest for a bit. We won't be leaving here until it gets dark, but I will get you something to eat and some coffee."

The man went out of the room and left Nathan, returning a few minutes later with a tray filled with bread, cheese and a cup of coffee.

As Nathan ate, he and the man talked. His name was Abdul Baari and he came from the town of Leeds in Yorkshire, though his family were originally from Lebanon. He had come back to visit relatives a couple of years ago and found himself getting caught up in the fight for Palestinian independence. He had then travelled to Iraq to help in the war there. Nathan asked whether he was still in Lebanon. The man laughed and told him no. He was still in Jordan, but hopefully not for much longer. Nathan learnt that he had friends in the brotherhood that occasionally did him favours, and he in return did some for them. Nathan was one of those favours. The tunnel he had come through from the warehouse was two streets away. If anyone had been tailing the ambulance, they would be watching a building that they would find to be empty if they raided it – and if they discovered the passage, there would be plenty of warning before they got to the hideout.

Once Nathan had finished the food, Abdul said he should rest and he would wake him when it was time to go.

CHAPTER SIX

I t was after eleven that night when Abdul helped Nathan into the car. It had a taxi sign on the top. When Abdul got in, he handed Nathan another couple of painkillers. "Take these, as we have a long journey ahead of us," he said. Nathan swallowed the tablets. Abdul started the car, making the headlights light up the darkness in front of them.

"Where are we headed?" Nathan asked, as they pulled away between darkened buildings. There didn't appear to be anyone else around.

"Well, my friend," Abdul said. "I was asked to get you out of the country, but since you have been asleep things have changed a little."

Nathan turned in his car seat. "What do you mean?" he asked.

"The news is saying that you have been kidnapped. There is a reward to help find you and to bring the kidnappers to justice." Abdul turned his head slightly to look at Nathan. "Someone wants you back."

"Perhaps I should give myself up and claim the reward," Nathan said. He heard Abdul laugh in the darkness.

The journey was spent talking about family and what they wanted to do, and how they thought things might turn out. Abdul said he was ashamed of Britain's part in the destruction of Iraq and its refusal to pressure Israel into giving the Palestinians their own country. He told Nathan that his family home in Leeds had been raided twice by the police, for no more reason than he was in the Middle East.

"You know what they call me in the newspapers in Britain?" he asked Nathan rhetorically. "A terrorist." He cursed. "Just because I have chosen to come and support my fellow Muslims, who find their country – be it Iraq, Palestine, Syria or wherever – under the rule of tyrants backed by the west or supported by the Godless people of Russia, who choose to fight their wars in our lands, killing our brothers and sisters. And I am a terrorist!" Abdul went quiet for a moment and then said, "You know, my brother, one day I hope to return to Britain to deliver just what they have said I am." Again he went quiet, then asked, "And you, my brother, what do you hope to achieve?"

Nathan thought about the question. "I am not sure," he said. "I hope I can improve people's lives through the provision of education and better living conditions, as well as improving the availability of health checks and medicine."

"That is very laudable, my brother," Abdul said, "and you can do that by fleeing in the middle of the night? You must be a magician." Nathan didn't answered, but understood what Abdul meant. "You have one drawback," Abdul continued. "You are American."

"Why should that be a drawback?" Nathan asked.

Abdul laughed out loud. "Come on, brother," he said. "You're an American. Do you think Arab governments are going to want you around? For all they know, you're a spy working for the C.I.A and if you're not, you will be embarrassing them by showing up how little they do for the refugees and their own people. If they don't want you, do you think your own government wants you running around the Middle East working with Muslims? Do you think they want you bringing to the attention of the wider world just how nasty the people the American government works with are, and what is really going on here?" Abdul paused for a moment. "I am not saying what you wish to do is wrong, my brother. I'm just pointing out that lots of people won't let you do it."

Nothing was spoken for a while as the car drove on into the night, not passing another vehicle on the way. Nathan saw that their journey was made on back roads, passing through small villages that were in complete darkness. He may have fallen asleep for a while, he wasn't sure, but he heard Abdul ask if he was hungry. He said no, but that he was thirsty. He watched as Abdul reached under his seat and pulled a bottle out. He passed it to Nathan and as he took a drink of water, the car slowed, pulled to one side and stopped.

Abdul wound his window down and some cool air rushed into the car.

"Where are we?" Nathan asked.

"Somewhere safe," Abdul said. "At least I hope so. Come on, let's stretch our legs." He got out, came round to Nathan's side of the car and helped him out. Nathan leaned on him as they walked a little way from the car into the darkness.

"You didn't say where we are," Nathan said.

"We are in the north. I am hoping someone comes along soon to meet us," Abdul said. They stopped by some rocks and Abdul helped Nathan to sit down on one. He sat beside him, with the car just visible in the distance. "You never told me how you know the brotherhood. It's not an organisation I ever thought would be helping an American."

Nathan told Abdul about his grandfather's background and the journeys he had made with him to the Middle East. The conversation was cut short by the sound of an approaching vehicle. Nathan saw Abdul pull a pistol from underneath his shirt, but made no move to get up. He placed a hand on Nathan's shoulder. "Sit still, brother," he said.

They saw the lights of a vehicle coming from the direction that they had been travelling in. It slowed when it reached their car, its headlights lighting it up. It stopped, but its engine continued to run. It was a van. Abdul and Nathan watched as the door of the van opened and a figure got out, walked to their car, appeared to look inside, then turned and looked around. There was no chance of seeing them in the darkness. The figure walked back to the van, leant through the side window and appeared to have a conversation. The door on the other side of the van soon opened and another figure appeared, but this one climbed onto the top of the van using the open door to help him. Nathan heard a voice call out in English, "Up the Villa."

Beside him, Abdul laughed and then shouted back, "We are the Leeds." Nathan had no idea what was going on but assumed it was some way of identifying themselves to each other. Abdul stood up. "Come on, brother," he said, helping Nathan up from the rocks and leading him towards the van. He saw the two figures approaching them.

It was Abdul who first spoke, "Nice of you to show up."

"We got a little lost," one of the men answered. His accent was also British but it was different to Abdul's.

"Better late than never," Abdul replied. "Any news?"

"Your friend," the man said, pointing at Nathan, "is a man many would like to meet, so I think its best we are on our way."

"Okay," Abdul said, "lend me a hand to carry him." The man took Nathan's other arm and they moved to the back of the van. The door was opened and Nathan was helped in. There were some blankets on the floor. Abdul got in with him and said, "Burn the car." The door was shut and they were in darkness.

A minute or two later, the engine started and the van moved off. "He's from England too?" Nathan asked.

"Nothing slips by you Americans, does it?" Abdul said,

with laughter in his voice. "He comes from Birmingham, which is in a part of England that we call the Midlands."

"And what was that 'Up the villa shout'?" Nathan asked. "Some sort of code?"

Again, Abdul laughed, "I suppose it is in a way. He supports Aston Villa, which is a football team – soccer, to you Americans – from Birmingham, but football fans just call them 'Villa'. I'm from Leeds and a Leeds fan. It's just something we use to identify each other."

They sat quietly as the van bumped along the road. Nathan was reminded of the story his grandfather used to tell him of his flight from Egypt. Nathan thought he now understood some of the feelings his grandfather had had then.

They drove for another two hours before the van stopped again. When the doors opened, the sun was just beginning to rise. He was helped out of the back of the van and found himself in the courtyard of a two-storey house. A high wall ran all the way round and when Nathan looked over his shoulder, he saw there were tall gates that hid the courtyard from the outside.

The man that had met them took his arm and led him to a house. Abdul and the other man followed. "We have arranged for a doctor to come and check your foot a bit later," the man from Birmingham told Nathan as they reached the door. It was opened as they got to it by another man. Nathan was carried through to a large sitting room and was placed on a sofa.

"This used to be the home of one of Saddam Hussein's regional governors," Abdul said, coming and sitting down beside Nathan.

"So we are in Iraq?" Nathan asked.

"We are," Abdul replied, "and you will be safe here for a while."

Nathan leaned his head back and rested it on the sofa. He thought how strange it was that only a few years ago he would have been hunting these men as the enemy and now he was being protected by them. Not only that, but he now thought of them as friends.

Nathan was seen by a doctor later in that day, who told him that his foot was healing well, but he should try and make sure he didn't walk on it too much. He left him some more painkillers to take. He slept in a large bedroom on the first floor in a very comfortable bed.

★★★

He woke to the sound of voices in the courtyard below. He slipped out of bed and hopped to the window where the sun was streaming into the room. He looked down and saw a car. Abdul and the man from Birmingham were talking to another man, who Nathan recognised straightaway as Rashid.

Nathan pushed open the window and called down, "Rashid, you're a long way from home!"

The three men turned and looked up at the window. Rashid smiled and called, "My brother, my home is now being looked after by Colonel Momani."

"I will send someone up to help you come down for breakfast," called Abdul.

Not long after the men were all seated around a large kitchen table, upon which coffee, fruit juice, eggs, bread and yogurt were laid out.

"So, my brother, how are you feeling?" Rashid asked.

Nathan told him that he was well and listened as Rashid related what had happened in the aftermath of the shooting. Rashid had left but Jamal had stayed because he was a doctor and had wanted to help. Rashid said Jamal had been arrested and, as far as he could find out, was still being held. Rashid had returned home knowing the Jordanians would pay him a visit, so he sent his wife and children away to stay with family and spent an hour burning anything he thought could be incriminating. At around 02.00, a phone call from a neighbour warned him that a number of cars were pulling up outside his warehouse. He left through a back door, climbed over the wall and disappeared into the night, just as he heard the front gates crashing in.

"So, you see, my friend, I too cannot go back to Amman now," Rashid said.

"I am sorry for causing you so much trouble," Nathan replied.

"What would life be without a little trouble?" Rashid answered. "In any case, I couldn't have gone on my trip to Lebanon without you." He smiled and drank his coffee.

"How did you know I was here?" Nathan asked.

"I don't think you realise sometimes," Rashid said, "but you have some very persuasive and powerful friends and Mr Hossaini is one of those. I thought I was well hidden in a safe house of some family friends, but a man turned up in the morning, sent by Mr Hossaini, to let me know where you would be taken. He said that I should make my way here. I don't know how he knew where I was."

"So you're off to Lebanon?" Abdul asked. "I have family there and I could do with a holiday. Do you mind if I come along?"

Rashid laughed and said, "My friend, you can come along, but I can't promise you a quiet holiday. I have to take some presents to friends there that others might not wish to see delivered."

Abdul laughed. "I always preferred an adventure holiday to a boring one on a beach," he said.

"Well, my friend, you are welcome to join us," Rashid said. He shook Abdul's hand across the table.

The man from Birmingham, who Nathan now knew was named Aashif, spoke, "I will come along if you have room for one more. I haven't had a holiday in years."

Everyone around the table laughed.

★★★

They left the house late in the evening. The sun just going down as they drove through the gates. Nathan was seated in the back with Aashi; all of them had a Kalashnikov rifle. Darkness soon fell. The conversation on the journey was taken up with a discussion on who would win the English Premier league. Nathan was the only one who couldn't participate as he knew nothing about football. Rashid, it turned out, watched the premier league all the time and was an Arsenal supporter. After driving for an hour, Rashid slowed the car and told the others that they were coming to the town of Rutba. He was going to turn off here and head north. It was flat, open desert. No marked roads, just tracks that locals and smugglers used when wanting to stay off the main roads heading for Syria.

There were a few lights on as they got to the edge of town, but hardly any people were moving about. Abdul pointed out an old Iraqi Army post, but there was no sign of any troops. Rashid turned left off the main road. They passed under what he said was the main highway going east to Ramadi and Baghdad, and continued on their way in the darkness. The conversation went back to football.

They had been driving north for five hours when Rashid pulled the car over to a stop. "It's time to rest," he said.

Abdul got out and went to the boot of the car. He came back with some bottled water and bread, and passed it out.

"Aren't you worried about being spotted by the army?" Nathan asked.

The other three laughed. "There is no army out here," Abdul said. He pointed skyward. "Your American drones and spy planes up there; they are the danger."

Rashid nodded. "I daresay some C.I.A man back in Baghdad is now looking at four men sitting and eating in their car in the western Iraqi desert wondering what they are up to." Aashif stuck his hand out the window and gave a one-fingered salute.

Everyone laughed.

"How much longer until we get to the meeting place?" Nathan asked.

"I reckon a couple of hours. We will meet someone there who will guide us to where we are going. Al Qa'im is one of the main crossing points into Syria, so it's best not to be seen driving round if you don't know where you're going."

After the food and water, they drove on. It was another hour before they came to a main road, where Rashid turned right and accelerated. This road was flat and made of tarmac. It made a nice change from the bumpy journey they had endured for the last few hours on the back roads. The next road sign told them they were now just six kilometres from Al Qa'im. Rashid pulled the car over again and stopped.

"Keep your eyes open," he said. "We don't want any unwanted visitors."

They had only stopped for five minutes when a motorbike, which was travelling from the direction of the town, slowed as it neared them and stopped fifty yards away from them. They watched as the rider got off the motorbike. He stretched his legs, then took his jacket off and turned it inside out. It was bright orange. Nathan jumped when Rashid suddenly pressed the car horn and started the motor.

He drove towards the bike rider and stopped when the car was level to him.

The rider came to the window and greeted them. After a short conversation with Rashid, he went back to his bike. Before mounting it, he turned his jacket back the right way so that it was a dull grey colour again and pulled away.

Rashid followed the bike and the group came to a main road junction, where they turned left. There were a number of other cars and lorries on the road, and they blended in with the traffic. After a couple of kilometres the bike turned right off the main road, passing a sewage and water treatment works, then turned left again. To their right, there were green fields and in the distance they could the Euphrates River.

"It reminds me of the west bank in Jordan," Nathan said.

"That's true," Rashid replied.

After another couple of kilometres, they came to the edge of Al Qa'im. Houses and shops lined the road and got denser as they got further into the town. The motorbike suddenly turned right and Rashid swung the car off the main road and followed. After another 100 yards or so, the bike stopped. The rider held his left hand out and pointed. Rashid came up behind him, turned the car left and they found themselves in front of a warehouse that proclaimed to be a wholesale fishmongers. The gates opened and Rashid drove in.

He switched the engine off just as the gates were closed by two men, both of whom had rifles slung over their backs. Another man, who was standing directly in front of them, was also armed but cradled his weapon, not seeing them as any threat.

Rashid opened his door and stepped out. Abdul got out next and came to open Nathan's door, helping him from the car. It was Aashif who spoke first as he stood stretching his legs. "If this is the best hotel you could find for a holiday, I want to go back home."

Abdul and Rashid both laughed.

A door opened behind the armed man and a figure came out. "Hey, brothers." Nathan recognised Tariq straightaway. "Glad you got here safely." He walked over and greeted them. "My Yankee insurgent," he said to Nathan as he embraced him.

Rashid introduced Abdul and Aashif to Tariq and they walked through the warehouse and out the back, finding themselves on the banks of the Euphrates River. "Now, this is a holiday," Aashif said, as they sat down at a table.

"So your journey was uneventful?" Tariq asked.

"Apart from Rashid's driving," Nathan answered.

"I am glad you are here," Tariq said. "When can I expect the trucks to arrive?" He looked at Rashid.

"I only have to make a phone call" Rashid replied.

"That's good," Tariq said. "I want to get the goods out of here quickly. Things are happening fast in Lebanon. It won't be long before it all flares up, so make the phone call, brother." He handed Rashid a large satellite phone. "Use this. It won't be traced and the signal scrambles, so it's hard for the American drones flying around to pinpoint it. Tell them to drive to this place in town," he gave Rashid a piece of paper, "and I will have someone meet them and bring them here." Rashid stood up and walked away from the group while he made the call. "So, brother, you have been in the wars I hear?" Tariq asked Nathan.

"I lost a couple of toes." Nathan lifted his leg up to show his bandaged foot. "It's healing well, but I won't be running any marathons for a while."

"From what I hear, you won't be going back to Jordan anytime soon either," Tariq replied.

A man appeared with some orange juice and glasses, which he put on the table. Everyone took a drink.

"You seem to know a lot that goes on," Nathan said.

"To stay alive, you should always know what's going on," Tariq said with a smile.

Rashid walked back to the group and sat down, passing the phone to Tariq. "They will be across the border this evening about 21.00."

"That's good. Now rest brothers, as I have a few arrangements to make." Tariq got up and left the group.

"You have some very powerful friends," Abdul said, looking at Tariq as he walked away.

"You can never have too many friends when times are hard," Rashid said.

They sat in silence, looking out across the slow moving waters of the river.

★★★

Just after 22.00, Nathan was talking to Tariq, who had returned in the late afternoon from making his arrangements. The others had gone to grab some sleep. The two of them were discussing the situation in Iraq, but Nathan said he couldn't see the American stance changing in the short term as so much had been invested in the war. Tariq said Iraq would never be the same. If anything, he thought that once the western troops left the country it would be divided up by ethnic and religious lines with years of trouble.

Tariq said you could already see the trouble spreading to neighbouring countries. He explained to Nathan that his groups aims were to attack the coalition forces head on, with ambushes, bomb attacks and damaging of infrastructure, so that the day-to-day running of the country would get progressively worse. Nathan pointed out that the lives of normal Iraqis would become worse and Tariq replied that everyone had to make sacrifices to drive the infidels from their lands. Anyone who helped the western occupiers was just as much a target as the western troops, and if the foreigners didn't leave their lands, they would take the battle to their countries. It was then that Tariq posed a question that Nathan had been thinking about himself for a number of weeks. What was Nathan doing in the Middle East?

Tariq said that Nathan's dreams to help the poor were admirable, but surely he now understood, with all that he had seen and the things that had happened to him, that it was impossible. Forces outside and inside the region had no wish to see the lives of the poor improved, as that would mean freedom and there were too many entrenched positions with the status quo suiting the super powers. Tariq said that Nathan had to decide whether he was willing to fight for the freedom of the people he wanted to help, as all his good intentions would come to nothing without people taking control of their own destinies.

Nathan said nothing, but Tariq was right. Who would he be fighting, though? America, the land of his birth and the home of his family? He needed to either leave the region or stay. It was not something he wanted to face up to just yet, but he knew the decision could not be put off much longer. He hadn't intended to take the path he now found himself on nor be around the people he now called friends. But they had accepted him for who he was. He knew he would be expected to stand beside them when it came to it.

Their conversation was interrupted by the approach of a man. He whispered to Tariq and went away.

"The trucks are arriving," he said. "Come, brother, we need to get them loaded quickly."

Nathan stood up. He had been given a walking stick to help him move around and he fell into step beside Tariq. As they walked, Tariq said, "Oh, one other thing, brother. You are still headlines in the Jordanian papers. Apparently they and the Americans are looking everywhere for you."

Inside the warehouse, two trucks had parked and now had their back doors open. Men were already loading boxes onto them. Nathan saw that many of the boxes had American Army stencils on them.

"We liberated them from an Iraqi military base outside Mosul," Tariq said, following Nathan's stare.

Abdul, Rashid and Aashif appeared. "Come on, you three," Tariq said. "Get your backs into the work." All three joined the other men loading the trucks. Nathan walked over to the stack of boxes and saw that they consisted of rifles, hand grenades, mines and ammunition. He saw larger ones that stated they were filled with anti-tank rockets.

"We are thankful to the American taxpayers for giving back just a little bit of the oil money they have stolen from my country over the years," Tariq said, coming to stand next to Nathan. "These arms will allow some of our Palestinian brothers to defend themselves and strike at the Zionist aggressors and their puppets."

It took a few hours to get the trucks loaded and when the back doors were finally closed, Abdul turned to Tariq and asked, "How heavy are your presents?"

Smiling, Tariq replied, "You have six tonnes on board, my friend. I hope that will keep my brothers in Ain-al-Hilweh happy."

"I think they will be over the moon," Abdul said.

Aashif laughed out loud and said, "The last person I heard say that was Harry Redknapp."

Everyone looked at the two Englishmen as though they were talking a foreign language, but the two laughed at each other.

"We will be moving off soon," Rashid said. "I want to be across the border before light. Do you have some scouts to send ahead of us?" He looked at Tariq.

"Of course, I will arrange it. Where do you intend to cross the border?" Tariq asked.

"I am going to head west before we cross," Rashid said. "I want to avoid Al Bukamal, which is the first town you come to when you leave Iraq from Al Qa'im. It's usually crawling with Assad's secret police. Once we have crossed into Syria and passed by Al Bukamal, I will rejoin the main road north when it gets near Al Jalaa. From there, let's hope we don't meet any trouble."

"How long do you think it will take to reach the camp?" Tariq asked.

"About three or four days if we are lucky," Rashid replied.

"Let's hope luck and Allah look down on us," Tariq said. He walked over to a table and picked up a box. When he came back to the group, he opened it and took out a satellite phone. "Take this, brother." He handed it to Rashid with a piece of paper. "When you get close to the camp, call the number on the paper and ask to speak to the Jewish doctor." They all looked at Tariq with surprised expressions. "Don't worry, friends, it's not something a Palestinian would be asked in the camp. They know whoever asks that particular question is bringing the goods they are expecting. You can make arrangements with them about how you will get into the camp."

CHAPTER SEVEN

They left the warehouse at 03.00. Tariq had arranged for two motorcycles to scout ahead just in case anyone was around, but the journey to the border was uneventful and they crossed into Syria just before four. Rashid drove the first truck with Nathan and another man called Hakim, who Tariq had sent along in case any trouble flared. Abdul was driving the second truck with Aashif and a man called Malik, who was another of Tariq's men.

Rashid seemed to have a knack of navigating them through the desolate, pitch-black terrain, on roads that barely deserved the name. They didn't travel at much of a speed, which was just as well as some of the potholes would have broken an axle if they had been travelling much faster.

It was a couple of hours before Rashid pointed out a few lights shining in the distance to the east. "Al Jalaa," he said, "we will turn east once we are well past the town, then join the main road north."

When dawn broke, they had been on the main road for an hour and were making good time. Abdul stayed fifty yards behind in the second truck. There were a few other vehicles travelling up and down the road but not many. Rashid said it would get busier as they day went on, which would be good as they could lose themselves among the traffic and not attract attention.

Just before they reached Al Mayadin, the trucks pulled off the road and they all got out. The sun was rising and everyone got down to pray, including Nathan. After prayers, they sat and ate breakfast. Rashid told them that they would drive into Al Mayadin but would turn off and head east to pick up the main highway towards Homs. He said they would break the journey at Palmyra, as he wanted to call in on family and check that arrangements to cross into Lebanon had been made.

The journey to Palmyra was without trouble and they arrived at a large villa on the outskirts of the town late in the evening. It was not far from the airport, which they could see in the distance. The two trucks drove into a courtyard and parked. A number of small children came from the villa and ran around excitedly. Rashid was the first out of the trucks and scooped up one of the small girls into his arms. He swung her around and she squealed in delight. Hakim helped Nathan from the truck and they walked over to join Rashid, who now had the other children around him wanting to be picked up and swung around. Nathan saw two men coming down the steps of the villa. Rashid saw the men and called out a greeting. He put the children down and embraced the two men, before introducing them to the rest as his cousins. They were the Syrian part of the family, he explained.

The two men shooed the children away and the group walked up the stairs and into the villa. It was large with high ceilings and nice furniture. The group carried on through the villa to the terrace at the back. One of the cousins called out for more chairs and three women appeared, dressed in full Muslim barques, carrying chairs. When the group were seated, tea, soft drinks and food were brought out by the women, who disappeared back into the house. The children could be heard playing in the background.

The cousins asked about the journey and how things were in Jordan. Rashid explained he would not be going back to Jordan for a while due to the trouble he had there. He asked about the preparations that had been made for crossing the

Syrian border into Lebanon. One of the cousins explained that they had had to change the crossing due to the Syrians closing the border due to brewing trouble in southern Lebanon. He said that they had found a crossing point further north and some local police had been paid to turn a blind eye. They would still have to be careful, however, as the Mukhabarat was very active along the border and they had been working with the Persians in Lebanon to catch smugglers and Jewish agents. The cousin explained that the Mukhabarat was not an organisation that could be bribed easily, even for them, so they had steered clear of any contact.

The situation in Lebanon was the main discussion and the cousins asked if the journey was really necessary. They could see nothing but war in the near future and explained that the Syrian media had been obsessed for the last month with stories of Israeli spies. There had also been daily announcements of traitors working for the Jews. Rashid assured his cousins that the journey was needed, telling them where he was headed and the reasons why. Nathan was surprised that Rashid was so open. He must have complete trust in his cousins. A moment later Nathan found out why.

His uncle, the cousins' father, had been arrested by the Syrian police two years ago. He had been held for a year on charges of smuggling and bribery, but after a year was released. The cousins explained that they had bribed two judges to make it happen, but their father had been tortured and beaten so badly that only a month after his release he died from his injuries. The cousins had always promised that they would have their revenge on Assad's thugs one day and avenge their father's death.

Everyone sat eating and drinking the coffee or tea, which was refilled by the women at regular intervals. Towards the end of the evening, the children were brought out to say goodnight. When they had gone to bed, talk turned to the wider Middle Eastern conflict and Nathan became the centre of the conversation. The cousins were fascinated that an American was working with the Arabs. Nathan was asked about his time in Iraq and why the Americans always took the side of Israel, Nathan did his best to explain that America, due to the big influx of Jewish immigrants in the early part of the twentieth century and their subsequent assimilation into American society, had long-standing ties that bound it to Israel. The group talked late into the night. Nathan started to feel he understood the deep-seated mistrust of America that he had found among most Arabs.

★★★

They restarted their journey early the next morning and headed down the main highway to Homs. One of Rashid's cousins, Raheem, was travelling with them and was in the first truck with Nathan and Rashid. Hakim had jumped into the back. Raheem was there because of the change to crossing the border into Lebanon. As they drove, the traffic got heavier and it was notable that there were a lot of military vehicles on the road –all heading east.

At midday, Rashid said they should stop and take some refreshments. He pulled off the road at the small town of Al Forqlus, which was only about twenty kilometres from Homs, and drove about 100 yards from the main highway. He stopped the truck outside a small cafe and the second truck soon joined them.

They all got out and stretched their arms and legs. The heat was stifling and all four of them walked quickly into the cafe where the shade provided some welcome relief. Rashid ordered some lemonade for them as they sat down. Abdul,

Aashif and Malik walked in and sat at the next table. Their conversation turned to football and Nathan was again surprised that everyone supported a team in the English premier league, knew all the players and all had their own idea about who would be champions. The cafe owner joined in the conversation as Rashid handed him the money for a second round of cold lemonade. Nathan suddenly heard Raheem tell them to look out of the window. All heads turned. Outside, a military jeep and a staff car had pulled up in front of the lorries.

Two soldiers jumped out the jeep and stood waiting, as a soldier got out of the front of the staff car and opened the back door. Two uniformed officers got out – one with the insignia of a major and the other, a captain. They walked towards the cafe, followed by the soldiers. Conversation had now stopped inside.

The soldiers entered. The two officers took a table against the wall on the other side of the cafe, while the soldiers sat at another table. The officers called for orange juice and ice to be brought over to them. The owner moved quickly, filling a pitcher with orange juice and ice and putting it on a tray with some glasses. He took it to the officers, who didn't offer to pay, but told the owner to get some drinks for the soldiers. He did so without comment.

The silence in the cafe was notable to Nathan and everyone did their best to avoid eye contact with the troops. The silence was broken by the major calling out, asking who owned the trucks outside. It was Raheem who turned to face them, saying that they were his. The officer asked him where he was going and Raheem replied, "Homs."

"What are you delivering there?" the officer asked.

"Machine parts for an engineering company."

The major nodded and went back to his conversation with the captain.

After ten minutes, Rashid stood up and Nathan, Raheem and Hakim joined him. They thanked the owner and made their way outside. Hakim was in front and made his way to the back of the truck. Nathan and the others were about to get inside when they heard a call and turned to see that the major and the other troops had followed them out of the cafe. Behind them, they could see Abdul, Aashif and Malik standing in the doorway.

"I forgot to ask something," the major said. "Where is it you have come from?"

"Palmyra," replied Raheem.

"And you have papers?" the major asked.

"They are in the truck."

The major asked to see them and told two of the soldiers to look in the back of the truck. Rashid said he would get them himself and opened the door to the lorry. Nathan watched the two soldiers disappear around the back of the truck, then turned back to face the major, the captain and the third solider. A second later, there was the distinctive sound of a Kalashnikov being fired and the two soldiers staggered back into view. They fell to the ground, followed by Hakim holding a Kalashnikov. Everyone froze for a moment in shock.

Rashid reached into the truck, pulled his own Kalashnikov out and turned to face the major and the other soldiers. Nathan saw the major reaching for his own gun and swung his walking stick, catching the major square in the face and knocking him down. Rashid levelled his rifle and fired before the captain or other soldier had time to do anything. They both went down and were probably dead before they hit the ground. Abdul came from behind and leapt onto the major, pinning him down. Malik joined him, pulling the major's pistol from his grip.

They all gathered round the major, who was kneeling with

blood pouring from his nose. Abdul had him by the collar of his uniform.

"What now?" Aashif asked.

"Well, he is not travelling with us," Abdul said, shaking the major and dropping him to the ground.

"He is nothing but a lap dog for Assad," said Raheem. "Give me the gun, Abdul." Abdul passed him the pistol. Raheem took the gun and fired it twice, the bullets striking the major's head. His body dropped lifeless at their feet.

"That's for my father," said Raheem.

Everyone climbed aboard the trucks and drove away from the cafe, leaving five bodies lying in the dust. Rashid said that they should get to Homs and find a place to stop and work out a plan. It would not be too long before the military and police were on the lookout, and they were bound to make the cafe owner tell them what had happened. He would have descriptions of each of them and their trucks.

The traffic was now heavy and moving slowly due to a column of transporter trucks that were carrying tanks along the highway. As they came to a junction, Raheem told Rashid to turn right. He swung the truck off the main highway and onto a smaller road that headed north.

"Keep following this road until you come to a T-junction and then turn left. We can get into Homs without having to use the main roads," Raheem said.

Nathan looked in the mirror and saw that the second truck was following them. They passed through a couple of small villages and after fifteen minutes came to the junction in the village of Sukkarah. Rashid turned left. There were fields on each side, where wheat was standing tall and moving lazily in the light breeze.

"Where are we going, Nathan?"

"When we get to the outskirts of Homs, we will head to

a big industrial area. We can lose ourselves there for a while," Raheem said. "I will make a couple of phone calls to some friends. We will need to hide until we decide what to do. The Syrians are going to be looking for us for sure."

Rashid reached under his seat. "Take this," he said, handing the satellite phone to Raheem. "If you're going to call someone, the chances are the phone will be tapped. This will give us a better chance of not being caught."

Raheem took the phone, switched it on and dialled. He waited for thirty seconds, then started talking. Nathan didn't know who he was speaking to, but heard him make arrangements to meet someone later in the day. He turned the phone off and handed it back to Rashid, who slipped it back under the seat.

"Follow the signs for the ring road," Raheem said.

Rashid nodded. "Why did we have to bump into that nosey major?" he said.

"Don't feel bad," Raheem said. "I quite enjoyed paying back some of what my father suffered. And what about our American friend – is he not a demon with that walking stick?" They all started to laugh.

Once Rashid had turned north onto the ring road, they fitted in with the slow traffic. They couldn't do more than ten kilometres per hour in some places because the traffic was so heavy. Every time they saw a police or army vehicle they expected to be stopped, but it would seem the alarm hadn't been raised yet. The second truck was only a few vehicles behind.

The traffic thinned out a bit and they started to move faster again. Raheem said to take the next main turning on the left and follow the signs for the north bus station. Rashid followed Raheem's instructions and turned the truck left. Abdul followed in the other truck. They drove along the road and came to a main junction. Nathan saw the sign for the bus station and pointed to it. Rashid turned right and they were soon passing the bus station, which looked crowded.

"Keep on going straight ahead," Raheem said.

Rashid carried on driving and came to a roundabout. They went straight on and large warehouses started to appear on either side of the road. There were also lots of trucks moving up and down the road, so they didn't stand out.

"A bit further on, you will see an old factory on the right. It was due to be knocked down," Raheem said, "but they haven't got round to it yet. I will tell you stop."

They carried on for another 500 metres before Raheem said to pull over. Rashid brought the truck to a halt beside the high, grey factory building. Most of its windows seemed to have been broken and there was a chain link fence surrounding it, with rubbish strewn around.

Raheem jumped out. The rest of the group watched as he went up to the gates and pushed them a bit. However, there was a padlock on them. He walked back to the truck. Raheem then guided Rashid as he turned the truck, so that he could inch his way back until the truck was pressing on the gates. The gates suddenly gave and flew open. Rashid drove through, followed quickly by Abdul in the other truck. Nathan leaned out the window and saw Raheem closing the gates. He pulled the chain and padlock back through so that it would seem they were still locked, but also put a large rock at the bottom to make sure they didn't open. He came back and climbed in.

They sat for an hour hidden from view. Everyone was on edge. Raheem went off to meet someone who was going to help with Malik. Rashid placed Abdul in one of the factory's rooms that looked out over the main road to keep watch. The rest of them sat together, leaning against the factory wall. All of them had a rifle with them.

What do you think Raheem is up to?" Aashif asked Rashid.

"Don't worry," Rashid said, "Raheem has been making deliveries and moving things about in this area for the family many times. He knows people and I expect he is sorting something out."

"We can't drive about in these trucks now," Nathan said.

"He will sort something out," Rashid said, standing up. "Let's have something to eat." He walked to the truck, opened the door and pulled a holdall out. "Something I was saving until we crossed into Lebanon, but we might as well tuck in now." He walked back to the others, put the bag down and unzipped it. He pulled out four large containers and opened them so that the rest could see inside. They were full of meat. "There's lamb in this one," he said, pointing, "and chicken and beef in the others."

All of them gathered around to eat. Rashid pulled some bread from the bag and passed it round. He got up and went back to the truck, returning with some bottles of orange juice. Aashif grabbed some bread, meat and a bottle of juice.

"I will take some through to Abdul." He stood up and disappeared through the door of the factory. Nathan found he was starving and ate like he hadn't eaten for weeks. Everyone was quiet as they enjoyed the food.

★★★

It was dark now. The sky was clear and full of stars. It was still warm but the heat was no longer oppressive. They were listening to Hakim telling them about an attack on the Iraqi military headquarters in Ramadi. There had been a meeting between the Iraqis and the local American Commander that day. A martyr drove a truck into the front of the building, blowing it up, and the rest of them had attacked from various points around the building. The attack lasted for several hours until they had to retreat as the Americans had brought up helicopter gunships to help. Hakim said that the Iraqis had fifty men killed, and the Americans lost two soldiers and many had been wounded. Nathan thought for a moment as Hakim continued his story. Two Americans killed? It felt strange that he thought of his fellow Americans as the enemy now and felt no remorse for the soldiers who had been killed.

His thoughts were broken by Abdul and Aashif coming out of the factory. Raheem and Malik were back, they said, and everyone stood up. Rashid went to the corner and peered round. A minute later, Raheem and Malik appeared. They had two men with them. The group gathered round and Raheem introduced the men. The taller man was a Syrian called Amir, while the smaller man, whose clothes looked two sizes too big for him, was called Sohail and was from Pakistan.

Raheem explained that the centre of Homs was crawling with troops and police. The television and radio was reporting a terrorist attack and everywhere was on high alert. They would have to dump the trucks and transfer everything to a new truck that he would collect later. In the meantime, they would have to remain here.

The Syrian, Amir, said that once they moved everything into the new truck, they should wait until at least 08.00 before they moved. There would be roadblocks all around the city, so it might take them some time to find a safe route out. However, there would be lots of traffic around so it would give them a better chance of merging in. Once they were clear of the factory, someone would make a phone call to tip off the army about the trucks being here and therefore hopefully distract them from hunting elsewhere.

A couple of hours passed before Raheem and Amir disappeared to go and collect the new truck. Nathan found himself sitting with the Pakistani Sohail and Abdul, who had been having a discussion about cricket – another sport that Nathan knew nothing about. The talk turned to what Sohail was doing in Syria and he explained that he had been at university in Damascus, studying electronics and engineering, but when the war had started in Iraq, he had joined the insurgency against the Americans. He had fought in a number of cities, putting his knowledge of electronics to good use in the making of bombs until he was looked on as one of the top bomb makers in the insurgency. His skills were in high demand. The Americans knew of him and had put him on their most-wanted list. He had come to Syria after being wounded in a gun battle close to the border.

Everyone took turns to watch the road while the others grabbed some sleep. It wasn't until about 04.00 when Raheem and Amir got back. They were driving a truck with Syrian Army insignia on it. Amir explained to the others that it had been acquired in a deal with a Syrian colonel, who received 20,000 cigarettes for the truck. It would allow them to move around without being stopped on the roads, but they would still have to avoid the checkpoints. Everyone joined in the transfer of the arms to the new truck and it was complete just after seven.

After the loading, they all sat and ate the rest of the food and drank the water they had left. Amir said he would arrange to pick up supplies when they were clear of Homs. Raheem said that they couldn't all travel in the truck, so a couple of cars had been left for them to use not far from the factory. They would go there first so that they could move in convoy. The cars would go on ahead to make sure that they didn't run into any unexpected checkpoints.

They pulled out of the factory just after eight. Amir was driving with Raheem beside him, and the rest were in the back of the truck. Traffic was very heavy as Amir guided the truck through the streets of Homs. After ten minutes, he turned into a street lined with shops that was not far from the centre. He slowed down, pulled up to the kerb and stopped, before jumping out. He went to the back, opened the doors and told everyone to get out. As they jumped down, he pointed to the side road, grabbed Rashid's arm and told him to drive the lorry. He would be in one of the cars and Rashid should follow him. Amir led the rest of the group up the side street to two cars. He got into one with Malik and Hakim, and Nathan joined Abdul, Aashif and the Pakistani Sohail in the other.

Amir led them through the streets, about fifty yards ahead of the second car and the truck. It seemed to Nathan that they were going backwards and forwards, as they didn't seem to be leaving the centre of Homs very quickly. Slowly, however, the roads became a little less crowded and they began to make progress. They came to a junction and saw Amir stop. They halted and watched.

A convoy of army vehicles passed in front of Amir's car. It was a big convoy and took at least five minutes to pass. They were just about to start moving again when they saw a police motorbike pull off from the back of the convoy and come to a halt beside Amir's car. In the rear-view mirror, Nathan saw Rashid pull the truck off the main road and into a side street. He turned to watch Amir, who was now out of the car and talking to the police officer with the motorbike. A police car came and parked in front of Amir's car. Two more police officers got out of the vehicle and strolled over to the car. Amir opened the boot, showing the motorbike officer that he had nothing in there.

Nathan saw one of the police officers lean into the car to speak to Malik and Hakim, then stagger backwards and fall to the ground. Amir pulled a pistol from under his shirt and shot the motorbike officer, who fell at the back of the car. The third officer ran and ducked behind the police car and could be seen firing at Amir's car.

Nathan watched as Hakim and Malik got out of the car, out of sight of the police officer. Both were holding Kalashnikov rifles and proceeded to fire at the police car. Abdul, who was at the wheel of the other car, gunned the engine and accelerated down the street towards the others. Just as they came to a halt, another police car came into view. They saw three officers jump out and begin firing at Amir and the others. Nathan grabbed the Kalashnikov at his feet, opened the door and fired at the second police car. He hit one of the officers and made the others duck down behind the police car. Suddenly, the front windscreen exploded and Nathan was showered in glass. He saw Sohail run from the car to a shop doorway and begin firing in the police's direction. Aashif and Abdul got out of the other side of the car and Nathan heard as they began firing their Kalashnikovs.

Nathan could see pedestrians flinging themselves into shops and hiding behind parked cars as bullets whistled past. He noticed that another two police cars had stopped on the opposite side of the road. Sohail was firing in their direction. Nathan stepped out of the car and tried to run to join Sohail, but his foot would not let him. He felt exposed as he hobbled as fast as he could. He saw dust kick up about five yards away from him and he knew he had to get under cover. He threw himself forward and rolled behind a parked car, landing next to two men who were hiding from the gun battle with their faces pressed to the ground. Nathan got to his knees and looked over the bonnet of the car. He could see yet more police cars and an army truck arriving.

Amir was firing at the truck, but Nathan saw him fall down. Hakim grabbed his collar and pulled him to the back of the car. He heard a shout in English and looked over to see Abdul waving his arm, shouting that they should retreat down the street. Nathan shouted the direction to Sohail, who nodded. Nathan then fired a burst at the closest police car, so that Sohail could duck and run past him to a doorway. Likewise, Sohail fired so that Nathan could fall back to join him. Nathan heard a whoosh and the air seemed to crackle, and a second later the army truck exploded. He looked over his shoulder and saw Rashid standing in the road, throwing a used and now empty missile to the ground. They used the few seconds of shock to retreat further down the street towards where the truck had been parked in the side street. As they did, Raheem appeared and fired another missile in the direction of the police vehicles. Nathan didn't see the outcome as he was running as fast as he could with the others down the street. His foot was hurting, but the adrenaline masked most of the pain. Rashid took Nathan's arm as they went around the corner to help him move a little quicker.

They stopped by the truck. The back doors were open and the box of anti-tank missiles was broken open.

"Well, this is a right mess," Rashid said, as Sohail joined them. They saw Raheem had stopped at the corner and was firing down the street. On the other side of the road, they could see Aashif and Abdul doing the same. Malik suddenly appeared, running past Raheem and into the cover of the side street. He stopped and stood beside Raheem, who spoke to him and came back to the truck as Malik took his place firing down the road.

"I'm sorry, my friend," he said to Rashid, "but I don't think we're going to make this delivery."

Rashid smiled and said, "Not to worry, brother, there will be others, but how do we get out of here?"

Raheem grabbed another anti-tank missile from the truck. "Bring some more of those to the corner," he said.

Sohail jumped onto the truck and handed Nathan and Rashid two more missiles, which they carried to the corner where Malik and Raheem were standing.

"We don't have much time," Raheem said. "They must have every army and policeman in Homs headed in our direction. Hakim and Amir are both dead. Malik and I will stay here for as long as we can, but the rest of you should get out of the area quickly." Rashid waved at Aashif and Abdul to run across the road and join them. Malik fired another missile off down the road and the two of them used the cover to sprint over and join the others.

"Get going," Raheem said, "but warn my brother that the Mukhabarat will be calling."

They said their goodbyes to Malik and Raheem, and started to run up the side street. Rashid stopped at the truck, opened the door and grabbed the satellite phone and a bag, which he put it in. Sohail called out and they all stopped. He was in the back of the truck and was pulling a box to the back. He threw it off and it broke open. It was full of U.S Army pistols and everyone grabbed one, throwing their rifles aside. Sohail threw a second box down, which broke and revealed ammunition and clips for the guns. Everyone grabbed a few and began to move off down the side street. Coming to an alley, they turned into it and trotted away in single file. The noise of gunfire became fainter. There wasn't much sunlight in the alley as the buildings were close together. Nathan wondered if they would get out of Syria alive.

CHAPTER EIGHT

Present day.

Nathan didn't sleep much and when his alarm went off at 03.30am, he was already awake. He rose, washed in the bathroom and walked back to his bedroom. He took a new suit from the wardrobe, dressed and then walked down to the kitchen to make some coffee. There, he found Abdul and Aashif drinking tea and cleaning Kalashnikov rifles.

"Good morning, brother," Abdul said. "It's a great morning to make history."

Aashif laughed. "He has been like that all night."

Nathan picked up the kettle and switched it on. "Is everyone else up?" he asked.

"Samir is out by the barns organising the loading of the coach," Abdul said. "Sohail is in the cellar finishing off the wiring up of the house."

"Let's hope he doesn't get his wires crossed before we leave or we might be in heaven before we expect," Aashif said, laughing out loud. Abdul joined in.

Nathan smiled at the two Britons, whose easy manner and constant joking he had come to like. That said, some of their British humour still left him speechless.

Sohail appeared at the kitchen door. "What's all the laughter?" he asked.

"Come in, brother, and have a cup of tea," Abdul said.

"Aashif was just hoping you weren't getting your wires crossed."

Sohail sat down and picked up a teapot from the middle of the table. He poured himself some tea. "Everything is set," he said, looking at Nathan as he added the milk to his cup. "As soon as you turn the key and lock the front door, all the explosives that I have planted on the farm will be live. When the front door is opened, it will set the timers running and they will go off at different times. The barns will explode within one minute of the door being opened and the main house an hour later."

Nathan poured the hot water from the kettle into his cup and stirred the coffee. He looked out of the window. Today was the day that all the planning would come to fruition. He had doubted that they would get this far without being discovered, but Tariq's ideas had proved correct. Individuals not connected to anyone weren't missed.

Samir walked into the kitchen. "Everything is loaded," he said. "All the men are ready and waiting."

Nathan nodded. "Well, let's drink up and get ready."

Each finished their coffee or tea and followed Nathan from the farmhouse. When everyone had left, Nathan stood by the door and carefully slipped the key into the lock and turned it. He heard the lock click and took the key out.

All of the men were standing outside the barn. Six of them were dressed in business suits like Nathan, and the rest were in jeans and shirts. Nathan and Abdul walked across and stood in front of the men. Nathan called out three names and the men stepped forward. Nathan embraced them and Abdul did the same. He then passed them the keys to the lorries they would be driving and gave them a mobile phone each.

"You know your mission," he said to them. All replied that they did.

Aashif shouted, "Allahu Akbar," and everyone else joined in. The three men walked away, two climbing into articulated lorries and the third into a 17.5-ton vehicle. Each was packed with high-grade military explosives and further loaded with fertiliser that Nathan had been buying. Using his expertise, Sohail had been able to combine it with other ingredients that would have caused a large explosion even without the military explosive.

Nathan called three other names and the men came forward. Each was given a set of keys. They then walked away and got into three vans, which looked just like any other Royal Mail van seen on the roads of Britain.

Nathan signalled the rest of the men and they all trooped forward and boarded the coach. On each seat was a Kalashnikov rifle and hand grenades, and there was a holdall on the floor. When everyone was aboard, Nathan and the others got on. Abdul slipped into the driver's seat and the others took theirs. Nathan stood in the aisle.

"Brothers, we are going to attack the heart of our enemy. Everyone must carry out their instructions without fear. Allah is with us." All the men cheered.

Nathan took his seat, picked up the pistol that was on it and slipped it in the inside pocket of his suit. He put the Kalashnikov into the holdall along with the hand grenades and zipping the bag up. There was a clipboard on the seat that he moved and propped up by the window.

Abdul turned in the driver's seat and told everyone to pull the curtains across the windows. Every man stood and pulled them, so that the inside of the coach was only lit by the light coming in through the front window. Nothing could be seen of the inside of the coach from outside. Abdul started the engine and the coach moved off. The two articulated lorries followed it, then the 17.5-ton lorry and finally the Royal Mail vans. The time was just after 04.15.

The convoy made its way towards Ludlow and then headed towards Kidderminster, before picking up the M5 motorway turning north, the M42 and the M40 for London. Traffic was still relatively light and Abdul kept the speed to a steady 60 to 65 miles an hour, staying in the inside lane. The time was 05.00.

The journey was made in silence. The men were either sitting and thinking their own thoughts or sleeping. Nathan closed his eyes as the drone of the motor made him sleepy. He heard Abdul call his name, opened his eyes and realised he must have drifted off to sleep as the sun was now bright in the clear blue sky. It was coming directly through the front windscreen. "We are coming up to the M25," Abdul said.

Nathan stood and walked to the back of the coach. He pulled the curtain aside and saw that the convoy was still following. He felt the coach move to its left as it turned off the M40 slip road heading for the M25. Nathan watched as all the other vehicles, except the 17.5-ton lorry and one of the articulated lorries and one of the Royal Mail vans, followed suit. He pulled the curtain closed, walked back to his seat and sat down.

"The others are on their way," Nathan said to Abdul.

"So we begin, brother," Abdul said. "I have a good feeling that God is looking down on us and protecting our journey."

They were on the northern section of the M25. The traffic was heavier but they were still travelling at 60 miles an hour. The other three vehicles turned south onto the M25 and joined the traffic travelling in the opposite direction. It was 06.50.

The convoy travelled on until it reached the A1 where Abdul took the slip road towards London. The two Royal Mail vans followed him, while the last articulated lorry stayed on the M25. It was 07.20. The traffic was very heavy on the A1 and the coach crawled along. Everyone was heading for work or was on the school run. It didn't matter, though. Nathan knew there was no hurry for them.

It was just coming up to 7.50, and the coach and the two Royal Mail vans had reached Holloway.

"Put the radio on," Nathan said. Abdul pressed the radio button and the sound of Radio 4 filled the coach.

★★★

Mohamed Bayoumi was from Egypt. He had fought for many years in Iraq and now he smiled at the thought of being part of history, and taking the fight for freedom to the home of the unbelievers and the murderers of his Muslim brothers and sisters. He was driving the articulated lorry on the northern section of the M25 and had just passed the A127 turn off. The traffic was heavy but was moving at a good speed. He grabbed the mobile phone he had been given, opened the message box and pressed send. The pre-written message was on its way to the assigned numbers. It read: "I am ten minutes from Paradise."

Nathan's phone went off and he checked the message. "It has begun," he said to Abdul and passed the phone to him. Abdul glanced at the phone, opened his window and tossed it out. Looking in his mirror, he saw it hit the ground and smash. It was quickly run over by another car. Samir came and sat next to Nathan.

"So we are on our way," he said.

"We will listen to the news and we will soon know," Nathan replied.

★★★

Taher al-Masri was driving the 17.5-ton lorry and was just coming up to the A2 turn off on the southern section of the

M25 when his phone went off. He opened the message and smiled. "I will be joining you soon, brother," he thought. He glanced in his mirror and saw the articulated lorry flash its lights as it peeled off and took the A2 towards London.

***

Mohamed Bayoumi had just reached the start of the Dartford Bridge over the River Thames. The traffic was heavy and he was in the inside lane, travelling at no more than ten miles an hour. He had other lorries in front of him and cars creeping slowly behind him, but no one was going anywhere fast. It was 08.05.

Taher was coming in the opposite direction and had joined the queue to use the Dartford Tunnel. The tunnel and the bridge were the main connections that linked the South and North to the East of London. It is the busiest river crossing in Britain, with over 130,000 vehicles using it every day.

Taher followed the traffic that divided up, with some taking the tunnel to the right. Taher stayed in the queue to the left. He had been through the tunnel many times with Abdul or Aashif, so knew exactly the point he wanted to reach before he carried out his mission.

***

Mohamed Bayoumi was smiling as he crawled up the incline of the bridge. A coach was alongside him on which a teacher was telling the pupils to calm down. They were on a daytrip to Chessington World of Adventure theme park as a reward for good results in their GCSE exams. Mohamed silently started to whisper a prayer as he reached the first set of high pillars that hosted the tension wires that held the bridge up.

He reached forward and flicked the switch just like Sohail had shown him to do.

The explosion could be seen for miles around and windows more than two miles away broke with its force. The traffic within 100 metres of Mohamed's lorry disappeared in a split second. The main pillar holding the bridge up was blown in half and the tension wires snapped quickly one after the other. A hole that spanned the width of the bridge was blown in it and the rest of the bridge span started to twist. Vehicles that had not been close enough to the explosion to be damaged were now tossed over the side of the bridge as the middle section collapsed into the River Thames 400 feet below.

★★★

Taher hadn't seen or heard the explosion. He was nearing the point in the tunnel that he knew was his destiny. The traffic was packed tightly around him and he glanced at the speedometer. It showed twenty miles an hour. He too started to recite a prayer as he leaned forward and flicked the switch on his dash. The force of the explosion vaporised anything that was not more than 50 metres away.

The explosion in the tunnel smashed the lining of its roof and sides. In seconds, the River Thames came crashing in and flooded the tunnel. Vehicles not destroyed in the initial explosion were now engulfed in a tidal wave of water that poured through the gaping hole in the roof of the tunnel. It tossed them around like matchsticks.

★★★

Sergeant Alan Mills was just walking back into the control room of the police river crossing, which was on the southern side of the river, near the entrance to the eastern section of the two tunnels. He had a cup of coffee in his hand and was thinking how quiet that morning's rush hour had been so far.

A bright flash caught his eye and before he could react, all the windows came crashing in. He was knocked over by the sudden rush of wind and glass caught his face. As he hit the floor, he could feel pain and the warm trickle of blood. After a few seconds, he picked himself up from the floor. He saw one of his constables pointing out of the window towards the bridge and he turned to look. For a few seconds, he could not take in what he was seeing. Most of the northern section of the bridge seemed to have disappeared, one of the large pillars was gone, and the middle section of the bridge seemed to be hanging down and held in place by just a few of the tension wires. All around him officers were moving forward to look out of the smashed windows. He saw that most of them were bleeding from wounds caused by the flying glass.

Sergeant Mills heard a shout and turned to see Inspector Richards behind him.

"What's going on?" he asked, but before Sergeant Mills could answer the whole building seemed to shake and flames came roaring from the tunnel entrance. Everyone was again thrown to the floor as a shockwave hit them.

★★★

At Scotland Yard central control, the big clock on the wall showed 08.15. A phone operator received a call saying that there had been an explosion on the Dartford Bridge. He was just passing the message to the officer in charge when all the phones in the room seemed to light up with messages. All were saying the same thing. The officer in charge called his superior with the news that was coming in.

The Commissioner of Police was in a meeting with all his senior officers on the ninth floor of Scotland Yard. The door to his office suddenly opened and a Commander burst in. He apologised for disturbing the meeting, but explained that reports were coming in of an explosion on the Dartford Bridge and in one of the tunnels. The Commissioner thanked him and told the officers present to go to their posts and find out what was going on. He put a call through to the Home Secretary.

***

Nathan and Samir were talking, when Abdul called out for quiet and turned the radio up. They listened to a newsflash that said there had been an explosion on the Dartford Bridge and reports saying that another explosion had been reported in one of the tunnels. Samir slapped Nathan on the back. "Brother, they have done it."

Nathan smiled back at him. "It's only the beginning."

The rest of the men on the coach spoke excitedly with each other as they continued to listen to the radio. Abdul turned the coach onto Holloway Road and moved slowly with the rush hour traffic. The two Royal Mail vans remained behind him.

***

The Home Secretary took the call from the Commissioner of Police and quickly called Downing Street to speak with the Prime Minister. He then put a call through to the Head of MI5 and arranged for her to join him at Downing Street for an emergency meeting. He called the Commissioner back and also told him to make his way to Downing Street.

CHAPTER NINE

It was 08.35. Khalid Al Yami could see the O2 leisure complex to his right as he moved along the A2 with the morning traffic and approached the southern entrance of the Blackwall tunnel. Apart from the Dartford Bridge and tunnels, it was the main connection for inner London from the north to the south. The traffic was very heavy and it had been stop–start for the last fifteen minutes. He was at the point where the three lanes started to merge into two and the traffic was at its heaviest – not that Khalid cared, as he knew his destiny was only a few minutes away. He thought about his family in Saudi Arabia, who he hadn't seen for many years since he had left to join the jihad in Iraq.

When he had left university, his father had wanted him to join the family construction firm, which was one of the biggest in the Saudi Kingdom and had made his family extremely wealthy. However, he had known that God wanted him to fight for his brothers' and sisters' freedom from the Americans in Iraq, so he had left the family home one morning without telling anyone where he was going and had never been back.

He saw the tunnel entrance coming up and sat up straighter, inching himself forward. The traffic was barely crawling as he entered it. He drove for another 500 metres or so when he came to a bend in the tunnel where the traffic slowed to a walking pace. He started to utter a prayer as he placed his hand on the switch on the dashboard. He closed his eyes and pressed it.

★★★

The Prime Minister sat at the head of the table and looked along it. He could see the Head of MI5 and her number two; the Home Secretary and the Justice Minister; and the Commissioner of Police with the head of the anti-terrorist squad. Also present were the Cabinet Secretary, the Minister for Transport, the Health Minister and various civil servants.

"Commissioner, would you like to start by bringing us up to speed on what we know?" the Prime Minister said.

"The information we have so far is that a lorry exploded at around 8.10 on the Dartford Bridge. It has destroyed the main span and brought down most of the northern section of the bridge. Not long after, there was another explosion in one of the tunnels crossing from the south to the north side. We don't know where precisely, but we can assume it was a lorry. I have officers analysing the CCTV footage to try and see what we can learn."

"Thank you, Commissioner," the Prime Minister said. He turned to the Head of MI5. "Is there anything you can tell us?"

"We have no knowledge of any planned attacks," she said. "GCHQ are running their way through all electronic traffic that has been intercepted in the last two weeks and we are checking on all known groups that we have had under surveillance – but this has come out of the blue as far as we are concerned."

"So we are totally in the dark about this," the Prime Minister said. He turned to the head of the anti terrorist squad. "Have you anything to add?"

"We haven't picked up any word of a planned attack," he said.

"What do we know of the casualties?" the Prime Minister asked.

"We fear it could run into the hundreds," the Home Secretary said. "With it being the rush hour, and due to the devastation these explosions have caused, I fear we might be looking at well over 500."

Everyone sat silently, taking in the number. "What about the transport situation?" the Prime Minister asked, turning to the Minister for Transport.

"I have spoken to the Highways Agency," the minister began. "The M25 has been shut in both directions, as well as two junctions to the north and south of the Dartford crossing. Traffic is at a standstill all over the area. On the north side, traffic is being sent down the A127 and A12 towards the Blackwall tunnel, but the reports we have say that the route is already overloaded and nothing is moving. On the south side, traffic is being routed down the A2 towards the Blackwall tunnel, but again everything is at a standstill. We are working on a plan that will see all traffic drive the whole length of the M25 to get from the north to the south and vice versa, but this will add hours to travelling times and also affect all other routes. We have also suffered very bad flooding in the Dartford area with the water coming from the tunnel."

"Not a very good picture," the Prime Minister said. "Do you have any news on casualties yet?" he asked the Minister for Health.

"We don't have any hard figures yet. I have spoken to the ambulance service, who have all available vehicles on route. All hospitals in London, Essex and Kent have been put onto serious incident alert with the recall of all staff. We will be opening a special telephone line for people to phone in if they have relatives they can't contact and who would have been using either crossing."

The Prime Minister ran his hand through his hair. "We need to get out a statement to the press." He turned to the Cabinet Secretary. "Organise that right away. I will make a statement to the press in an hour, when we will hopefully know a bit more about what has happened." The Cabinet Secretary nodded and scribbled in his notepad. "Right, everyone, I want us to reconvene in forty-five minutes, so you can brief me on the latest news before I speak to the press." Everyone started to stand around the table. When the Commissioner's phone went off, he took the call.

"Prime Minister," he said, as everyone looked at him. "I have just heard that there are reports of a massive explosion in the Blackwall tunnel." The time was 08.45.

★★★

Abdul was at the wheel of the coach and was whistling to himself as he waited for the traffic lights to change. He knew this part of north London well from the years he had spent running the haulage company. The lights turned green and he pulled away. Kings Cross and St Pancras railway stations were to his right as he drove up Euston road. The news was still on the radio and the reports of the devastation the explosions had caused were being updated by the minute. Aashif came to the front of the coach and was sitting behind Abdul, and across the aisle from Nathan and Samir.

"You know I had dreamed we could do this," he said.

Samir turned to look at him, with a smile on his face. "We are going to teach these dogs just what our brothers and sisters have been suffering for years at the hands of their soldiers."

Abdul looked in the mirror as he passed the junction of Euston road and Judd Street. He saw one of the two remaining Royal Mail vans turn off to the left. "Another brother is on his way," he said, looking back over his shoulder at Nathan.

Nathan nodded his head. *So far so good*, he thought, but he knew the police would be checking CCTV for clues about the lorries that had been used in the explosions. They were not so stupid that they wouldn't find out that more was to come, but he and the others had gambled that the current confusion would hide their main target.

***

It was 09.30 and everyone had again gathered around the table at Downing Street. They had been joined this time by the Minister for Defence.

"Well, Commissioner," the Prime Minister began, "I have been watching the news on the television, but what can you tell me?"

"We now know an articulated lorry blew itself up on the northern section of the Dartford Bridge," the Commissioner began, "which caused it to collapse. Roughly two minutes later, another lorry exploded in the Dartford Tunnel running from the south side going north. We are not sure what type of vehicle yet as we cannot get into the tunnel, which has cracked open and has been flooded by water from the River Thames. At around 08.40, we presume another lorry exploded in the Blackwall tunnel. Because of the age of the tunnel, it has been devastated by the explosion. It has cracked open and the River Thames has flooded into it. We have not been able to gain access to either tunnel yet to ascertain what has happened exactly."

The Prime Minister turned to the Health Minister. "What news of casualties?" he asked.

"We are gathering reports from all hospitals," the Health Minister replied, "but the ambulance service have said that they have run out of vehicles to transfer the casualties, and are using police vans and other vehicles that are available. In total, so far, we have 265 confirmed dead, Seventy bodies have been pulled from the River Thames and over 300 casualties have been taken to hospital. Many are in a critical condition. And now, with the explosion at the Blackwall tunnel, the service is completely stretched, and as the traffic is so bad, they are having trouble getting through. I expect the casualty count to rise as we still haven't been able to get into the tunnels."

The Prime Minister sat quietly for a moment. "Have you been able to get any information on who is responsible yet?" he asked the Head of MI5.

"We are checking all groups and any intercepts," she said, "but so far it looks like a very well planned operation has gone under the radar. I have been in touch with the Americans and our European partners to see if they have any groups that may have shown up as planning something this big, but at the moment I have to admit that we are completely in the dark."

"What is the transport situation?" the Prime Minister asked.

"It's dire," the Transport Minister began. "All the plans to divert the traffic towards the Blackwall tunnel from the M25 have had to stop because of the explosion there. Traffic in east and south London and all approaches is at a standstill, and all roads in the Kent area are blocked. Traffic is being turned around on the M25 and sent back to go all the way round, but most of the M25 is solid with traffic."

"Defence Minister," the Prime Minister said, "I want you to work with the Commissioner and the Health Minister. Put army units, helicopters and any transport that is available at their disposal. I want the three of you to get together and come up with a plan to get the casualties to hospital quickly. I have a news conference shortly but we will meet again in four hours. I want to hear that some positive action has taken place. The public will expect us to show leadership. Don't disappoint them."

***

Absimil had been parked up in the Royal Mail van for over three hours on a trading estate in West London. He had watched his two brothers carry on their journey around the M25 when he had pulled off and he knew they would have completed their martyrdom by now. He had been to this place a dozen times before. The Englishman, Aashif, had brought him here. He knew exactly what his destiny was as he turned the key to start the van.

He had grown up in Somalia. His family clan had been from the northern part of Mogadishu and from a young age he had fought gun battles with government troops who tried to force his family from the area. He had joined an Islamist group shortly before his sixteenth birthday. He had fought in Kenya and had travelled to Iraq when the Americans invaded to help his fellow Muslims there.

He turned the van onto the dual carriageway, which was heavy with traffic and creeping along slowly. He smiled to himself. *Today I will strike a blow that will be felt around the world and give hope to my oppressed brothers and sisters in Iraq, who are not forgotten.* The van was packed with 700 pounds of military grade explosives. There was a Kalashnikov rifle by his feet in case he was stopped by the police, but he had taken the route a number of times and he had always been waved through any checks.

***

Abdul turned off Marylebone Road into Park Crescent. The traffic was moving but, as always in central London, no one went anywhere fast – not that he cared. There was no rush.

"Everything is going well so far," he said over his shoulder to the others. They had all been listening to the radio, which was still giving out reports about the Dartford crossing and the

Blackwall tunnel. The Prime Minister had come on to give a statement about cowardly attacks on the country, which had made them all laugh.

"They think it's finished," Aashif said. "They are in for a shock."

"Let's hope we can speak to him personally about his attitude to the people of Iraq and Palestine later," Nathan said, which made them all laugh again. Abdul turned into Portland Place heading south, with the last of the Royal Mail vans still behind him.

CHAPTER TEN

The Prime Minister finished his statement to the press. He hadn't taken any questions, but had said he would give a fuller briefing in a few hours. He sat in his office with the Cabinet Secretary, his political advisor and a number of other senior civil servants. How different it was from yesterday when he had attended the state opening of parliament by the Queen. All the pomp and ceremony of the occasion, and now he was dealing with what looked to be the worst terrorist attack in the country's history.

He knew he would have to stand up in parliament and make a statement to the house in the afternoon. It was supposed to be the big debate on the Queen's speech, but his advisors had said he should let the house have their say on the day's events and postpone the debate for another day. The Cabinet Secretary had arranged for all the leaders of the other main political parties to come to Downing Street at 11.00 for a meeting and be briefed on what was known.

The phone on his desk rang and the Prime Minister picked it up. He listened to the Home Secretary tell him that the army had now been mobilised to help with the evacuation of casualties from the sites of the explosions, using all the available helicopters. Troops had been sent along with heavy equipment to help in the rescues and recovery of those trapped in the tunnels, but it was taking some time due to the road network being completely at a standstill. He also said that the police were using the CCTV network on the roads to try and track where the vehicles used in the explosion had come from.

The Prime Minister thanked him for the update and said to keep him informed of any more news. The time was 10.30.

★★★

Absimil smiled as he rounded a roundabout heading towards Heathrow Airport. He joined the queue waiting to enter the tunnel that led to the airport complex. The last time he had been here, Aashif had been with him and he had shown him the exact point where he would reach his destiny. It was where one of the main runways ran over the tunnel and where he would be able to cause the greatest damage. He was proud that he had been chosen to do this. Absimil entered the tunnel. Two police cars were parked to one side but paid him no attention. The traffic was moving slowly. The cars and coaches that moved around him were full of people.

Captain Henry Chester had just watched the Alitalia plane take off and told the first officer to increase the engine power of the British Airways flight to South Africa. He released the brakes and the plane started to move forward. The speed increased as the engine power rose. They were about 400 yards along the runway when he suddenly saw the runway seem to rise up in front of him, followed by a fireball. He screamed at the first officer to reverse thrust as he slammed on the brakes and fought to hold the plane in a straight line. The plane shuddered as the engines screamed from being at full pelt. Captain Chester slammed into reverse, but knew that they would not stop in time. He noticed as they neared the flames that part of the runway had disappeared. He felt the front of the plane suddenly dip and then dive into the hole that the explosion had created.

★★★

The leaders of the opposition parties had left Downing Street. The Prime Minister was sitting in his office, going over the wording of the next statement he would be making to the press with the Cabinet Secretary and his advisors. The phone rang and the Cabinet Secretary picked it up. He listened and held it out for the Prime Minister. It was the Commissioner. The Prime Minister took the phone and listened for a few minutes.

"Come to Downing Street straightaway," he said and put the phone down. Turning to the Cabinet Secretary, he said, "Get everyone back here now. There has just been another explosion, this time at Heathrow." The time was 11.30.

★★★

Abdul carried on driving south down Portland Place. He looked in his mirror and saw the last Royal Mail van turn off to the left into Duchess Street. "The last brother is on his way," he said.

Aashif looked across at Samir and Nathan. "We are nearly there, brothers," he said. "I can't wait to get going."

Nathan looked back. "Don't worry, Aashif," he replied. "We will play our part, but there's no rush. We have time to rest and get ready before we strike." He sat back in his seat. He knew that the day had only just begun for them and the spare time they had would be spent resting. He wanted everyone relaxed and ready.

★★★

Everyone had arrived at Downing Street for the meeting. "Can someone tell me what is going on?" the Prime Minister began. "Do we not have any idea who is behind this attack?" He waited for an answer but none came. He waited a moment longer. "What can you tell me about Heathrow, Commissioner?"

"The CCTV has been studied and we are trying to work out which vehicle was used," the Commissioner said, "but it has caused a terrible loss of life. A British Airways jumbo flying to South Africa was in the middle of its take-off and crashed into the crater created by the explosion. The reports I am getting say the plane exploded. It was fully fuelled for the flight and the authorities at the airport say they don't think anyone on the plane has survived – and, of course, we don't know how many people were in the other vehicles that were in the tunnel when the bomb went off." The whole room was silent.

After a minute, the Prime Minister asked, "How many people were on the plane?"

"Three hundred and ten," the Commissioner said.

"My God," the Home Secretary uttered.

"We need to know what's going on," the Prime Minister said, looking at the Commissioner. "Have you been able to find out any more about the lorries involved in the first explosions?"

"We only have the first vehicle, the articulated lorry, that exploded on the Dartford Bridge," the Commissioner replied. "I have trained officers going through the CCTV from the M25 to follow its route, but it will take time as we want to be sure we get it right. We are going through the same process at Heathrow. The fire brigade are fighting the fire, but with all the vehicles in the tunnel and the plane fully loaded with fuel, they can't tell us how long it will take to bring the fire under control."

The Prime Minister turned to the Head of MI5. "Do you have any news on the group or individuals who might be involved."

"In all honesty, Prime Minister, we don't have any leads," she said. "A few groups from abroad have claimed responsibility, though. We are checking them out and anyone who has any connection to them in this country will be visited."

"I can't believe we don't have any clues," the Prime Minister said.

"I am sorry, sir, but just like 9/11, this has come out of the blue."

The Prime Minister shook his head and turned to the Health Minister. "What news of the casualties?"

"It's not good," he said. "The news from Dartford is that we now have 572 confirmed dead." Everyone took a deep breath at the number. "We also have 700 injured, some very seriously. Divers have gone into the tunnels at Dartford and Blackwall, but we haven't really started to recover the dead from them yet, and now we have the Heathrow incident. The ambulance service and hospitals are fully stretched in London and the surrounding areas. We are using army helicopters to fly the injured as far as Hampshire, Milton Keynes and Cambridge."

The Prime Minister turned to the Transport Secretary. "What news do you have?"

"We have closed the inside lane to all traffic on the motorway networks except for emergency vehicles," he said, "but the traffic around London is basically at a standstill. This evening's rush hour is going to be a nightmare. Heathrow is now closed, meaning no take-offs or landings. We have all other airports around the country on alert, so traffic around them is gridlocked with vehicles being searched. We have put extra police into all railway stations and the underground."

The Prime Minister sat back. "So, what next? Is it over?"

No one answered straightaway, then the Commissioner

said, "We don't know. We are at this moment raiding any groups we have had under surveillance around the country, but have found no information about anything this big being planned. As to whether it's over, we really don't know. We have to hope that we get something from the CCTV. I've called in help from all police forces around the country as we are fully stretched. All my officers are now on duty and we have extra patrols out across London – but we can't be everywhere and we don't have any ideas who we are looking for."

★★★

Abdul was sitting at the traffic lights at Oxford Circus, waiting to cross into Regents Street. Nathan stood up and called three names. The three men were dressed in business suits and they stood up and walked to the front of the coach. Each were carrying their holdalls. Nathan embraced each one and Abdul opened the doors. Nothing was said as the three men left the coach and disappeared into the crowds on Oxford street. Abdul shut the doors just as the lights went green and he drove forward into Regents Street.

The news was still playing on the radio and a report came through about the extent of the devastation that had been caused. Abdul drove down Regents Street until he reached Piccadilly Circus. He followed the traffic and turned into Coventry Street. He pulled to one side and stopped after 50 yards. Another three men dressed in suits got up from their seats and came down the aisle of the coach with their holdalls. Nathan embraced them, "Good luck, brothers," he said. Abdul opened the doors and watched as they got off and turned into Panton Street, heading for Leicester Square.

Abdul pulled away from the kerb as the door closed and

carried on down Coventry Street. "Well, everyone is on their way now," he said.

"They will do their part," Samir said.

"I have a good feeling Allah is guiding us to success," Aashif said.

"Make sure all the curtains are still drawn across the windows," Nathan said to Samir, who got up and went back down the coach checking.

★★★

Commander Eric Sinclair had been head of the anti-terrorist squad for eighteen months and had been involved in the capture of numerous terrorists who were plotting to attack targets in Britain. However, as he sat with some of his senior officers in an office on the fifth floor of Scotland Yard, he knew that today's events had been a wake-up call.

"Well, what have we found out?" he asked.

"We were able to get the number plate reading from the CCTV of the lorry used on the bridge. It was bought over eighteen months ago from a used commercial vehicle site in Birmingham," Chief Inspector Richards replied. "I have officers on their way there to interview the owners and workers to see if they recall the sale and the purchaser."

"But it must have been kept somewhere out of the way," the Commander said. "Eighteen months is a long time to hide a vehicle that size, and if the others involved in the subsequent explosions were also lorries, it means it must have been a big warehouse or some private land out of the way. Have we managed to track the lorry on the bridge?"

Another officer answered, "We have traced it back to the M4 junction where it joined the M25. We are in the process of getting all the CCTV from the M4 to look at."

"And have we learnt anything yet?" the Commander asked.

"I have men analysing the pictures," the officer replied, "but we don't have anything concrete to say yet. However, I am sure that once we have gone over it carefully we will know more. At the moment, we are just trying to track its journey."

"Okay, but I want some more detailed answers in an hour," the Commander said. "We know it wasn't an isolated incident and we have four explosions. With the timings, this operation has been meticulously planned. These vehicles must have come from the same place. What do we know of the amount of explosives used?"

"From the initial examination of the damage to the bridge," the Chief Inspector said, "the forensic team have said it was high grade military explosive, but with a commercial fertilizer based bomb. They say the amount of military explosives used must have been well over five tons."

"Are you serious?" the Commander asked.

"Yes, sir," the Chief Inspector said. "I have spoken to the forensic teams working at the Dartford and Blackwall tunnels and they have said they think similar amounts were used in those explosions."

"You're telling me that we have terrorists who have gotten hold of fifteen tons of military explosives?" the Commander asked.

"It's more, sir," the Chief Inspector said. "We have the bomb at Heathrow to count yet."

"Have there been any reports of large thefts of explosives?" the Commander asked. "This amount can't go missing without someone noticing."

"None," the Chief Inspector said. "We have contacted all our European partners, Interpol and the Americans, but none of them have had any reports of such large quantities being stolen. The forensics have taken samples from the bridge and have said that once they should be able to tell us where it was manufactured and we can then look for a trail."

"We need to get things moving and fast," the Commander said. "We don't know if there are any more driving around out there."

CHAPTER ELEVEN

Abdul parked the coach on the Embankment, where there were at least another eight coaches all parked up along this stretch of road. Each had dropped tourists off to have a wander round London, and now the drivers were resting before picking them up again and resuming their journeys.

Nathan stood up and reminded the rest of the men on the coach to keep the curtains closed and to use the time to get some sleep. He told them it was going to be a long day and a long night. The time was 12.35.

Abdul slipped out of the driver's seat, pressing the button to open the doors as he did, and stepped out into the warm June sunshine and stretched. Nathan and Aashif left the coach to join him.

"Things are working out just how we planned," Abdul said to the other two.

"So far," Nathan said, "but we have to hope the next part does what we expect it to."

"Don't worry, brother," Aashif said. "Allah is keeping us safe. We will fulfil our mission."

"Come on," Abdul said and walked around to the front of the coach. He knelt down like he was tying his shoe, while the other two blocked him from the view of anyone walking by on the pavement. He reached forward and pulled off the number plate of the coach, exposing the original. He stood up and threw it into the coach. The three of them walked to the rear of the coach and proceeded to do the same. Luckily, the driver of the coach behind them was not in his driving seat or he would have seen what was going on. They then walked back to the door and boarded the coach. Abdul picked up the first number plate and tucked them both under the driver's seat.

"Time to rest, brothers," Nathan said as they took their seats.

★★★

The three men who had got off the coach in Oxford Street proceeded to make their way to Selfridges. They entered and went straight up the escalators to the restaurant. Two of them found seats, taking the third man's holdall as he went to the counter and ordered three coffees and three cream cakes. After paying for them, he walked back to the table and sat down. He looked at his watch. It was 12.40.

"There's no rush, brothers," he said. "We have half an hour before we begin."

The three well-dressed men attracted no attention from any of the other diners.

★★★

Commander Sinclair took a phone call from Chief Inspector Richards. He listened as the Chief Inspector told him the latest news from the search on the lorry. He explained that they had tracked the lorry's journey along the M4 and had now discovered it had come from the M40. They were getting all the CCTV from that motorway. He also said that it had seemed to be travelling with another couple of lorries and they were cross-checking to see if either of them had been on the CCTV from the Dartford or Blackwall tunnels. The

Commander then asked about the forensics on the explosives and the Chief Inspector said there was no news yet but would make a call to find out how they were getting on. When he got off the phone, the Commander immediately put a call through to the Commissioner.

★★★

The Prime Minister walked into the packed press room at Number 10 Downing Street at precisely 13.00. Cameras flashed as he stood behind the lectern. "I am going to make a statement about what we know of this morning's events. I will be taking a few questions afterwards. The Prime Minister then read the statement that he, the civil servants and political advisors had put together. It lasted ten minutes. When he had finished reading, he looked around the press room and saw the lead political editor from the BBC with his hand up. He pointed to him.

The reporter stood up. "Did the government have knowledge of a planned attack? And could you give precise numbers of the dead and injured?"

The Prime Minister said, "No, the government, police and the security service had no knowledge of any attack of this scale. I will not be going into figures for the dead and injured until we have a clearer picture."

He turned and scanned the room. He saw a familiar face from Channel 4 and pointed to her. She stood up. "Is it true that the number of dead could reach over 1,000?" The Prime Minister repeated that he wouldn't be going into numbers, but that there had been a significant loss of life. He also reaffirmed that the emergency services were doing everything they could to deal with the appalling consequences of a cowardly terrorist attack against innocent people.

He pointed to the news editor from Sky News. "Do you think the attacks are over?" The Prime Minister said they could only hope that it had ended.

He took a few more questions but didn't give any detailed answers, and said there would be a further press conference that evening at six. He turned and walked back through the doors behind him, which were quickly shut.

The time was 13.20.

***

The three men in Selfridges finished their coffee and cream cakes. One leaned back and said that it was time to begin. The man on his right leant down, unzipped his holdall and took out a parcel the size of a bag of sugar. It weighed ten pounds and was packed with explosives. He placed it on his lap and pulled off some tape, which exposed a sticky glue. He then pulled a wire that went into the parcel. He put his hand with the parcel under the table and firmly put it against the underside. He held it for five seconds and took his hand away. The parcel remained stuck to the underside. The men stood up and walked calmly from the restaurant to the escalators. No one took any notice of them as they left the store.

***

Commander Sinclair sat in the Commissioner's office. Chief Inspector Richards was next to him and a number of officers were also around the table.

"We have had no more explosions," the Commissioner began. "What do we think? Is it over or are there more to come?" He looked directly at Sinclair as he said it.

"We really have no idea," Commander Sinclair replied.

"So, tell us what we do know," the Commissioner said.

Commander Sinclair noticed the change in the Commissioner's voice. It sounded like he was being blamed for not knowing what had happened. "So far, my officers have tracked the lorry that exploded on the Dartford Bridge to the M40 motorway. They are now working their way through all the CCTV from the M40 to follow it back. Hopefully we will find out where it came from."

"Anything else?" the Commissioner asked.

"We have discovered," Sinclair said, "through tracking the lorry, that when it came down the M4 motorway it was in convoy with the lorries that exploded in the Dartford and Blackwall tunnels. We wound the CCTV back from the tunnels and were able to identify the lorries that were used as the same ones that accompanied the articulated lorry from the bridge."

"Do we have any information on any other vehicles?" the Commissioner asked.

"At this moment we are looking at all vehicles that were moving along the motorway at the same time as the lorries," Sinclair said. "I hope to be able to give a better answer to your question in the next hour, but what we do know is this attack has been well planned and is not some amateur undertaking. Forensics have told us that over five tons of military explosives were used in each of the bridge and tunnel attacks."

"What?" The Commissioner said, startled by the amount. "Five tons, in each explosion?"

It was Chief Inspector Richards who spoke next. "They also said it was backed up by tons of a fertiliser-based explosive. We haven't been told about the amount used in the Heathrow explosion, but it must have been a very significant amount."

"This is getting more worrying by the minute," the Commissioner said. "You're telling me that we have a group of terrorists who have been able to get their hands on tons of military explosive and no one has noticed."

No one answered. Chief Inspector Richards broke the silence. "From our initial study of the CCTV footage of the Heathrow explosion, we don't suspect a heavy goods vehicle was used. We are using data from the speeds the traffic was travelling at as they entered the tunnel to the time of the explosion. We should, hopefully soon, be able to identify the vehicle."

"That is all well and good," the Commissioner said, "but what is the answer to my question regarding the explosives?"

It Commander Sinclair who answered, "We have checked with the Ministry of Defence and they assure us that they haven't lost or had any explosives stolen. We have also spoken to Europe, America and even the Russians, and they all assure us they have not lost the amounts used in the explosions. Forensics are working to identify the type of explosive used and as they believe it is military, we should be able to identify the country of origin."

"I want top priority given to that," the Commissioner said.

***

Nathan walked down the coach and sat down next to Sohail.

"How are you feeling?" he said.

Sohail opened his eyes and a smile came to his face. "I am at peace, brother," he said.

"Not long until we get our turn," Nathan said.

Sohail laughed. "I can't wait," he said. "We still have some surprises in store for them. You know, brother, I never expected us to get this far. When we were back in Iraq and you told us of the plan, I thought we would have been caught or killed by now."

It was Nathan's turn to laugh. "I had the same thoughts, but here we are, sitting in the heart of the enemy's capital. They have no idea we are here or what we have in store for them."

"It's a long way from running through the back streets of Damascus ducking bullets," Sohail said.

Nathan smiled. "You're right, brother," he said, "but we're not running now."

★★★

The three men who had been dropped off in Coventry Street had made their way to Leicester Square, but didn't stop there. They carried on until they reached the start of a bustling Covent Garden at lunchtime. They, like their three fellow fighters in Oxford Street, had been into a few shops, leaving a small carefully hidden package each time. They had just come out of the fifth shop, when two men approached them.

Constable David Gosling was part of the West End central robbery team. He and eight other officers were working Covent Garden. There had been a rise in crime at lunchtime, particularly in pick-pocketing and street robbery. He was standing with Constable Mike Green, when they had noticed the three well-dressed Middle Eastern-looking men because they all had suits on. They would not have looked out of place in the City, but in Covent Garden they stood out like a sore thumb. Everyone else was dressed in light summer clothes, t-shirts and jeans.

Constable Gosling and his partner had been watching them for ten minutes. They were going in and out of various shops, but never seemed to buy anything. What also made him suspicious was the holdalls they were carrying. He suspected they were shop lifters, so he had alerted central control and the rest of the team were now zeroing in on his location.

Gosling crossed the road as he saw the men leave a large clothes shop. Mike Green was just behind him as he stepped onto the pavement and held up his hand.

"Excuse me, gentleman, may I have a word with you?" The three men stopped. "I am a police officer and I would just like to ask you a few questions." He held up his warrant card.

★★★

Mohamed Al-Bayati was from Iraq, and from a young age had been involved in fighting wars. In fact, he had never known a peaceful day except for the last six years when he had been spirited out of Iraq to run a small shop in Morocco. Then, three years ago, he had been contacted and told his time had come. He had found himself smuggled into England to a farm. Last night, he and the other two had been told their part in the planned attack. The three of them had spent the evening studying the map, which was in the inside pocket of his suit, and the list of shops they were to visit to plant the bombs the little Pakistani had made, Once they had done that, they were to make their way to the Court of Appeal on the Strand and attack it. Now, however, two men stood in their way.

None of the men answered Constable Gosling, which made him wonder if they spoke English. "Do you mind if I take a look inside your bag, please?" he said to the man standing directly in front of him. He was a big man and Gosling hoped he wasn't going to put up a fight.

Mohamed understood English perfectly, but shrugged at the policemen. He turned to the other two and told them in Arabic that the men were police and that they would have to kill them. He turned back to the policemen.

Constable Gosling heard the first man say something to the other two in a foreign language. He turned his head and said to Constable Mike Green, "I think we might need an interpreter if we nick these three" and turned back to the men. "I want to look in your bag, please," he repeated, pointing at the bag.

Mohamed nodded and placed the holdall on the floor in front of him and stepped back slightly. He saw the first policeman kneel down and start to unzip the bag. In stepping back, he shielded the third man, who unzipped his bag and pulled his Kalashnikov rifle from it.

Constable Gosling was on one knee pulling the zip open. He pulled the bag apart, and for a second didn't take in what was in the bag. He expected it to be full of stolen clothes, but what he saw was a Kalashnikov rifle, hand grenades and some small brown packages. He turned his head to say something to Mike Green.

As Mohamed saw the policeman unzip the bag and pull it open. He moved to one side. The fighter behind him had the Kalashnikov out and aimed at the police.

Constable Gosling turned his head to speak to Mike, but before he could say anything he saw him fly backwards. He heard the cackle of what seemed like a machine gun and turned his head quickly back to the three men. One of them aimed a rifle at him.

★★★

Alice Parker had been a police officer for eighteen months. She loved working the streets of London and had been part of the robbery team. She heard on the radio that Dave and Mike had stopped three men who they suspected of shoplifting. She and her partner, Constable Sean Woods, were the closest and turned the corner of Bedford Street into Kings Street.

About fifty yards up the road, she could see Mike and Dave. Dave was kneeling down and looking into a bag. What she saw next stopped her in her tracks. One of the men seemed to have some kind of rifle and she saw Mike fall backwards to the ground. The man then aimed at Dave and fired. Dave slumped forward across the bag on the floor. One of the other men grabbed Dave and slung him aside, pulled a rifle from the bag and zipped it up before lifting it onto his shoulder.

Alice didn't know how long the scene in front of her had played out for. It could have been just seconds, but it seemed like minutes. She shouted, "Stop! Police!" and saw the man with the rifle turn in her direction. She saw the bright flash of the gun's barrel and instinctively threw herself to the ground. There was screaming all around her. She didn't know if someone had been hit or was just screaming from what they had seen. She heard Constable Woods put out an emergency call of an officer down and armed men shooting. She saw the men break into a trot, making their way up Kings Street towards the centre of Covent Garden. She noticed they all had rifles in their hands now.

★★★

Commander Sinclair was seated with Chief Inspector Richards going over the reports and trying to work out where the lorries might have come from. They had a map of the United Kingdom in front of them on the desk, marked with what they knew so far.

"The lorry that exploded on the bridge was bought in Birmingham," the Chief Inspector said. "The M40 comes from that direction, so are we looking for a place in the midlands as the base?"

"I don't know," the Commander said. "The planning that's

gone into this is so complex that this could just be another thing to throw us off."

The phone on the desk rang and Sinclair picked it up. He listened for a moment and said he would be right there. He put the phone down. "Two policemen shot in Covent Garden. Reports say three gunman armed with rifles. I will call the Commissioner; you get down to the operations room and I will meet you there once I have spoken to him."

"We don't know if it's related to the terrorist attacks," Richards said.

"That's true, but let's not take any risks," Sinclair replied, picking up the phone. Richards left the office to make his way to the operations room. Sinclair quickly got through to the Commissioner and related what he knew. The Commissioner said he would also meet him in the operations room.

The time was 13.35.

★★★

Alice Parker made her way with Constable Woods to where their two colleagues were lying. It was clear as soon as they got to them that they were both dead. Alice could hear the sound of police sirens getting closer. As she looked up, she caught sight of the gunmen.

"I'm going to follow them," she said to Woods, who was kneeling beside the body of Dave Gosling. Alice got up and ran across the road, pushing her way through a crowd of people. She got on her radio and reported what was happening and the direction the gunmen had taken.

Mohammed Al-Bayati and his two companions reached the top of Kings Street and turned into the centre of Covent Garden. It seemed like the shooting just down the street hadn't happened, as everyone here was wandering about shopping or sitting outside bars and restaurants. He paused and spoke to the others. Each unzipped their bag and took out a couple of hand grenades. Mohammed turned back, raised his Kalashnikov at the restaurant opposite and fired a long burst.

★★★

Felipe Gonzales carried the tray with the drinks and food that was for table seven. He had been working at the restaurant for five months since he moved to London from Spain, where he had lost his job when the economic troubles had taken hold. He was living with his partner in a small flat in Islington and was working a double shift today. They needed the money as they had started to decorate the flat.

As he dodged between the tables, the sound of police sirens echoed around the piazza. *Not another robbery*, he thought. A diner had had her bag stolen a few days ago while she ate. He glanced around but didn't see anything. He reached table seven and felt, what he thought was, someone punching him in the back.

Madeline Evans was visiting London. She hadn't seen her best friend, Christine Marks, for three months due to work. They had spent the morning shopping and gossiping, and were now sitting in the lovely June sunshine waiting for their order to arrive. She saw the handsome waiter approaching and nudged Christine.

"I wouldn't mind taking him home with me," she said.

Christine laughed at her friend. It had been great catching up and she realised just how much she had missed their time together. As the waiter got to them, he appeared to trip and fall across the table onto Madeline, who screamed.

★★★

Chief Inspector Richards had just taken a report off the duty officer in the main operation room and read it. He passed it to Commander Sinclair.

"Looks like we have trouble," he said.

Sinclair read the report with a sinking feeling. *How could this be happening*, he thought. He had not seen one assessment of the likelihood of a terrorist attack on this scale in the last year. "Do we have confirmation that it is only three terrorists?" he asked.

"Yes," Richards said, "we had an officer not more than 50 yards away who saw the murder of the two officers. They are just getting the CCTV cameras aligned and we should have a live feed to Covent Garden."

Suddenly the Commissioner appeared at their side with two other senior officers. He asked to be brought up to date on what was known. Sinclair went over things and he had just finished when all the screens ahead flickered. All turned their heads to the bank of television screens that lined one wall and all burst to life with different angles and sights of Covent Garden. One of the screens showed a bar with people laying or hiding behind tables. The duty officer asked for the picture to pan out. The picture widened to show three men standing brazenly in the middle of the piazza, shooting in different directions.

"Where are the armed police?" the Commissioner said.

The duty officer turned. "They are just getting into position, sir," he said. "We had to make sure we cut off all their exits and get as many people out before we went in."

Everyone watched the screen. They saw the men begin to walk forward, shooting at anyone who moved and throwing hand grenades into shops as they passed them.

"Get me the senior officer in charge down there," the Commissioner said.

The duty officer walked back and took his headset off. "He is on the line, sir," he said and passed the headset over.

The Commissioner took them and put them on his head. "This is the Commissioner. Who am I speaking to?" he said.

"Hello, sir, this is Commander Tendali," a voice came back.

"Commander, I want the firearm teams to go in now. It's turning into a massacre," the Commissioner shouted down the line.

"We don't quite have everyone in position yet, sir," Tendali said.

"I don't care," the Commissioner shouted down the line. "Get your men in there and engage now."

"Yes, sir," Tendali replied.

The Commissioner handed the headphones back to the duty officer and turned his head to look at the screen. "This is unbelievable," he said to no one in particular.

The time was 13.50.

***

Aashif had been leaning back in his seat with his eyes closed, listening to the news on the radio. He sat up sharply when a news flash came on.

"Brothers, listen," he called out.

Nathan, Samir, Rashid, Abdul and Sohail moved forward, taking the seats behind the driver. Aashif leaned forward and turned up the radio. The news flash talked about an ongoing incident involving the shooting of two policemen and a large number of the public. It said that three gunmen were on the loose, but the police had them trapped in the centre of Covent Garden.

"Something must have happened," Rashid said.

"It doesn't matter," Nathan said. "It sounds like they are causing a lot of problems."

"Nathan's right," Abdul joined in. "As long as they are causing mayhem."

"It sounds like they are doing that alright," Samir said.

"Things should start kicking off soon," Nathan said.

Aashif laughed. "I think it already has, my brother."

CHAPTER TWELVE

The three men who had left the coach at Oxford Circus and had gone to Selfridges now returned to the place they had gotten off the coach. They had spent their time walking in and out of the shops in Oxford Street. There was a constant sound of police sirens and other emergency vehicles filling the air. Every so often, a convoy with blue lights flashing would come speeding by. Armed police stood alert at different points around Oxford Circus.

One of the men left the other two and made his way into a shop. The others walked onto Regents Street and waited by traffic lights to cross the road. When the lights changed to red and the traffic stopped, the two crossed, passing two armed police officers who were scanning the crowd and vehicles as they went by. The men stopped by a window display, put their holdalls on the floor and unzipped them. The crowds walking by paid no attention.

They both reached into their bags, took out a number of hand grenades and put them into their suit pockets. They both then pulled their Kalashnikovs from the bags, lifted the holdalls onto their shoulders, turned and, without waiting, fired at the backs of the two policeman who were standing no more than ten feet away.

The police officers were both dead before they hit the ground. Some of the bullets that didn't strike them carried on into the road. A bus that was passing was in the line of fire and its front window shattered. The bus driver was hit twice in the head and his limp body fell forward onto the steering wheel. The vehicle careered out of control and mounted the pavement, mowing down people waiting to cross the road. It eventually buried itself into a shop window. The other officers around Oxford Circus didn't know what was happening as the noise of the traffic had not allowed them to hear the gunfire. There was a lot of screaming going on from the injured and people that were shocked by what had happened.

Police Constable Daniel Kazmierzak was on his radio reporting the accident. He watched his partner jump the crash barrier to go and find out what had happened, and was amazed when he saw him fall backwards to the ground. He went to move forward to help, but as he did the big glass pane window of the shop behind him shattered. A woman standing beside him fell to the ground and for a second his mind couldn't work out what was going on. Instinct made him crouch down and scan the area. He was lucky, as he soon heard the sound of bullets ricocheting off the lamppost and traffic lights just above his head. He caught sight of two men across the road, who appeared to have rifles aimed in his direction. Just as he adjusted his machine gun to return fire, a white van stopped in front of him and shielded him from the gunmen. He used the cover to move. As he did, he put out an emergency call of gunmen firing in Oxford Circus, with an officer down and injuries to the public. He moved to the front of the van, taking up a firing position and telling the driver to get down. He looked across the road but the men had gone. Three other armed officers from his unit came running across to join him.

★★★

The Prime Minister was sitting with his advisors and drafting the speech he would be making to the House of Commons later. He knew it would be carried live by all the television and radio stations, so it had to engage the public as well as being a statement to the House on the situation. They had been working on it for a while and had been changing it as reports from the morning's explosions gave grim updates of the number of casualties. The door to the meeting room opened and his Private Secretary came in. He reported that there appeared to be a terrorist attack in Covent Garden and the Commissioner was on the phone.

The Prime Minister quickly picked his phone up and pressed the flashing button. He heard the Commissioner's voice and listened silently. Everyone in the office looked in his direction. After a few minutes, he said, "I will leave this line open. Keep the reports coming in. My secretary will relay them to me." Putting the phone down, he told his Private Secretary to stay in constant contact with the Commissioner and bring him any updates. The Private Secretary left the room.

The Prime Minister turned to the rest of his team who were gathered around the table and explained what he had been told about the attack in Covent Garden. It was still going on, with armed police engaged in a shootout with the terrorists. The Commissioner had told him that there were a lot of casualties among the public. As everyone digested the news, the door suddenly opened and the Private Secretary came back in. The Commissioner has just said that there appears to be another terrorist attack in Oxford Circus. The Prime Minister sat back in his chair. "Get me the Home Secretary right away," he said.

★★★

Constable Alice Parker had reached the top of Kings Street and stopped at the corner. She could hear gunfire and the sound of screaming. She stole a look around the corner and watched the gunman disappear into the main piazza of Covent Garden.

She didn't follow but encouraged people who weren't injured to run to her and get round the corner to safety. She did that for a couple of minutes. The gunfire coming from inside the piazza was constant and she could only imagine the terrible scene inside. She heard a shout from behind her and saw eight armed police officers, all dressed in black. She held up her warrant card as the first one reached her and pointed out where the gunman had gone. The officer told her to stay back and move any public away from the area. They then ran past her towards the piazza.

Alice moved back away from the corner and the noise of the screaming. She could hear the whine of police sirens.

At the other side of the piazza was Sergeant Dan Evans. He had been in the Metropolitan Police Firearms Unit for six years and had never, in all that time, fired a shot in anger. Yet here he was, crouched behind a car and reloading his machine pistol for the second time. Two gunman were firing down on his unit from the first floor of the piazza. About thirty yards away, a police car was ablaze. He watched as it drew up. An officer got out just as one of the gunmen appeared and threw a grenade. It bounced once and went through the open door of the car. In a second, it exploded. He watched the officer get blown ten yards across the road. His body lay still where it had fallen. He knew the other officer in the car didn't stand a chance of survival.

He finished reloading and took a quick look over the bonnet of the car. The gunmen never seemed to stay in one place for long and seemed be taking up positions that always afforded them a good vantage point. He knew these men weren't amateurs.

★★★

Abdul Rahman Ali was probably the oldest of the group assembled by Tariq, who he had known for many years. He hadn't hesitated when he had been asked to join a special mission. He had fought in wars in Kashmir, Chechnya and Iraq, and now, at fifty-two, he knew he was ready to fulfil his destiny. He felt exhilarated and hadn't felt this way since fighting house-to-house against American marines in Ramallah in Iraq. His two fellow fighters had gone to the other end of the building, shooting and throwing hand grenades into any shop or restaurant they passed. He could hear they had engaged the police in a gun battle, as there was a lot of incoming fire.

He waited in a position overlooking the entrance they had first come through. He was surprised to see two columns of four black-clad policemen moving slowly through the entrance below him. *How could they be such idiots?* he thought. *They should have waited until they could attack from all sides.* He shook his head in disgust. *Even the Americans hadn't been this stupid.* He pulled the pins from two hand grenades and released the triggers. He waited a few seconds, then threw them down and ducked into hiding. One. Two. Three. The air shook with the explosions. Jumping up, he quickly sprayed bullets from his Kalashnikov into the entrance. No fire was returned. Ducking down again and crouching, he ran twenty yards to a shop doorway. As he stopped, he saw a group of people inside. He levelled his rifle and fired a burst into them. Screaming came from inside, but he turned his attention back to the entrance. He could see five black bodies laying still.

★★★

The Commissioner was watching the pictures being beamed in from Covent Garden. He saw a number of policemen shot as they moved forward to engage the gunmen. Commander

Sinclair was shocked at what was going on in front of his eyes. The duty officer approached them.

"Sir, I would like your permission to withdraw our men until we can assess the situation," he said.

The Commissioner didn't reply right away. His mind racing at what to do next. "We can't leave the public to their fate," he said.

"Sir," the duty officer said, "we have had twelve officers killed already. My men on the ground have said it would be suicide to try to get into the piazza."

"Perhaps we should call in the army," Sinclair said.

The Commissioner looked at him. "Okay, pull your men back, but keep firing on the gunmen. Don't let them slip away," he said. "Sinclair, get onto the army."

Chief Inspector Richards walked across the operations room to join them. Sinclair saw him and said, "What's the news from Oxford Circus?"

"The gunman ran off down Regents Street. We are searching CCTV to try and find where they went, but it's a pretty confusing situation," Richards said.

The Commissioner took his eyes from the large screen. "What is the news of casualties?" he asked.

"So far, fourteen dead with many seriously injured," Richards replied, "but they say the number of dead is likely to rise as there are people trapped under a bus."

The time was 14.00.

★★★

Debbi Fitzgerald glanced at her watch. 14.00 – only an hour and she would be finished for the day. She had worked in Selfridges' restaurant for five years and enjoyed her job, as it afforded her the time to get home and pick up her kids from school. It also allowed her a bit of extra money. She walked around and cleared the tables. It had been a busy lunchtime, but it was starting to ease off. There were mainly tourists in now, including a Japanese family, some Germans and a large group of noisy young Italians weighed down with shopping bags. They were enjoying some downtime from their shopping trip. Debbi had just reached the table with the Italian youngsters on it, when, for a split second, her eye caught a bright flash.

The bomb under the table had been timed for 14.05 and the ten pounds of explosives detonated. The young Italians and Debbi were the first casualties. Their bodies were instantaneously shredded by the force. The rest of the restaurant was completely destroyed. No one sitting in it survived the explosion.

The kitchen area was severely damaged, with staff laying dead or injured. The main gas pipes attached to the cookers were fractured and a fire quickly took hold. Within a minute, the whole top floor of the department store was ablaze.

All along Oxford Street, in different shops, another seventeen bombs exploded. People were screaming and confusion reigned.

***

Superintendent Graham Days was standing with some of his senior officers in the centre of Oxford Circus. Behind him, the fire brigade and ambulance service were trying to recover the dead and injured from beneath the bus that had crashed. There were a number of other bodies lying around that had been covered in white sheets. The latest news form the CCTV operators was that they had picked the gunman up in Argyle Street. The Superintendent had just told the officer in charge of the armed units to move his men to intercept them. Suddenly, the air was filled by the sound of an explosion. Instinctively, everyone ducked. A coffee shop not more than 50 yards away had exploded.

As the Superintendent stood up straight, he could see that there were a number of shops and stores further up the street that also appeared to have exploded.

"Get this area cleared!" he shouted.

Officers started to corral the large crowd away from Oxford Circus, pushing them down towards Tottenham Court Road. The third man from the group of gunman slipped out of the shop he had been standing in while the mayhem outside played out. His holdall was slung over his shoulder as he joined the thousands of shop assistants, office workers and shoppers being pushed away from the dangers in Oxford Circus.

Sayid Haddad got further into the centre of the crowd being moved down Oxford Street. He could hear police shouting for people to keep moving and thought of what he had been told about the operation last night. It had excited him, but he had had doubts that things would work out. Yet, here he was, about to carry out his part, and everything he had been told had come to pass. He could hardly move his feet now with the crush of bodies around him. He reached into his pocket and pulled out the small phone the Pakistani had given him. He remembered exactly what he had to do. He pressed one, two, three and his finger hovered for a second over the send button. He pressed it. In the holdall, 90 pounds of explosives were triggered.

★★★

The Commissioner left Scotland Yard with Sinclair and arrived at Downing Street at 14.15 for a meeting with the Prime Minister and other ministers. Constant news was relayed to them about the situations in Covent Garden and Oxford Circus.

"Right everyone," the Prime Minister began. "I want to know precisely what is going on." *I wish we knew*, Sinclair thought. "Commissioner, can you bring us up to date on what's happening."

The Commissioner sat up straighter. "Following the bombings this morning, we now have two ongoing situations in Covent Garden and the Oxford Circus . We have contained the gunman in the central piazza in Covent Garden and, with the help of the army who have arrived on the scene, we hope to be able to bring it to an end." The Defence Secretary, who was sitting beside him, nodded in agreement. "The situation in Oxford Circus is more fluid," the Commissioner continued. "The gunman have slipped away from the scene and officers are trying to track them down, but we have also had a number of bombs go off in shops all along Oxford Street. We also appear to have had a suicide bomber explode himself up in the centre of the crowds being moved out of the area. At the moment, we can't give any figure as to casualties, but officers on the ground tell me they are likely to be very high. My officers are fully stretched. We have extra armed patrols on the underground and the mainline railway stations. Vehicles crossing the bridges over the Thames and using the Rotherhithe tunnel are being stopped and checked. Extra officers are patrolling the City area and guarding major buildings. We are also trying to keep the traffic moving, but my information says that it is getting close to standstill in the centre of the capital, which is making it hard for emergency vehicles to get anywhere fast. On the bombs, forensic experts are analysing the explosives used so we can ascertain the country of manufacture, then we can start to track where it was acquired. We think that the bombs in the tunnels and on the bridge used over 5 tons of military grade explosives, which was also mixed with tons of a fertiliser-based bomb."

The Prime minister was taken aback by the latest news. It seemed that every hour brought further bad news. "You're telling us that terrorists have gotten hold of tons of explosives? I take it the army hasn't lost that amount?" He looked at the Defence Minister.

"No, sir, we have all our explosives accounted for," the Defence Minister replied.

"So I take it we think it was smuggled into the country," the Prime Minister said, looking back at the Commissioner.

"That is the premise we are working on."

"Do we still have no idea who is behind this?" he asked, looking directly at the Head of MI5.

"Sir, we have checked through all intercepts from groups here and abroad," she said. "We can't find any chatter about a big attack, certainly nothing on this size – and as for who is involved, we are in the dark."

"You're telling me we have no idea whatsoever?" the Prime Minister asked.

"None at all, sir," she said. "I wish I could tell you something different."

"I have to make a statement to the House and to the country, and I have to tell them we don't know who is attacking us?" The Prime Minister looked around the table, waiting for someone to answer. None came. "What news on the casualties?" he asked, turning to the Health Minister.

"It's not good, Prime Minister," he said, looking down at the notes in front of him. "The figure we have for the bombings this morning, including Heathrow, is 1,347." There was an audible gasp from around the table. "We expect that to climb as the divers in the tunnels at Dartford and Blackwall are still recovering bodies. We also still believe that not all of the victims who fell into the Thames from the bridge have been found. So far, there are 2,600 injured, and many of them very seriously. We now also have these situations in central London. All of the hospitals in London are at full capacity, so we've had to use hospitals as far away as Cardiff and Manchester. The ambulance service have called in all available vehicles from the counties surrounding London, but this has had a knock-on effect because day-to-day emergency calls are taking much longer, so we may have people dying who would normally be saved."

"Thank you," the Prime Minister said. "What is the news on the transport situation?"

The Transport Secretary sat up straight. "The motorway network coming into the capital from all directions is grinding to a halt. The police and the Highways Agency are working on contingency plans, but tonight's rush hour is going to be calamitous. There is nowhere for vehicles to go. The east side of London is at a standstill, and traffic coming up through Kent from the Ports of Dover and Folkestone is being diverted from the M25 on to the M26 and back onto the M25, then sent all the way round. This is doubling the traffic on the route, so nothing is moving very fast. All other routes that run parallel to the M25 are full, so local areas have also come to a standstill, which, in turn, is making things extremely difficult for emergency vehicles. I have asked the train operators to run extra trains and Transport for London have said they will run the underground through the night, but this situation will be around for months, maybe years, until we get the tunnels and the bridge repaired. We are assessing the situation at Heathrow, but I don't think it will be operational for a few weeks – even when it opens, it won't be able to operate at full capacity. Flights are being diverted to airports around the country and to France and Holland. I don't want to raise the subject of cost when so many people have lost their lives, but the economy will take a big hit, which could run into billions of pounds."

The Prime Minister looked around the table. "I think everyone understands how bad the situation is and I have heard nothing that tells me it will improve. I will be in the House of Commons all afternoon, but I will reconvene here at seven this evening. I want to hear some answers to questions. The country will be demanding that."

Everyone stood up to leave the meeting room. The politicians headed for Parliament, while the police and the MI5 officers went back to their offices. The Prime Minister found himself alone. He knew his speech to the House of Commons today would be the hardest he would ever have to make. He looked down at his notes and saw the number of people who had been killed. He still couldn't comprehend it, and knew that it was likely to rise. He wanted to give the country some hope, but there didn't seem to be any information to assure them it was over.

His thoughts were broken by a knock on the door. His Private Secretary entered. "Your car is here, sir," he said.

The Prime Minister stood, straightened his tie, picked his notes and walked from the office into the hallway. He passed through the world-famous black door with number ten on it and out into the warm, bright June sunshine. On the other side of the road, behind crush barriers, hundreds of journalists and cameramen were standing. They shouted questions and cameras flashed, but the Prime Minister ignored them all. He climbed into the back of the Jaguar and it pulled away, taking him to Parliament.

The time was 14.45

CHAPTER THIRTEEN

Abdul Rahman Ali was sitting with his back against the wall. He had just rolled his last hand grenade down the stairs, which led to the first floor of the piazza. The wound in his leg was starting to bleed more and more. He knew he didn't have the strength to move far. His consolation was that he had killed the enemy who shot him. His two fellow fighters had put up a great fight at the other end of the piazza, but he had seen one killed and knew the other one, like himself, had been wounded. He could hear boots moving on the stairs again and poked his Kalashnikov around the corner and fired a burst. The bullets ricocheted off the wall. He turned his head to look for his friend, who he could still hear shooting. He then saw two black figures carrying machine guns appear from a shop, aiming their guns at him. *How did they get there*, he thought.

★★★

"It's time to move," Abdul said as he started the coach and pulled out into the traffic that was moving along the embankment. Everything on the coach was quiet, except for the radio that was still giving out the news of the attacks,

★★★

Since turning off Euston Road, Kamal Ahmed had driven across London and had been parked up in the Royal Mail van, waiting for the right moment. His part of the operation did not have a time when it had to be carried out. He had come to this spot at least twenty times before, with the American and the big Englishman, Aashif. The people who had built the tall glass building, which he knew was called the Shard, must have thought it safe from attack. It was surrounded by big bollards that stopped vehicles getting close enough to cause extensive damage, but the American had spotted a flaw. There was a hotel halfway up the building. Every so often, a big limousine would arrive and two of the bollards directly in front of the building would go down. It allowed access, so that the rich guests could step out of their car and straight into the building.

Kamal had watched a few vehicles go through this procedure and then park inside the bollards. He then saw another big Rolls Royce, whose lights indicated that it was turning in. The bollards started to go down and Kamal started the van, pulled out and quickly got behind the Rolls Royce. When the bollards disappeared into the ground, Kamal followed the Rolls Royce into the parking area in front of the reception.

Earnest Sarpong had lived in England for ten years, having come from Africa with his family, and now worked as part of the security at the Shard. He usually worked nights, but had swapped shifts this week, as he was taking his wife and two children on the London Eye that evening as a treat. His radio bleeped and he heard his name called. He was told to go to the front of reception as a Royal Mail van had pulled in there. He was to tell the driver that deliveries were made round the back.

Kamal was smiling as he stopped behind the Rolls Royce. He watched the driver get out, walk round and open the back door. A woman in a fur coat got out. Suddenly, he heard a tap on his window. He turned his head to see a black man in a security uniform, signalling for him to wind down the window. Still smiling, he reached forward and flicked the switch on the dashboard.

The Royal Mail van was packed with half a ton of military explosives, which had been surrounded with twenty-two large propane gas cylinders. The explosion tore through the reception area, killing anyone standing in it, and then carried on up through the first twenty-six floors. The propane cylinders, some of which exploded straightaway while others flew through the air like unguided missiles, were thrown out by the initial explosion. They travelled in all directions before landing and exploding, causing even more damage in the area.

There are 11,000 panes of glass in the Shard and, within a few seconds, 6,000 had shattered, sending glass showering into the streets of the surrounding area.

★★★

Susan Read had just got off the train at London Bridge, having travelled up from Kent. She was meeting her husband, who worked at Guys and St Thomas Hospital. He was finishing early and they were planning to have a day wandering around London. She had phoned him when she had heard the news of the terrorist attacks, but he had said not to worry as they would still be able to do something. They hadn't had the chance to spend too much time together lately. The train had been packed with people due to the roads being gridlocked. She had listened to people talking about the news and the number of people killed.

As she walked along the platform with the crowd, there was a sudden tremendous bang. Everyone on the platform stopped as one. All eyes turned towards the Shard, which towered over the station. It seemed to shake before her eyes as she looked up. For a minute, she thought she saw rain – or was it snow? People all around her started to scream, and in a moment she realised she was one of them. Her hands went to her face as she felt extreme pain. She tasted blood and suddenly couldn't see. She fell to the ground like most of those around her.

★★★

Harry Smart was checking tickets at the barrier of those leaving the station. Suddenly, the whole station seemed to vibrate and echo, and then there was a bang. It was so loud that it hurt his ears. For a second, he stood rooted to the spot and then he heard screaming, which seemed as loud as the initial bang. He ran towards the noise, up the stairs leading to platform two. As he reached the top, he stopped. Before him, he saw scores of people on the ground covered in blood and glass. Others were standing but looked as though they had been cut to ribbons, with blood pouring from their faces and bodies.

★★★

Chief Inspector Richards walked into Commander Sinclair's office.

"Another one," he said, as Sinclair looked up.

"Jesus, when is this going to stop?" Sinclair replied, throwing the pen he was holding onto the table. "Where?"

"The Shard," Richards said. "The first reports say that there are many dead and injured, and the area around the Shard is completely devastated."

Sinclair sat back. "How could we not have heard anything?" he said.

Richards shrugged. "We do have something, though." Sinclair looked up in expectation. "We have worked out that the lorries from the bridge and tunnels travelled in convoy with three Royal Mail vans, one of which we now know was used in the explosion at Heathrow. I expect we will find that the bomb at the Shard was also contained in a Royal Mail van."

"But that leaves one more," Sinclair said.

"Yes, I have put out an alert. That's not all," Richards said, coming to the table and putting a picture on it. "This is a still from the CCTV on the M4." Sinclair picked it up. "You can see there's a coach leading the convoy, which we have tracked all the way back to the M42. It is leading them to the M25. It pulled off onto the A1, heading for London."

"A coach? You're not telling me they're using a coach as a bomb?" Sinclair asked, looking up from the picture.

"What would be the point, unless they needed a coach to get into a particular area," Sinclair said. "You better alert Victoria Coach Station and all tourist spots."

"We've got the registration number from the pictures, so every policeman in London is on the lookout for it now. All Royal Mail vans will be pulled over and checked," Richards said.

Sinclair picked up his phone. "Well done, I will call the Commissioner and let him know what's happening."

★★★

"Order, order," the speaker of the House of Commons called out to a packed Parliament. The members were standing all around the chamber or sitting tightly together on the green benches. "We have a statement from the Prime Minister." The house went quiet as the Prime Minister stood up.

The time was 15.00.

"Thank you, Mister Speaker," the Prime Minister began. "The whole House and the country will join me in sending our condolences to the family and friends of those killed and injured in today's terrorist attacks." There was a loud chorus of

"Hear, hear". "I would like to take this opportunity to tell the house and the country just what we know." He leant forward and turned over a page of his notes. "This morning, at around 08.00, a lorry exploded on the Dartford Bridge, causing it to collapse with a great loss of life. This was followed by two more large explosions: one in the Dartford Tunnel and another in the Blackwall Tunnel. These have also lead to significant casualties.

"Later, a bomb exploded at Heathrow, causing another great loss of life." He turned another page and looked around the House, which was silent. All eyes were fixed on him. "I have had meetings with the security services and police, who have said that they had no knowledge of any plot on this scale being planned." There were a few shouts from around the chamber and the speaker called for order. When it was quiet again, the Prime Minister continued, "There have also been attacks in Oxford Street, where at least seventeen smaller bombs have exploded in shops. A number of terrorists also launched an attack on the public with machine guns and the police are, at this moment, hunting for them. There was also a suicide bomber who blew himself up among the crowds being ushered away from the scene."

The Prime Minister stopped for a moment. He looked around again. He had never seen the house so concentrated or so quiet. "There was also an attack by terrorists in the Covent Garden area, and again the casualties among the public and police were high, but this has now been ended with three terrorists being killed." He turned another page "However, in the last few minutes, we have had reports of another large explosion at the Shard. I have been informed that there are many casualties." A murmur ran around the house at the latest news and the Prime Minister waited.

"Our emergency services are doing all they can. All

hospitals in London and the surrounding area are dealing with hundreds of seriously injured people, but I have to tell the House that the number of people reported to have been killed has risen to 1,370." There were gasps all around. "We can expect that figure to climb with the latest attacks. I will keep the House updated as soon as I am made aware of them."

He stopped, picked up a glass of water and took a sip. There was still complete silence. He put the glass down, turned another page of his notes and continued, "I want to assure the House and the country that the government is taking all steps to try and find the people responsible for these attacks and bring them to justice. We have been in touch with our allies abroad, who have pledged to help us. I know the country as a whole will be shocked and saddened by today's events. It is an attack on everything we hold dear." He looked around the House, then sat down.

The speaker called, "Order," as a number of voices became raised. "The leader of the Opposition," he shouted and she stood up, looking across at the Prime Minister.

"I would like to associate myself and all my colleagues with the Prime Minister's condolences to the families and friends of those killed or injured," she began.

★★★

Abdul turned his head as the coach sat at the traffic lights of the junction with Westminster Bridge and the Embankment. "There are a lot of police around."

Nathan and Rashid, who were sitting side by side in the front, scanned the pavements. There were a lot of police, but this was expected. "Don't worry, brother. We are here now and we will be knocking on the door soon to be let in – police or no police," Rashid said.

The lights turned green and Abdul turned right into Bridge Street, heading towards Parliament Square. Big Ben towered over them to their left.

Samir nudged Sohail. "Look, brother, wouldn›t you like to see the view from up there?" he said.

Sohail looked up. "Dreams can come true," he said and Samir laughed.

"Everybody get ready," Nathan called from the front of the coach as it turned into Parliament Square. Every man pulled their Kalashnikov from their bags along with some magazine clips and hand grenades, which they slipped into their pockets. The coach continued along Parliament Square. There were lots of tourists around enjoying the June sunshine and taking pictures. Every 100 yards, Nathan could see policemen dotted among them.

They went through the traffic lights and drove between Westminster Abbey and the Houses of Parliament. Abdul could see the large metal barriers that surrounded Parliament ahead. No vehicle could get close enough to cause great damage. He pulled the coach over just before the barriers began and blocked the traffic behind him, which had to pull into the other side of the road to get past.

Nathan stood up as soon as the coach stopped and picked up the clipboard, Samir and Rashid stood up, too. Abdul pushed the button to open the door.

"Thank you for travelling with Paradise Tours. I hope we see you again," he said, hearing the familiar laugh of Aashif behind him.

Nathan smiled. "You will do, brother," he said. "Good luck." He stepped out of the coach, with Samir and Rashid following him. Outside the entrance to the Houses of Parliament, Nathan saw five armed police. It was more than usual, but they had predicted that security would be beefed up. The three of them began the fifty-yard walk towards the doors.

***

Sergeant Edwards was in charge of the armed unit guarding the doors that led to the central lobby and into Parliament. He had noticed the coach stop and looked on as three men got off and came walking towards them.

"Looks like some lost tourists," he said, and his officers turned to look. A tall white man in a suit holding a clipboard was leading. "We better get them shifted or the road will be blocked." He could see that traffic was already building up behind the parked coach.

Nathan saw the police watching them as they approached. When he reached the doors, he asked, "Could you help us? We were meant to have a meeting with our local MP, who was going to give us a tour of Parliament, but our driver doesn't know where we should park."

Sergeant Edwards let go of his machine pistol and it swung free to his side as he stepped forward to help. "Well, sir, you will have to move the coach. If you go down the road another 100 yards." he said, pointing, "there's a barrier. You can pull in there and the police will direct you." As he turned back, he saw that the hand that held the clipboard now had a pistol.

Nathan had watched as the policeman pointed and turned to give him directions. He had used the time to throw the clipboard down and pull the pistol from his pocket. He aimed at the policeman and he fell to the ground. Samir and Rashid also pulled out their pistols and caught the police by surprise, shooting them where they stood. Before they could react, the three men moved forward quickly. They stepped over the bodies of the dead policemen and into the main entrance.

Abdul had been watching from his seat in the coach. As soon as he saw the first policeman fall, he shouted, "Go!" Aashif and Sohail, who had Nathan's and the others holdalls with them, were the first off the coach. They were quickly followed by the rest of the men, who sprinted towards the doors.

When Nathan and Samir entered the main entrance, two more policemen were there but both were unarmed. Samir shot them and the sound of gunshots echoed around the central lobby. Everyone stopped still, looking towards the entrance.

The time was 15.20

★★★

Police Constable Craig Davis was giving directions to French tourists outside Westminster Abbey opposite Parliament when he saw a coach pull over and block the road. He didn't go to the driver straightaway but finished with the tourists. By this time, the traffic was already backing up towards the traffic lights at Parliament Square. He crossed over and walked along the driver's side of the coach.

Abdul watched the last of the men disappear through the doors of Parliament. He sat up and was ready to pull away, when he saw a policeman coming towards him in his mirror. He smiled.

Constable Davis got to the driver's door and looked up. He banged on the window and saw the smiling driver look down at him. "Move the coach," he said. The driver seemed not to understand. "You can't park here," Davis said, but the driver shrugged. Davis was losing his temper. He could hear car horns being blown in frustration from behind the coach.

Abdul continued to smile down at the policeman, who

was telling him to move the coach. *In good time, my friend,* he thought to himself. *I will move just when I'm ready.* He glanced back at Parliament, where the bodies of the five policemen still lay where they had been shot. *Funny,* he thought, *no one appeared to notice.* People walked along the street and paid no attention, but he knew the CCTV would have spotted it.

He saw the policeman walk around the front of the coach, waving his arms and telling Abdul to move. Abdul slipped the brake off and pushed his foot down on the accelerator. The coach jumped forward and, just for a second, he saw a surprised look on the policeman's face.

Constable Davis saw the coach move forward just as he got to the front. He held out his hands in front of him in an attempt to try and stop the vehicle. *The driver can't have seen me,* he thought, but when he looked up, he saw the smiling face of the driver looking down at him. Abdul felt a bump as the coach ploughed into the policeman and knocked him backward. He then felt the wheels bounce.

Abdul looked into his side mirror and saw the legs of the policeman being crushed by the back wheels of the coach. Turning back, he could see the shocked faces of pedestrians who had seen it all happen. He drove along and swung the coach across the road, smashing into a London taxi. Abdul then put the coach into reverse and sped backwards. Turning the wheel, he accelerated forward again and went back the way he had come. He had a last look towards the doors where Nathan and the others had disappeared through. The bodies of the policemen still lay outside. He noticed a couple of people kneeling beside the policeman he had run over.

★★★

Natalie Bennett was proud to be one of the few female members of the armed unit tasked with guarding Parliament. She was standing just outside the security barriers and was looking down the road. Suddenly, she heard an emergency call from central control. It said that gunshots had been heard inside parliament. She saw the other officers in her unit come over from the security cabin and heard her Unit Commander shout something. She turned and saw him waving to her to join the team. They began to run along the road in the direction of the main lobby entrance. As she ran with her team, a coach sped by and a second later she heard a crash. Looking over her shoulder, she saw the coach had hit a taxi. *Traffic can deal with that*, she thought and carried on running with her fellow officers towards the main lobby doors.

★★★

Rashid and Samir and two other fighters had been systematically shooting anyone in the main lobby area. Bodies were lying where they had been shot and blood was already pooling across the floor. People who had been wounded were screaming, but the gunmen were walking around and shooting them one by one.

Nathan and Sohail had piled eight of the holdalls together. Each holdall held 90 pounds of explosive. Above the sound of gunfire, Nathan wished Sohail good luck in his mission. He called over the group of four men who were going with Sohail and they all picked up two bags up each and followed the little Pakistani. They soon disappeared down a corridor.

Aashif appeared. "Some police are coming," he said.

Nathan looked up. "Put two men on the door."

Aashif waved two men to join him and disappeared back around the main entrance. Within a few seconds, Nathan heard the sound of Kalashnikovs being fired. Aashif reappeared, smiling.

"I don't think they will be rushing to get in this way."

Nathan picked up his holdall. "Come on, let's say hello to the Prime Minister."

***

Natalie Bennett, with her team of six, had run alongside Parliament and now drew level with the pathway that led to the main lobby doors. To her left, she saw four people kneeling beside a policeman in the road; to her right, the bodies of five officers lay on the floor near the main doors. Their machine guns were beside them. Her Commander held up his hand to indicate for them to stop, but before he could say anything three men appeared from the doors and started firing at them. Natalie threw herself down behind the metal barriers, as did the rest of her team. The sound of bullets hitting metal filled her ears. She looked towards her Commander and saw he was holding another officer who had been shot, while another colleague lay bleeding a little further along. Turning her head, she saw people running along the street. Her ears now became attuned to the sounds of screaming. There were at least five bodies lying on the other side of the road. She noticed that the people who had been kneeling beside the policeman in the road were also lying flat and not moving – out of safety, she thought, and and not because they had been shot.

CHAPTER FOURTEEN

Edward Sears, Liberal MP, had, with the rest of the House of Commons, just listened to a Scottish National Party MP make a speech, which criticised the government and said it had had no knowledge of the attacks. There was a lot of noise, with MPs on both sides shouting and heckling. The speaker called for order, as the Prime Minister was on his feet and waiting to respond.

Edward had been an MP for nine years and a Captain in the Army before that. He had doubts about the government denying any knowledge, but was willing to give them the benefit of the doubt. He knew from his experience in the army that even with the best of intelligence, something always came about that you didn't expect.

He was squashed between fellow MPs and hoped he would get called to make a speech later on. He sat back in his seat that was positioned near to the main doors – as far from the speaker as you could get. He could just about hear the Prime Minister above the shouting as he gave an answer to the Scottish Nationalist MP's question.

The speaker stood again to call for order, as the noise of heckling and shouting of abuse across the House became louder. The Prime Minister sat back down until the speaker had taken control. *It's getting crazy*, Edward thought. *No one is going to hear a thing, and God knows what the public watching on television will make of it.* Then, right in front of him, the main doors burst open and men carrying what he recognised as Kalashnikov rifles appeared. He froze in his seat when they started shooting.

***

Nathan, Samir, Rashid and Aashif stood outside the main doors that led to the House of Commons' chamber with seven other fighters. Two bodies of men dressed in old-style regalia lay on the floor in front of them.

"Well, brothers, we are here," Nathan said to the others. "Let's make them pay for the evil committed against us." He and Samir pushed on the doors and they swung open, revealing a packed house. They ran in. Samir immediately started to fire his Kalashnikov and the others followed quickly.

***

The speaker was feeling exasperated. The noise abated for a moment but then restarted as soon as he sat back down. He would have to take action and throw MPs out of the chamber if it continued. The country wanted to hear clear debate about the day's events. He knew passions were high, but this was not the spectacle he wanted to be shown on the television.

The Prime Minister was on his feet trying to respond to the last speaker, but even he was having trouble hearing him and he was only twenty feet away. He rose to his feet, shouting at the top of his voice for order. As he did, he scanned the whole house. His eyes caught the main doors opening and the group of men rushing in.

The speaker felt two sharp stabs in his chest, which threw him backwards into his chair. Looking down at where the pain was, he saw blood. He raised his hand to touch it and felt himself slowly slipping off the chair. He made a grab for the armrest, but was unable to stop and toppled forward.

***

Christian Sharp was in control of the live television pictures being broadcast from Parliament. He and his team had expected a lively debate, but the noise and disruption was unbelievable. He was calling out which camera to cut to when the Prime Minister sat back down and the speaker rose for the umpteenth time to call for order. The camera focused on the speaker. Christian watched, readying himself to move back to the Prime Minister when suddenly the speaker stumbled back into his chair and slipped down to the floor.

One of his assistants called out that there were demonstrators in the chamber. Christian looked to the screen his assistant was pointing at, but for a moment didn't believe what he was seeing. The men who had broken into the chamber appeared to be carrying guns.

"Cut the pictures!" he shouted.

All across the country, on all networks, the live pictures went blank.

★★★

Nathan ran along the central aisle with Aashif and Rashid. They had seen MPs disappearing around the back of the speaker's chair and out of the chamber through a door that led to the voting lobbies. Rashid fired a burst from his Kalashnikov at the fleeing backs of the MPs. He saw a number fall and the rest of them freeze. Samir and the others fired up into the galleries above, where the press and public were seated. Those not hit ducked and crawled away out of the doors. MPs all around the House were crouched down and trying to make themselves as small as possible.

Edwards Sears was one of those crouching down, but his army training kicked in when he saw the man in front of him shooting up at people in the gallery. He leapt forward and knocked the man over. The rifle span out of the man's hands. Edward rolled away from the man, grabbed the gun and turned back towards him. He saw the man begin to rise and fired without thinking, seeing the man fall backwards.

Samir saw one of the fighters fall out of the corner of his eye. He saw an MP grab the weapon that had dropped from the fighter's hand and fire. Samir was only a split second slower, shooting the MP holding the Kalashnikov. He then turned back and, in a rage at the shooting of his fellow fighter, shot three more MPs sitting on the benches in front of him.

Nathan reached the speaker's chair, pulled the dead body of the man dressed in a black cloak out of the way and jumped up onto it. The shooting stopped and there was silence, except for the agonised cries of those who had been wounded.

★★★

Abdul came up to the lights at Parliament Square and turned left, smashing two cars out of the way as he did so. He accelerated until he was level with the green in front of Westminster Abbey and turned the steering wheel hard to his left. He mounted the pavement, knocking over a group of tourist taking pictures, and bounced up the kerb. He passed between two tall trees, flattening the railings. People turned to see what the screaming was. The coach ploughed through more of the people standing around, who had previously been enjoying the sunshine on a trip to the abbey.

Abdul slowed slightly as he manoeuvred the coach to the angle he wanted. He saw people scattering as he accelerated again. The main doors of the abbey were getting closer and he felt the wheels jump as more tourists fell under the coach. His whole attention was on the doors. He slammed on the brakes and the coach skidded across the ground. Three people were just coming out of the building and, for a second, Abdul saw the surprised looks on their faces before the coach smashed into them.

Abdul was thrown forward at the sudden impact and the coach was brought to a halt. The seat belt cut into his shoulder. There was silence for a moment and then he heard screams. He sat back and waited.

★★★

The Commissioner had just taken a call that told him terrorists had broken into Parliament. Officers were currently involved in a gun battle with them at one of the doors. His phone went again and an officer told him that television pictures showed the terrorists had got into the main chamber.

The door to his office opened and Commander Sinclair and a number of other officers came in. "Have you heard the news?" Sinclair said.

"Yes," the Commissioner replied. "You better get in touch with the army." Sinclair nodded to Richards, who was at his side. "Everyone take a seat."

Richards left the office while all the others took their seats around the Commissioner's table. When everyone was sitting, he continued, "What is going on? Someone please tell me."

★★★

Tariq was sitting in a house in Tikrit in central Iraq, which had once been owned by a brigadier in the Iraqi Army under Saddam Hussein. He was watching the BBC on satellite television and could not believe that all the planning had come to such a great conclusion. He had seen the live pictures of the debate about the attacks in London go blank, followed by a news flash that there had been a terrorist attack on Parliament.

The men sitting with him cheered and patted each other on the back. They had had no idea why Tariq had called them earlier in the day to meet him. They had expected he had planned a big attack on the government, but when they arrived he had invited them to watch television with him. He had told them that they would see just how far they could strike at the enemy. True to his word, they had watched as news after news of attacks in London had come through. He explained how long the mission had been planned for and they were truly surprised that not one of them had heard a whisper about it. Tariq picked up a satellite telephone and dialled a number. He told the person on the other end of the line to deliver the letter.

***

The Commissioner and his senior officers, including Sinclair, had all made their way to the operations room. They had been joined by a number of army officers. The television screens had the live feed of pictures from inside Parliament. They also had the sound, and they watched and listened to what was happening.

***

Nathan called for quiet. He stood in front of the speaker's chair.

"We are here to deliver a message," he began. "Your country, along with other godless ones, has raped our lands, killed our brothers and sisters, and stolen our resources for centuries." He waved his arm around. "So you can live here, enrich yourselves and make plans to kill more of us, using your army whenever you decided it suited you. That is all at an end. We have today repaid some of the atrocities you have inflicted on us. Your people now know just how our brothers and sisters felt watching their loved ones pay with their lives because of your decisions. Our children were murdered by your soldiers. Your crocodile tears mean nothing to us. You have no right coming to our lands, saying who should govern us, telling us you know best, backing tyrants who torture us and turning a blind eye when it suits you. We decide who governs our lands, not you. We decide how we are governed, not you. Allah is our guide, not you." Nathan looked around. He saw his men with their guns trained on the crouching MPs. "I want you all to listen carefully. Everyone on this side," he pointed to his right at the government benches, "you will all move across to the other side when I tell you. Anyone who does not follow the order immediately will be shot." He waited for a moment to let his words sink in. "You sitting there," he pointed to the government front bench, which included the Prime Minister, "will stay where you are."

★★★

Police Constable Natalie Bennett was still crouched behind the metal barrier. Every so often she and another officer would return the fire that was coming from the main doors. Things had got a lot harder because the men inside had thrown hand grenades at them. The barriers had so far offered sufficient cover and they had not been hurt. One unfortunate officer lying nearby had died from gunshot wounds and another was propped up against the barrier.

She listened to her Unit Commander, who was giving information of what was happening on his radio. Up the road, she saw three black armoured Land Rovers moving slowly towards them. They seemed to take forever to reach their position.

When they finally did, they parked with their backdoors away from the shooting. More black-clad police officers jumped out, crouched and ran to the barriers, keeping low as the men in the entrance fired on them. Natalie heard the bullets pinging off the Land Rovers. Her Commander said that they were pulling back and they should help their injured colleague to the Land Rover. The newly arrived officers started a sustained barrage of fire towards the doors to pin down the men inside. Natalie and the rest of her unit helped their wounded colleague to the back of the vehicles and put him inside one. They all jumped in after him.

★★★

The Commissioner, along with all the others watching the television screens, was taken aback when they heard the voice of the man standing on the speaker's chair.

"He's American," he said. "Someone get onto the American Embassy and find out what's going on."

They continued to watch. The time was 15.40

★★★

Abdul was sitting quietly in the driver's seat of the coach. He started to recite a prayer as people gathered around. He knew the building he was about to destroy had crowned the kings and queens of Britain and was at the centre of the religion of the disbelievers. When it had been brought up as a possible target at their meetings, he had volunteered straightaway. It represented everything he despised about this country.

Abdul looked at the clock on the dashboard. It was 15.45. He took the mobile from his pocket and dialled ten, nine, eight. The space where luggage was usually loaded was packed with 900 pounds of explosives. His finger hovered over the send button. "*I will see you in paradise, Aashif,* he said quietly to himself.

The explosion tore through the doors of the entrance. The North tower was obliterated and anyone within 50 yards was killed instantly. Inside the abbey, the explosion travelled along the main aisle and into the roof, destroying centuries of work and bringing down brick and masonry onto those below. It showered the roads and pavements around the abbey, injuring many more.

★★★

In the House of Commons, the sound of a large explosion was clearly heard. Nathan looked down at the others and Aashif smiled back at him. He turned back to the MPs pointing to those on his right, "Everyone on this side move across now." As one, all the MPs on the government side rose and started to quickly move across the floor to the other side of the chamber, those seated beside the Prime Minister stayed still.

As more and more MPs crossed over, the other side started to get crowded. People were pushed further and further back, squashed together like sardines. Near the entrance, Samir and two of the fighters were shouting and pushing those moving too slowly. One MP received a blow to his back from a Kalashnikov. The pain caused him to turn. He was about to say something, but the fighter took his turning as a threat and shot him dead. The gunfire and the brutality of the act had the effect Nathan desired. The MPs were nearly climbing over each other to get away from the gunmen. When all the MPs except for the front bench were packed together on one side, Samir told one of the fighters to go and tell the men at the front entrance to join them.

***

"What are they doing?" the Commissioner asked no one in particular.

Sinclair offered his opinion. "They might be rigging up explosives," he said. "Having them packed tightly like that would maximise the casualties."

"Have your men arrived yet?" the Commissioner asked the Army General, who was watching the television.

"They will be at Parliament within ten minutes," he said. "Now, if you'll excuse me, Commissioner, I will go and organise things. Please keep in touch and pass on any more information you have." As he was about to leave, a duty officer came across.

"Sir," he said to the Commissioner, "there has been another big explosion."

"Where?" the Commissioner asked.

"Westminster Abbey," the duty officer said. "Reports say a coach drove up to the North entrance and exploded."

The Army General turned and left without saying anymore. The Commissioner watched him go and felt helpless. What was there that he could do?

Sinclair came to his shoulder. "Sir, we have officers inside the building. They are making their way towards the central chamber. Should I tell them to continue or hold back?"

The Commissioner looked at Sinclair, then back at the screen. The MPs, except for the Prime Minister and his front bench, were now tightly packed together. If they had rigged explosives, any attack might set them off.

"Tell them to hold back," he said. "We will let the army make that decision."

★★★

Bradley Simmonds had been the lead correspondent for Reuters in Iraq for fourteen months. He, along with everyone else in the Baghdad office, had been watching the events in London. The televisions in the office were all tuned to different stations: CNN, SKY, Al Jazeera and the BBC. He heard a voice call out his name from the door and turned to see a young man he recognised who worked at reception. He waved to him. The man crossed the floor and gave him an envelope, saying that it had been hand-delivered. Bradley thanked him and turned it over. His name was written on the front.

He tore the letter open and pulled out seven sheets of A4 paper. He noticed six had lists of names printed on them, with a country next to each name. The seventh sheet was a letter, which he read it and then read again.

It said it was from the Islamic Front of Iraq. Bradley knew this group to be one of the most active and ruthless groups fighting against the Iraqi Government. They also had ties to terrorist groups in Syria and North Africa. The letter said it was responsible for the attacks in London and that they wanted Bradley to pass on the lists of jailed freedom fighters to the British and American Governments. All these people would have to be released or the fighters in London would execute the Prime Minister, along with every other member of the government.

The letter stated that it would then prove its authenticity. It said that the base used to organise the attacks was a farm in Shropshire and it gave the address. Bradley shouted for quiet, then read the letter to the rest of the office. When he was done, he started issuing orders to people to get onto the

London office and to get the American Embassy on the phone. He gave the letter to a fellow journalist and told him to make a few copies, then send one to the British Embassy and one to the American Embassy. He should then scan it and send it to Reuters' London and New York offices, and put it out on the wire that a demand for the release of imprisoned terrorists has been received in exchange for the lives of the British MPs. Everyone started to move.

***

Sohail and his group were wandering through the corridors of the Houses of Parliament. They had heard the explosion and Sohail knew that Abdul had fulfilled his mission. Sohail didn't want to fail. He held out a map that was supposed to lead them to their target, but it didn't seem to be leading them there. They had shot scores of people dead that they had come across, but he was still lost. Their target had been the Elizabeth Tower that housed Big Ben. He had planned to rig the explosives and bring it crashing down.

As he reached the end of another corridor, he looked out of the window. It overlooked a courtyard. The main road ran alongside it and the entrance led to an underground car park.

When he had been researching Parliament, he had read of an attack by the IRA that killed a conservative MP by a bomb attached to his car. It exploded as he drove down the slope. From the window, he could see police directing hundreds of people out of the building, onto the road and away from the danger. He told his men to drop their bags and shoot down onto the fleeing people below. They immediately smashed the windows and started to fire into the crowd.

***

After a little rest, Constable Natalie Bennett and her unit were helping to evacuate people from Parliament. She was standing by the railings and directing everyone out of the gate, up towards Whitehall and away from danger. Every so often she turned her head back towards the entrance down the road, where her unit had been pinned down, one of her colleagues killed and another left in a serious condition. Two police-armoured Land Rovers were still sitting in place where they had stopped and she could see armed officers crouching down behind them. The body of a police officer still lay in the road, with scores of civilian casualties on the pavement on the other side.

A group of people ran out of the gates and she told them to keep running up the road away from danger. Suddenly, she heard gunfire and saw a number of people fall inside the courtyard. Two police officers, who were standing at the top of the slope of the car park, also went down. She scanned the windows above and saw machine guns firing down. She moved to get under cover. It was just in time, as bullets struck the ground where she had been standing. She aimed upwards and let off a burst from her machine gun. She couldn't see if she had hit anyone, but it gave her satisfaction to know she was fighting back.

★★★

Sinclair had left the operations room with Richards and gone back to his office. "Well, some good news," Richards said. "The two terrorists who started shooting in Oxford Circus have been cornered."

"Where are they?" Sinclair asked.

"They're in the Liberty department store," Richards replied, "but they have left carnage in their wake. So far, according to the senior officer, there are forty members of the public dead there and many more seriously wounded – but that's without whatever's happening inside the store."

Sinclair sat back in the chair. "Why didn't we get a clue that something was going to happen?"

Richards didn't answer. He was just as mystified as his boss. There was a knock at the door and an officer came in. He handed Sinclair a message. Sinclair read it and passed it to Richards. "A breakthrough at last," he said, opening a draw in his desk and pulling out a map that he spread across the table. "According to that," he pointed at the message, "they came from a farm in Shropshire." He traced his finger across the map. "Here, and the motorway network is not too far away."

Richards put down the message. "That would certainly fit in with the tracking we did."

Sinclair picked up the map and began to fold it. "Get onto the midlands unit and have them raid the place right away, but tell them to be careful." Richards picked up the phone.

Sinclair walked over to the office window. Looking out, he could see the Houses of Parliament in the distance. There was also a pall of smoke rising from the bomb that had exploded at Westminster Abbey. He had no idea just what was coming next. The day had been so confused. He had to think hard about all the explosions and attacks to try and remember just how many there had been. He finally turned away from the window. "Any more news on the terrorists in the Liberty department store?"

"We have officers in there," Richards said. "Apparently, they are on the first floor, but are heavily armed so it's taking time to get to them."

"What about casualties?" Sinclair said, sitting back down.

"Not good," Richards replied, "but I don't have detailed figures. The officer in charge has said that there are many dead inside the store."

The phone on the desk rang and Sinclair picked it up. He listened for a few moments, then said, "We will be right there," and put it back down. "We have to go to the Commissioner's office. Bring all the reports we have about today's events."

CHAPTER FIFTEEN

Nathan was standing with Rashid and Aashif in front of the speaker's chair. He knew they were being watched by the police.

"We give it half an hour," he said to the others. "Tariq would have sent the message by now and I'm sure that the police will try and make contact with us soon." He turned to look at the MPs, who were packed tightly together on his left. "Aashif, you have the list." Aashif nodded. "Start to sort out the Jews."

Aashif walked away, passing in front of the Prime Minister and his cabinet colleagues. He stopped and addressed the packed ranks. "Listen," he shouted, "I am going to call out some names. Those called will come forward and sit here." He pointed to the floor space in the centre aisle and began to call out names.

Samir had spoken to the two fighters, who had been at the main entrance. He gave them instructions and they left the chamber, again taking two holdalls with them. Samir and another fighter closed the main doors to the chamber. Nathan spoke with Rashid, who called three fighters to him and left through the door behind the speaker's chair. He then watched as the men and women whose names were being called out start to make their way out of the packed seating area to the front. Aashif had them sit next to each other on the floor, so that a long line was starting to form.

Samir walked down the chamber towards Nathan. As he passed the Prime Minister, he heard a voice say, "What are you doing?" He stopped and turned. It was the Home Secretary.

"Who gave you permission to speak?" Samir shouted at him.

The Home Secretary, who was not used to being spoken to like that and did not seem to realise the danger, continued, "I asked what you are doing."

Samir stood looking at him for a moment as Nathan walked to join him. "You ask what we are doing," Samir said. "Are you stupid? What does it look like? And, I repeat, who gave you permission to speak?"

The Prime Minister, who was sitting on the Home Secretary's right, put a hand on his arm to quieten him, but the Home Secretary continued, "What is the point of all this?"

Nathan was now by Samir's side. "I think he does not understand English," Samir said, looking at Nathan.

"We made our statement," Nathan said. "Outside, our demands have been passed to the governments of various countries – yours included. Although, with you being in here, you wouldn't know that. It will be up to the people outside whether you live or die."

The Prime Minister said nothing, but the Home Secretary spoke again. "You have no hope of succeeding."

Samir levelled his Kalashnikov and fired. Two bullets hit the Home Secretary in the head and his body fell lifelessly across the Prime Minister. "You won't be around to find out," Samir said. There were screams and groans from all around the chamber. "Anyone else who speaks without being spoken to will be shot."

Nathan looked up. He knew the cameras were watching. "You have seen that we will not be messed around. You have two hours to tell us our demands are being met," he called out. Samir grabbed the Home Secretary's shirt collar and pulled his body off the Prime Minister, dropping it to the floor.

Nathan turned to the Prime Minister. "Do you think we will win?" he said.

"I have no idea," the Prime Minister replied.

"Come on, now," Nathan said. "You have seen what we have achieved already. Surely you don't doubt we will triumph."

"I can't see what you have achieved except misery and pain to thousands of people," he said.

Nathan took the seat next to him, where the Home Secretary had just been seated. "Precisely," he said. "It is exactly what you and all the Western governments have been doing to the people of Iraq and the whole of the Middle East. You want to know what our demands are?"

The Prime Minister turned his head to look at Nathan. "What are they?" he asked.

"The release of 1,000 freedom fighters held by governments all around the world." Nathan looking directly into the Prime Minister's eyes and continued, "Do you think that will happen?" The Prime Minister made no reply. "Come on, you can talk to me. We are close friends now. My friends and I have waited years to meet you. Aashif, over there," Nathan pointed to Aashif, who was standing behind the line of seated Jewish MPs, "is from Birmingham. He was called a terrorist because he fought for his fellow Muslim brothers and sisters in Iraq. Surely that's not right? Now, I ask you again, as one friend to another, do you think we will succeed?"

The Prime Minister swallowed, then said, "No, I don't think you will."

Nathan smiled. He heard Samir laugh. "Your government won't negotiate with terrorists, is that right?" Nathan asked.

"That is the British Government's position," the Prime Minister replied.

"The British Government's position," Nathan repeated, "but I have the British Government in front of me, so perhaps we can come to some deal now. I am sure you don't want to be responsible for any more deaths, do you?" The Prime Minister said nothing. Nathan continued, "You have the power now to save the lives of hundreds of people. Don't you want to do that?"

"I am in no position to speak for other governments," the Prime Minister replied, shaking his head.

"Spoken like a politician," Nathan whispered into the Prime Minister's ear. He sat back. "But you can speak for the British Government, so why don't you have a meeting now?" He gestured to the other members of the government seated alongside him. "Decide what your position is. I will give you fifteen minutes." Nathan stood up. "Go on, make a decision."

The time was 16.15.

★★★

Sinclair and Richards arrived at the Commissioner's office. They were shown into it and led to a large meeting room. Around a table in the centre were seated sixteen other people. The Head of MI5 and the Head of MI6 were there, as well as some other senior police officers, the army general he had seen earlier and two other army personnel. There were also others who he had never met before. He and Richards took the two remaining empty seats, which were positioned about halfway down the table.

"Everyone is here," the Commissioner began. "I won't worry about introducing everyone, as I want to get straight down to things. I would like to start with a briefing of what we know." He looked at Sinclair. "Would you begin?"

"Sir," Sinclair answered, looking down at the papers in front of him and scanning the information. He looked up. "The group claiming responsibility for the attacks is the

Islamic Front of Iraq. It was they who sent the demands to Reuters in Baghdad. In the message was the address of a farm in Shropshire where they say the operation was planned. We have officers on their way to raid the site.

"The two terrorist who launched the attack in Oxford Street are now surrounded in the Liberty department store just off Regents Street. We hope to bring that to an end soon. Reports of the explosion at Westminster Abbey say there has been a significant loss of life and the building has been badly damaged. The fire brigade have reported that they have the fires caused by the bombs in Oxford Street under control, but Selfridges is not yet safe to enter in order to ascertain the full extent of the damage or casualties.

"The bomb at the Shard has caused widespread damage – not only to the building itself, but to the surrounding area. Again, there is a great loss of life. Covent Garden has now been declared safe, but there were a great number of casualties. The bombs from this morning are still being assessed, but the feeling is that the tunnels and Heathrow will not be useable for months, if not years." Sinclair stopped reading and looked up.

"Do we have any news on the number of casualties yet?" the Commissioner asked in a low voice.

Sinclair shuffled the papers in front of him. He looked down, then looked up again. "We don't have the full extent, sir, as we haven't yet assessed the Shard and Westminster Abbey explosions, and the situation in the Liberty department store and Parliament have not finished."

"But do we have some idea without those?" the Commissioner asked.

Sinclair again moved the papers around in front of him. He glanced down at the latest figure. "Sir, the latest casualty figures from all emergency services gathered in so far, from all the sites, is 2,362. Over 1,709 are injured – some very seriously."

"And these figures are without the latest bombs?" the Commissioner asked.

"Yes, sir," Sinclair replied.

The Commissioner coughed to clear his throat. "I think everyone around this table realises the situation we are in. We don't have anyone from the government with us, for obvious reasons, but the head of the civil service has come along." The Commissioner pointed to a man on the other side of the table to Sinclair. "He will be able to give us an idea of what the government's thinking would be. I want us to get an understanding of these people and what action we intend to take, as we have so far been on the back foot. I want us to change that—"

"Sorry, Commissioner," the Head of MI5 interrupted. She sat forward. "I hope we are not going to make any hasty decisions just so it would seem we are doing something."

"We will make any decisions collectively," the Commissioner continued, looking at her. "I hope we will all be of the same mind. Now, if I could ask the General to bring us up to speed on what the army are doing."

The General sat up straight. "Thank you, Commissioner. I have senior officers on the ground around Parliament who have assessed the situation. A squadron of the special boat service have entered the building from the Thames side. They have managed to evacuate staff that they found hiding. We know that the terrorists are not just in the main chamber, but are wandering the corridors and shooting indiscriminately. I have dispatched a unit of the SAS to find and neutralise them. Two further units of the SAS are ready to attack the main chamber once we have worked out what they are up to. We have secured the roof and, at this very time, another unit is making its way to the central lobby. Once all my men are in position, we have to decide whether to attack."

The Head of MI5 again spoke, "General, the whole of the government are being held hostage. I don't think we should do anything rash."

The General turned and looked down the table. "We don't intend being rash, just clinical."

"Thank you, General," the Commissioner said. "Now, if I could ask Sir David Greville to give us the thoughts of the government."

The man sitting opposite Sinclair laid his hands on the table. Sir David Greville had been head of the civil service for six years, was a lifelong civil servant and this was the second government he had served. "Commissioner, the government's position has always been not to negotiate with terrorists, but I don't think we have been in a situation like this before. We are talking about the government and all the elected MPs of the country being held hostage. I have to agree with the Head of MI5. This is not a situation to rush into. We could have a constitutional crisis if the leaders of all parties and many MPs are killed. The question may arise of who should run the country."

"Thank you," the Commissioner said and looked further down the table. "What is the view of the foreign office?"

A well-dressed man with a deep sun tan looked around the table, before speaking, "We have spoken to our allies, especially those holding any of the names that appear on the list handed to Reuters' Baghdad office. Some have said they may release, while others have said under no circumstances. I hold no great hope that we can persuade many of them. The Israelis and Americans have flatly said no, but the Europeans may be more amenable. Even so, considering the short amount of time that their demands allow us, I see no chance of success."

"So we need to buy ourselves some time?" the Commissioner asked.

"I think we should try and make contact with them," the Head of MI5 said. "See if there is any way we can bring this to a close without more killing – or, at least, try."

A knock on the door interrupted the discussion and an officer entered. He walked to the Commissioner and handed him a note. He then turned without waiting for a reply and left the meeting room. The Commissioner read it and looked up at the others around the table. "The Home Secretary has been shot dead," he said. Not one word was spoken around the table at the news. The Commissioner put down the message. "Can we have some ideas of how we should tackle this situation?"

It was the General who spoke first. "I think this proves that we must not wait much longer. Our units will be in place soon and they should be allowed to carry out their mission straightaway. The more time we give the terrorists to get organised, the harder things become."

"I have to disagree," the Head of MI5 said. "We need to make contact and get a dialogue going. We are talking about the whole of the British Government being held hostage."

"I don't think we should rush things," Sinclair joined in. "I agree that we must try and open some kind of conversation with the terrorists."

The man from MI6 spoke, "We know there's not much chance of foreign governments agreeing to release the prisoners on the list that has been passed to us, so I don't think we should wait. We need to take action as soon as possible."

Sir David Greville leant forward. "I think we need to consider the consequences of any action we decide to take, because if things go wrong," he stopped, and let the silence hang in the air, "the Head of MI5 is right. If something was to happen to the whole of the government and the opposition, the country would basically be left with no leadership. In that vacuum, anything could happen. I, for one, would like to see some negotiation with the terrorists if at all possible."

The Commissioner drummed his fingers on the table. He knew there was no way the people around the table were going to agree, but they had to leave this meeting with a plan. He looked around the table. "We need to do something," he said. "I want us to come up with a plan."

***

Sohail decided that if he couldn't bring the Elizabeth Tower and Big Ben down, he would do as much damage as he could instead. He and his group retraced their steps back the way they had come, passing open office doors that showed dead bodies that had been shot where they had been working. He stopped when he came to a junction of corridors and looked at the map. Although he didn't trust it now, he hoped it was somehow right. It showed that they were in the centre of Parliament, on the first floor.

Kneeling down in the centre of the corridor, he wired up four of the holdalls that held explosives. He checked the time. It was 16.20. *Twenty minutes should do*, he thought. He set the timer, stood up and waved the four fighters to follow him. They moved along the corridor, turned a corner and continued on their way, passing more open doors that showed their handy work. They came to a corner. Sohail turned it and saw, about halfway down, the backs of eight black-clad figures. He immediately opened fire and was joined by two other fighters who had turned the corner after him. Sohail saw two of the black-clad figures fall and the rest throw themselves into cover through open doors. He and the other fighters retreated back around the corner.

He knelt down and told two fighters to keep shooting

down the corridor. Sohail decided this place was as good as any to plant the rest of his explosives, so he and the other two fighters piled the bags together. He heard the sound of the Kalashnikovs firing and the return fire of the black figures as he began to wire up the bags. It only took him a minute, as he knew every wire and switch by heart. Just as he finished, he heard the shout, "Grenade!" and ducked behind the bags. There was a loud bang and he heard a scream as the fighter to his right caught the force of the blast and fell down. Sohail told one of the others to return the favour and the man threw two of his grenades down the corridor. The sound of them exploding followed quickly and two of the fighters resumed their firing.

Sohail stood up. He had set the explosives for ten minutes. He called the others to join him. They moved the injured fighter to the corner, gave him his rifle and a number of grenades, and Sohail wished him good luck. He told him to hold the infidels off as long as he could. Sohail turned and, with the other three following, ran down the corridor away from the fighting. They came to a junction of corridors. Sohail didn't want to go back the way they had come, as he knew the other bags he had wired up would be going off very soon. He turned right in a different direction. He still had the map, but didn't bother to look at it now as he had lost all trust in it.

CHAPTER SIXTEEN

Tariq had the satellite phone to his ear as he looked out of the window across the rooftops of Tikrit. He had a warm feeling inside. Everything that he had hoped to achieve with this attack had come to pass so far. However, he knew the end game was just beginning. He had discussed it with the others over many nights during the planning stages. Every scenario had been gone over, but now, having reached their goal, there were only two left. Everyone knew that the demands were unlikely to be met, but they would ask anyway. If they were refused and there was a further loss of life, people would ask why the prisoners hadn't been released and more people hadn't been saved. If they did release them, they succeeded. It was win–win. He heard someone pick up the phone.

***

Bradley Simmonds was at his desk. All around him, his staff were gathering any information they could find on the Islamic Front of Iraq. He had fielded calls from the New York and London offices, asking for more information on the group. He felt his mobile vibrate in his pocket. He took it out and glanced at the number, It said "No caller ID." He shrugged and answered it.

"Mr Simmonds, my name is Tariq. You got my letter earlier today, telling you of a property we owned in England."

Bradley put his hand over the phone and shouted for quiet.

Everyone turned towards him and stopped talking. "Sorry, what was your name?" Bradley said.

"Mr Simmonds, please let's not have any games. You don't work for the CIA. If you did, we would have killed you already. We know about your lovely flat in the green zone you share with your Japanese girlfriend. If we thought you were a spy, you would be dead. However, all your reports have been fair, so I have chosen you to be our conduit to the infidel governments."

Bradley had heard the name of the man on the other end of the line quite clearly. He knew he was one of the most wanted men in Iraq. "What is it you want?" he asked.

"That's better, Mr Simmonds. Now we have shown that we are who we say we are, I daresay the English police are at the farm. So far, though, I have seen nothing that says any of the names on the list are going to be released. If that doesn't start to happen soon, we will take further action in London to show that we are not to be trifled with. Mr Simmonds, you will pass our message directly to London. Make sure it is given to the highest authorities." Bradley heard laughing coming down the line. "Sorry, Mr Simmonds, for laughing, but I know you can't give the message to the government as they are otherwise engaged. Instead, make sure it goes to the top of the police force. Ensure this is done, Mr Simmonds. I wouldn't want anything to happen to you or your lovely lady." The line went dead.

Bradley sat for a moment. He felt chilled. The voice on the other end of the phone had been calm and polite, but there was a menace to it that frightened him – and he had been in some war-torn, dangerous places. Bradley placed his mobile on the desk. All his staff were still looking towards him. "Someone get me a direct line to the London office."

★★★

Tariq turned away from the window and looked at the men sitting around him. "Okay, brothers, let's disperse. I will be in touch in a day."

The men rose to their feet and bade him goodbye. When they had all left the house, Tariq went out into the back garden, walked to the far corner and opened a door. It led into a back alley, where a man on a motorcycle looked up. Tariq climbed on the seat behind him and the motorbike sped off through the back alleys of Tikrit. Tariq knew he would never return to that house. Too many people knew it existed now and word would find its way to Baghdad. The Americans or Iraqi special forces would soon come knocking.

***

The SAS men were slowly making their way from room to room while firing at the gunmen at the end of the corridor. They were now only twenty feet away and the shooting stopped. The captain in charge of the unit signalled two of his men to move forward. They had their backs against the wall as they slowly edged nearer the corner. When they reached it, one held up a mirror and used it to look around. He could see one man lying on the ground with a Kalashnikov at his feet. He sprang around the corner and fired two bullets into the body. His partner joined him and scanned the corridor ahead. "Clear!" he shouted, and the rest of the unit came up to join them.

The captain knelt down to look at the dead body. He glanced to his left and saw two black holdalls. "Check the bags," he said.

The timer had just reached zero as the SAS trooper knelt down to look inside. The explosion killed all of them, sending their bodies, along with tons of the Westminster building, into the River Thames.

★★★

Rashid and the other fighters came back into the chamber from behind the speaker's chair, closing the doors behind them. "We have set things up," Rashid said to Nathan, who nodded. They were suddenly shaken by the sound of a large explosion. Dust and the odd bit of masonry came down from the ceiling above. Everyone seemed to duck momentarily.

"What you reckon?" Nathan said to Rashid.

"I'm not sure. Could be Sohail or maybe the army have brought up some heavy armour to break in," Rashid replied.

Nathan looked at the time. It was 16.30. He walked over to Samir, who was standing in front of the government benches and watching the Prime Minister talking to the ministers around him. Rashid followed.

Samir nodded as they came and stood next to him. "They have been chattering away like old women," he said.

Nathan stepped forward. "Prime Minister, have you come to a decision? Will you negotiate with us?"

The Prime Minister looked up as all his colleagues sat back. "We are willing to discuss things and settle this without any more loss of life."

"A wise decision," Nathan said.

★★★

The Commissioner was still going around the table and asking for the thoughts of those present, when the door opened and an officer hurried in. He stood by the Commissioner. "Sir, there's been an explosion in Parliament," he said. "I think you should see what's happening."

"Is it in the main chamber?" the Commissioner asked.

"No, sir," the officer replied, "but it was a big explosion

and has taken out a large section of the building on the south side overlooking the Thames."

The officer went to the door and called out. Two policemen entered, pushing a large widescreen television into the room. It was placed behind and to the left of the Commissioner.

"This will give pictures of the live feed from inside the main chamber in Parliament," he told the Commissioner. He switched the television on and the picture appeared. "We still have the sound and can hear everything they say, but they haven't revealed very much about themselves. We have a few names that we are checking out, but not much more."

***

Nathan sat down next to the Prime Minister. "So, do you have any proposals to put to us?" he asked.

"You know we don't have any say over what other governments do with imprisoned terrorists," the Prime Minister said.

"I think I asked what your proposals were," Nathan replied. "What other governments do or don't do is neither here nor there – although you and I know that you could sway governments with promises of help or other things." Nathan smiled, and he heard Samir and Rashid chuckle. "Let's not beat around the bush, Prime Minister. You know our demands. A list has been delivered with the names of 1,000 freedom fighters from here and abroad. They have to be released. You will then arrange for a plane to take myself and my friends to safety. We will not negotiate on any of these points."

"You must understand that those things cannot happen quickly," the Prime Minister replied.

"We are not stupid, Prime Minister, but we will expect some action to be taken," Nathan said.

"You can't honestly hope to be successful," the Prime Minister said. "What will you have achieved? You are asking the impossible."

"Prime Minister," Nathan began, as he stood back up, "I had hoped you would be more pragmatic, but you still talk like you are dealing with some local issue that will be forgotten tomorrow." He turned. "Samir, get the list off Aashif."

Samir walked down the aisle to Aashif, who was standing with another fighter behind the Jewish MPs on the floor. Samir took the list from Aashif and came back to Nathan, who turned to the Prime Minister. "It would seem that you think you are in control of the situation. I know your security forces are watching and listening to everything we do." He waved his hand above at the cameras. "I would have thought you would be willing to concede that we hold the bargaining chips – or maybe you have a superiority complex and don't think we are worthy of negotiating with. Perhaps you think you can buy more time before your special forces attack. Unfortunately, however, you and your friends watching are sadly mistaken." Suddenly, the whole chamber shook to the sound of a large explosion. It was much bigger than the first they had heard not so long ago. Again, pieces of the ceiling cascaded onto them.

"That sounds like another part of your famous old building being destroyed," Nathan continued, "but let us get back to our demands. You, the British Government, can set the ball rolling by agreeing to our demands. I am sure you can lean on other governments to help. We all know there are ways." Nathan looked at the Prime Minister, who made no reply. "I can see that all your countrymen and women killed today don't really mean anything to you."

"That's not true," the Prime Minister said, his voice rising.

"But you are willing to risk more of them being killed than agree to our demands," Nathan said, "or is it that they are faceless people you have never met. The workers of your country who you only speak to when you want their vote."

"You have murdered them, not me," the Prime Minister answered.

"Ah! So it's murder," Nathan said, smiling down at the Prime Minister. "I thought the term you used was collateral damage. When your planes or drones or even your soldiers kill innocent people, you don't say it's murder. It's collateral damage – and you say how sorry you are. Well, myself and my friends are sorry for the collateral damage we have caused. Is that alright with you? We have apologised."

"There is no comparison," the Prime Minister said.

"No comparison," Nathan shouted. "Are you saying the lives of women and children in Iraq or Palestine, or anywhere else you send your troops to, are not equal to your women and children?" The Prime Minister said nothing. "Well, let's look at things another way," Nathan continued. "Samir, what is the name at the top of that list?"

Samir glanced down at the paper he was holding. "Sir Henry Blackmore," he called out.

The Prime Minister glanced to his left. Two seats away, the Foreign Secretary looked up. "Ah, Foreign Secretary," Nathan said, looking in his direction, "you are the architect of British Foreign policy with the Prime Minister. From our research, you have known each other for a long time. You even went to the same school. So, Prime Minister, would you call the Foreign Secretary a close friend?"

"Yes, we are close friends. That's no surprise to anyone."

"Did you know that his grandfather was Jewish?" Nathan asked.

"Yes, I did, but what's that got to do with anything?"

"Well, it could explain why you turn a blind eye to the murder of thousands of women and children in Gaza by the

Jews' bombing, or the murder of our brothers and sisters in the West Bank, or, of course, the ethnic cleansing of Palestinians from areas so that the Jews can build settlements and take over the area. You do nothing. You even use your veto in the United Nations to stop criticism of Israel. Now, Foreign Secretary, stand up and walk over there."

The Foreign Secretary stood up and walked past the Prime Minister to the line of seated Jewish MPs. As he reached them, Aashif grabbed him and threw him to the floor. "Now, Prime Minister," he continued, turning back to face him, "all those people killed this morning – which we have agreed were collateral damage – you knew none of them. However, the Foreign Secretary here is a close friend. He also happens to be someone who backs the State of Israel against our Muslim brothers and sisters in Palestine. He is our enemy and your friend." Nathan looked up and waved his arm. Aashif stepped forward and levelled his Kalashnikov at the back of the Foreign Secretary's head. "If he was to be killed, would he be collateral damage or would you save your good friend by agreeing to our demands? You won't agree if it's the lives of people outside, the normal everyday working people of this country, but what about your close friend?"

The silence hung in the air. The eyes of every MP were on the Foreign Secretary, who sat with his head down. Aashif was behind him, holding the Kalashnikov just inches from his head.

The time was 16.45.

★★★

Sohail and the other three fighters were thrown to the floor by the second explosion. Alarm bells were ringing out and thick smoke was drifting along the corridors. Sohail told the others

207

to follow him and they all crouched down to stay below the smoke. Sohail led them further away from the explosion and came to some stairs. As he started down them, he thought he heard voices and stopped, holding up his hand. His men froze behind him. Sohail strained his ears and he again heard voices from below. He couldn't make out what was being said, but there were certainly people on the stairway. He inched back up the stairs, the fighters just behind him. He wanted to get back down to the ground floor, but didn't want to get involved in another fight. The smoke was getting thicker. There was clearly a fire taking hold where the last bomb had exploded.

***

"Wait," the Prime Minister called out.

Nathan turned towards the Prime Minister. "So, do we have a deal?"

"Yes," the Prime Minister uttered, his voice breaking. "We will do a deal."

"That's good," Nathan said. "Seeing we trust no one but you, we will release you to make the arrangements. Everyone in here is in your hands – their lives will be saved or lost on your decisions. We see you care about your friends, so we will allow you to go. Stand up." The Prime Minister stood. Nathan continued, "There are a number of things you need to do quickly. First, all police and any troops in the building must be withdrawn. If we see any, or anyone starts attacking us, we will kill everyone in here." The Prime Minister nodded. "Secondly, you will arrange for a coach to take us to an airport, where a plane will be waiting and will be fully fuelled to take us where we wish." The Prime Minister nodded again. "Thirdly, you will arrange for the release of all our brothers and sisters held in British jails to be brought to the airport to get on the plane with us. Do you understand our demands?"

"Yes, I do," the Prime Minister said.

"You have until 19.00," Nathan said, standing in front of the Prime Minister and looking straight at him. "If the coach is not there at that time, we will carry out our threats. I will call you using one of your minister's phones." Nathan waved to Rashid, who came and took the arm of the Prime Minister. Nathan looked up at the cameras above. "You heard that," he shouted. "The Prime Minister is being released. Withdraw your forces from the building now and we will allow the Prime Minister to walk out of the main door in five minutes. We don't want to find anyone in the building. Also, just so you know, we still have a few surprises for you outside. We will demonstrate once again how vulnerable you are."

★★★

The Commissioner and the others had been watching and listening to everything that had gone on. He turned to the officer who had brought the television in. "Get the message out that all police officers in the Parliament building are to pull back and leave now."

The officer nodded and quickly left the room.

"You are not going along with that, are you?" the General said.

The Commissioner looked at him. "I just heard the Prime Minister say he agreed with those demands and until he tells me any different, that is what I intend on doing."

"You should give the order for the SAS to pull back, General," the Head of MI5 said, as she looked down the table.

The General turned his head. "This is ridiculous. We are in a situation that demands action. We can't possibly let them walk out of there."

"The Commissioner is right," she said. "We all heard the Prime Minister agree to those demands. You must give the order for your troops to pull out."

Sinclair could feel the tension in the air. He knew there was never going to be complete agreement over what they should do, but with the Prime Minister being released and saying he would meet the terrorist's demands, it had taken the need for any decision-making away. He saw the look of relief on the Commissioner's face.

The General looked around the table. Everyone returned his stare. "Okay, I will give the order." He turned and told one of his officers to give the order. The officer rose from his seat and left the room.

It was Sinclair who spoke next, "The American terrorist made a threat that they would demonstrate how vulnerable we were. I am assuming that means another attack."

"He may have meant something in Parliament," the Commissioner said.

"No, Commander Sinclair is right," the Head of MI5 spoke out. "The threat was clearly a demonstration that they can still hurt us."

"Sir," Sinclair spoke directly to the Commissioner, "the vehicles that travelled in convoy have all been accounted for. They were used in all the big explosions, except one – a Royal Mail van."

"So you think it's another big bomb?" the Commissioner asked.

"Yes I do, sir," Sinclair said, "and with your permission, I would like to go and start the search for it."

"Get on your way," the Commissioner answered. Sinclair, with Richards beside him, stood and hurried from the room.

"Commissioner, may I suggest," the Head of MI5 began, "that you have a vehicle outside the main doors to pick the

Prime Minister up. It should take him straight to Downing Street and we should all make our way there to meet him."

"I was just going to do that," the Commissioner answered, with annoyance in his voice. "I will arrange it now and everyone should make their way to Downing Street."

The time was 16.55.

★★★

Sinclair reached his office. He had Richards make a number of phone calls to call a meeting of senior officers. It would take them ten to fifteen minutes to arrive. In the meantime, they would go over everything that had happened and look for some kind of pattern. Sinclair pulled out all the files, pictures and information they had on the day's events. He then laid out the pictures of the vehicles, which had been blown up from CCTV, across the table. Above each vehicle, he placed a picture of the target of their explosion. It left one Royal Mail van.

CHAPTER SEVENTEEN

Gunnar Anderson had been sleeping. He sat up and rubbed his eyes, looked at the clock on the dashboard and was happy to see it hadn't yet passed 17.00. He was annoyed with himself, though. He should have stayed awake, but the day had been long and the waiting around had made it seem longer. There was a parking ticket on the window. Gunnar smiled. *Not one I will be paying*, he thought.

He had grown up in Stockholm and his family had lived in a big social housing estate on the outskirts of the city. His father had been a bus driver and his mother had worked as a cleaner. Life had been unremarkable and at school he had found nothing that interested him. In the end, he hadn't even bothered to turn up, instead spending the time wandering into the city centre. He had then started to commit crime in order to get money. It wasn't long before he was arrested a number of times and found himself in and out of prison.

It was during his third prison sentence that he met a Swede who was a Muslim. They had shared a cell together. The Muslim was there because he had been part of a demonstration outside the American Embassy that had turned violent. He had been convicted of assaulting a police officer. The two months spent in his company had changed Gunnar's outlook on life.

When he was released he had not returned home, but instead went to live with Mohamed and his brother. He had converted to Islam and had soon joined the demonstrations against Israel and America. He went to prayers daily and became a trusted and respected member of the small group.

He never went back to see his family. After a year, he and Mohamed had travelled to Turkey and crossed into Iraq to join the fight against America. It was there that he had joined the Islamic Front of Iraq and had met Nathan and the rest of the group.

All day he had heard the radio giving out reports of the attacks and the successful taking of Parliament, and now it was his turn to follow the path that had been chosen for him. The time had come.

★★★

Rashid and Samir had the Prime Minister between them as the doors to the main chamber were opened by two other fighters. Nathan stood just behind them. "Remember, Prime Minister, 19.00. The coach must be there by then and if not, we will kill everyone in here and there will be more attacks outside."

The Prime Minister nodded. Rashid and Samir led him into the lobby, where bodies still lay where they had been shot. The Prime Minister was taken aback by the number.

As they reached the main entrance, Rashid quickly glanced outside. He saw nothing but some police cars parked in the main road. "Go," he said to the Prime Minister and pushed him outside.

The Prime Minister stepped over the dead bodies of the police officers who had been killed in the initial attack and made his way to the waiting police car. It was sitting beside the black Land Rovers with its blue lights flashing.

Rashid watched the Prime Minister walk away from the building and turned back to go to the main chamber with Samir. Suddenly, he heard a shout, and he and Samir turned to their left. They saw Sohail and three other fighters emerge from a corridor.

"Ah, the magician," Rashid said, smiling, as they walked over and embraced. "Come, you will have to tell everyone what you have been up to." He put his arm around Sohail's shoulders and they walked back to the main chamber.

★★★

The five o'clock news was just about to start on the BBC. Kay Sandford and Bill Secombe had been on air since the first attack on the Dartford Bridge, and it had been decided that they would stay on air to keep continuity until a change was made at 18.00.

All day, they had interviewed political personalities, terrorism experts and foreign political figures to get some insight and background into what was going on. Although tired, both felt that today was one of those days that changed everything. Being at the centre of such an event was what their careers were all about.

News had just been passed to them that the Prime Minister was being released. They would lead with that story, followed by the latest from Westminster Abbey and the Shard. They would also be reporting on the fire that had broken out in the Parliament building itself, which was blazing unchecked as the fire brigade couldn't get near to it with the terrorists inside. Sitting with them, waiting to be interviewed, was an ex-Foreign Secretary and a woman from the American state department to give their opinions on the terrorists' demands.

The floor manger held up his hand and counted down from five. As the music from the opening credits could be heard in the background, Kay sat up straighter. The floor manager pointed at her. "This is the five o'clock news with Kay Sandford and Bill Secombe. We continue with the latest from the sites of the explosions that have torn through London today. We lead with the news that the Prime Minister has been released by the terrorists. We will shortly be going to one of our correspondents near the Parliament building for the latest, but first a round-up from the sites of the explosions."

★★★

"Any ideas?" Sinclair asked. He glanced around the group, who were looking at the map.

"I can't see a pattern," Richards replied, "except for the fact that they've attacked some of London's most important and iconic infrastructure. Apart from that, I can't see anything."

"Could it be another attack on a bridge?" asked one of the officers.

"We have every vehicle crossing every bridge over the Thames being checked," Richards said. "Anyway, nothing is moving very fast because of the traffic problems. Any Royal Mail van would stand out."

"Are we sure it's a Royal Mail van? Could they have changed vehicles?" another officer asked.

"It's a possibility," Sinclair said, "but I doubt it. The amount of explosives used in these attacks would make it hard to change vehicles, and so far it's been all those that travelled in convoy from the farm. I don't see them changing their pattern now. By the way, what's happening at the farm?" He turned to Richards.

"It's been sealed off and, after all the explosions so far, army bomb disposal experts are going in to check things over first. It might be some time before we know anything."

"So where is this van?" Sinclair said.

★★★

215

The Prime Minister sat with a large glass of scotch in his hand. A doctor had checked him over, but the Prime Minister had dismissed him quickly. He wanted to get on with things.

"Prime Minister, what do you propose we do?" Sir David Greville asked. He was seated on the Prime Minister's right.

"We will start making arrangements for all convicted terrorists on the list to be brought to..." he paused. "Which airport will we use to fly them from the country?"

"We will use RAF Northolt," the Commissioner answered.

"We will have them taken to RAF Northolt," the Prime Minister continued. "I want a coach outside Parliament at 19.00. Have all our police and troops been withdrawn from the Parliament building?" The Commissioner and the General both nodded. "Right, let's get things started." The Commissioner spoke to a couple of officers, who then got up and left. An army officer beside the General also got up and left.

"We have to end this without any more loss of life," the Prime Minister said.

"Sir," the General said, "I think you are making a big mistake giving into their demands."

"Sometimes, General, it's not possible to do what you think is right," the Prime Minister replied.

"I don't think we should be giving in either," the Head of MI6 said. "We are making a rod for our own back. Terrorists all around the world will now target Britons, knowing we are likely to concede to their demands."

"Can't you see this is different?" the Prime Minister asked.

"The Prime Minister is right," the Head of MI5 joined in. We are in a situation that has to be brought to an end peacefully. If this is the only way to do it, then we should do it."

"I think it's a mistake," the General said. "You might as well invite every terrorist to come to Britain. It's stupid."

"General," said Sir David Greville, "the Prime Minister is in a situation that no one has faced before. We must be practical. I think the decision is the right one in the circumstances. Any attack on Parliament might lead to a greater loss of life than we have already. The quicker the situation is brought to a close, the better."

"I have made the decision," the Prime Minister said. "If I thought there was another way, I would choose it. For the moment, we will follow the instructions of the terrorists. Do I make myself clear?"

★★★

Gunnar Anderson looked in his side mirror. Nothing was moving in the street. He remembered coming here twice before with the American and the British brother, Abdul. They had explained to him how they had walked around the building looking for its weakness a number of times until they found the flaw in its defences.

The whole building had bollards, metal and concrete around it. At the front was a locked metal gate that stopped vehicles getting near the new, gleaming front entrance. It was only opened for VIPs and was closed immediately after. The bollards were at the edge of the pavement, so as to prevent any vehicle getting close. It was the same around the back, except for one place.

A hundred yards from where Gunnar was parked, he saw a large metal door. It was big enough to allow lorries to enter. The thing the American had pointed out was how often the door was left open, with staff walking in and out for a smoke. There was security there, but it was lax, and on his second visit to the site he and the American had watched for an hour as the doors had remained open. People had wandered in and out, and vehicles had come and gone. Today, too, the door stood invitingly open. He saw two women standing in the evening sun smoking, and a security man in a Hi-Vis jacket was chatting to them. Gunnar glanced at the time. It was 17.10. He turned the key and the engine burst into life.

★★★

The General left Downing street and climbed into the back of his car. He saw the Head of MI6 coming out and called, "Could I give you a lift?"

"I have a car, thanks," he said.

"I will drop you off. I want to talk about things," the General said.

The Head of MI6 hesitated, then said to the man with him to follow them. He walked over and got into the back of the General's car. The cars pulled away and turned into a deserted Whitehall. Except for the police, there was no one else around. All traffic had been banned from the area and so they sped up towards Trafalgar Square. "This is a stupid decision," the General said.

"I agree," replied the Head of MI6. "We shouldn't ever show any weakness and now the Prime Minister's decision has left us vulnerable to attacks all around the world by terrorists."

"There must something we can do," the General said. "I don't want those murderers flying out of the country after what they've done."

"I don't think the Prime Minister is going to change his mind," the Head of MI6 said, leaning back in his seat. "Do you have any ideas?"

The General smiled. "I think we are of the same mind," he said, "but I don't think we can discuss things with any of the others. They all seem to be backing the Prime Minister."

The Head of MI6 turned his head. "I agree."

Trafalgar Square was deserted as the car turned left, speeding off down The Mall with Buckingham Palace in the distance.

"I have a couple of thoughts," the General said, "and I know you would have the expertise available to help."

★★★

Gunnar pulled away from the kerb and drove steadily towards the open gate. Everything seemed normal. As he neared, he saw the security man glance over and he pressed the indicator to show he was turning in. He saw the security man wave in his direction and turn back to continue his conversation with the two women. Gunnar slowed, swung the wheel over and drove through the gates.

He was surprised how big it was inside as he passed from the sunlight into the semi-darkness inside. He saw another two security officers on his right and waved his hand at the two faces that watched him pass. He drove another 20 yards until he was sure he was directly under the main building and then stopped. He leaned forward and flicked the switch on the dashboard. The clock said 17.12.

★★★

"Thank you for coming to talk to us about the day's events," Kay Sandford began, twisting in her seat to talk to Malcolm Davis, the ex-Foreign Secretary who had retired three years ago as an MP. He now wrote and lectured on foreign affairs. "What do you think might happen next, now that the Prime Minister has been released?"

Malcolm Davis smiled back at Kay. "He is going to have some tough decisions to make—"

There was a sudden rumble, then everything around them seemed to be thrown into the air – themselves included. Kay Sanford saw her co-presenter, Bill Secombe, crushed by falling lights just as she felt a blow to her head.

***

The bomb tore through the BBC building, moving up three floors and destroying everything in its path. The main news room was completely devastated. The new front of the building blew out glass like small missiles in all directions. No one in the underground goods entrance survived. The two women smokers and the security man were blown across the street, their bodies instantly shredded. The building collapsed in itself. Floors weakened and tumbled down on each other until they came to rest on what had been a Royal Mail van.

***

Nathan sat on the government benches in Parliament. They had moved everyone to the one side now, except for the seated Jewish MPs, who were still sitting in a long line on the floor. Sohail had explained to them what he had done, cursing the useless map that had not allowed him to carry out his mission. Samir and Rashid came and sat beside Nathan.

"Do you think the Swede has carried out his attack yet?" Samir asked.

"I think he may have," Nathan said. "He was told any time after five."

"I hope he has," Rashid said. "The puppets at the BBC never give us a fair hearing, as its controlled by the Jews."

"I think I will call my friend, the Prime Minister," Nathan said. He took a phone that had once been the Foreign

Secretary's from his pocket. He pressed a number and it rang twice before Nathan heard the Prime Minister's voice. Nathan switched to loudspeaker.

"Ah, Prime Minister," Nathan said. "So nice to hear your voice again. Have you started making the arrangements?"

"Yes," came the reply, "but it may take some time to get all of the prisoners to the airport. They are all around the country."

"You can use helicopters to fly them there," Nathan said. "I am not looking for excuses. You have our timetable. When the coach is parked outside Parliament, the driver will leave it. You will ensure that no police car comes near us and that all roads are clear. Which airport are we going to?"

"RAF Northolt," the Prime Minister replied.

"Why not Heathrow or Gatwick?" Nathan asked.

"Heathrow is not working at the moment," the Prime Minister said, "and Gatwick was too far to travel."

"I can understand not using Heathrow," Nathan replied, "but an RAF airport? You are not planning anything silly, are you?"

"I can assure you that we will not interfere with your plans in any way," the Prime Minister said.

Nathan looked at the others, who had been listening. "You would be silly to do so. We will be taking a number of MPs with us, including the Foreign Secretary. They will be released when we reach our destination. The pilots must be Arab. No others are permitted. I will be in touch again. Some of my men will be searching the building soon, and if they come across any police or troops, we will start to shoot the MPs."

"Everyone has been withdrawn from the building," the Prime Minister replied, "but can the fire brigade start to tackle the fire that has broken out?"

"No, no one is allowed near the building," Nathan said, raising his voice. "If we see anyone, we will start killing the MPs. I will call you again." Nathan ended the call.

"Things are looking good," Samir said.

"We will be on our way back to Iraq soon," Rashid said.

"Do you have the airport coordinates in northern Iraq that Tariq gave us?" Nathan asked.

Rashid took a small notebook from his pocket and tapped it. "In here, brother."

***

The phone on Sinclair's desk rang and he picked it up, listened for a moment, said thank you and put it down. "There has been a big explosion at the BBC building, so I think we have found our last vehicle." He looked down at the map and placed the Royal Mail van on the site of the BBC. "Richards, you better get onto whoever is in charge down there and get some reports." Richards nodded. He and the other officers left the office. Sinclair picked up the phone and put a call through to the Commissioner.

***

A civil servant entered the meeting room at Downing Street and passed a note to Sir David Greville. He read it and dismissed the man, who left the room.

"Prime Minister, there has been a big explosion at the BBC building," he said. "First reports say that the building has been badly damaged with a great loss of life."

The Prime Minister took a long drink from his glass of scotch, then said, "I want to get onto the television to speak to the country. I have to let the people know we are taking charge of the situation."

"I think that is a good idea, sir," said Sir David. "A lot of people would have been watching the television when the

BBC was hit, and will be wondering what is going on. We must give them some hope that all this is coming to an end."

"Make the arrangements," the Prime Minister said, "and make sure it happens before 19.00. I want to explain what we are doing to end all this madness."

Sir David got up and left the office. The Prime Minister was alone. He took another sip, emptying the glass and placing it on the table in front of him. He thought about all the MPs still trapped in Parliament. After the latest bomb at the BBC, he was determined that no one else would be killed.

★★★

Nathan sat with Rashid, looking across at the MPs.

"Do we stick with the plan?" Rashid asked.

"Yes," Nathan said, "I don't think we will be interfered with when we leave, and Sohail has just connected to the internet using one of their tablets." He pointed to the MPs. "The Swede was successful in his mission at the BBC. Reports say the building has been destroyed and the BBC news was blacked out, although it's now up and running from another building now. Even so, we have shown again what we can do." Nathan looked up and pointed. "They will be listening to us and I want to tell them," he raised his voice, "that if we are attacked when we leave on the coach, we will bring more destruction to your city and you will have the blood of your fellow countrymen on your hands."

★★★

Sir David Greville came back into the office. "Sir, the American Ambassador is here." He stood aside and a man the Prime Minister recognised came into the room.

"Ambassador, good to see you," the Prime Minister said, as he stood up and held out his hand.

"I am sorry it's in such circumstances," the Ambassador said, shaking the Prime Minister's hand. They both sat down.

Sir David was the only other person in the room. "Could I get you a drink, Ambassador?" he asked.

"No, thank you," the Ambassador replied.

"I will have a scotch," the Prime Minister said. Sir David poured the drink and placed it on the table beside the Prime Minister.

"The President wanted me to come and see you personally," the Ambassador said, as he pulled a folder from his briefcase. "The man who appears to be leading the attack is an American called Nathan Bush. This is all we know of him." He pushed the folder across the table. "In brief, he served in the marines and had a distinguished career until some trouble in Iraq. He then spent time in the Middle East, supposedly doing charity work, but the CIA had him on their radar as he was mixing with terrorists. They tried to get him back to the United States when he was wounded in Jordan, but he fled the hospital and disappeared. They've since heard rumours of him being part of a terrorist cell, but about six years ago he vanished. It was thought that he had been killed. His turning up as leading this attack was just as much a shock to us."

"Thank you, Ambassador," the Prime Minister said. "We will make sure the file gets to the right people. Now, are you willing to release the terrorist names on the list that you are currently holding in prison?"

"We will not, Prime Minister," the Ambassador replied. "The President said to apologise, but the American people will not tolerate the release of any prisoners we hold, who may then come back and kill more American citizens around the world.

We feel it would leave us exposed to hostage-taking with yet more demands for prisoners to be released. I am sorry."

"I understand," the Prime Minister said. He took another drink from his glass of scotch, put it down, stood up and came around the table.

The Ambassador got up from his chair and held out his hand. "I am truly sorry we can't help."

The Prime Minister shook hands with him. "I understand," he repeated. His voice was tired. He watched as Sir David showed the Ambassador from the room, then he walked over to the window that overlooked the garden at the back of Number 10. The garden was in full bloom, with the June sunshine bringing the colours to life.

He heard the door open and turned to see Sir David re-enter. "I didn't really expect the Americans to agree to any releases," the Prime Minister said, walking back to his seat.

"It was hardly likely," Sir David replied, "but I have just been given a note. The Italian Government said they are willing to release their prisoners once all the hostages are freed."

The Prime Minister nodded. "Send a thank you to the Italian Prime Minister. Have we had any other government's official responses yet?"

"No, nothing official, but off the record, not too many are sounding like they will go along with things," Sir David replied.

The Prime Minister sat back down. "I want to know how the preparations are going. Get everyone back here for 18.00, and I want to make a statement to the country at 18.30. Organise it with the broadcasters."

"Yes, Prime Minister," Sir David said and he left the office.

The Prime Minister looked at his watch. It was 17.40.

CHAPTER EIGHTEEN

Tariq had made his way to another safe house. It had been hidden among the back streets of Tikrit. He was now seated on large cushions with two of his closest allies in the insurgent war, and was explaining what had happened. They then discussed the next phase.

"You will travel north," he told the oldest of the two in front of him. He handed over a sheet of paper. "Gather all the local fighters and take them to the old air base. Make sure it is secure and await the arrival of the plane. When it has landed, separate the hostages and disperse them to different locations. Our brothers on the plane should be brought here." He pointed to the map.

"But we will have more than one plane arriving," the old man replied. "The news said that 1,000 were to be released."

Tariq laughed. "My brother, we knew that would never happen. The British will release theirs, as they want their MPs released safely. If some other weak governments free some of our brothers and sisters, all the better, but that was never our real aim. The demands were just a ruse. We wanted to show that we could strike at the heart of the enemy and we have. If our brothers can return safely, we will have triumphed. All Western countries will think twice before they attack us. They will know that it is not just their soldiers who are in danger, but that we are capable of bringing death to their doorstep."

The old man smiled and stood up. "I will do as you bid."

Tariq watched him leave the room. He had no doubt his orders would be followed. The old man, who looked so gentle and friendly, was a ruthless operator who had assassinated many Iraq collaborators and commanded the respect of all the fighters under Tariq's command. Tariq turned to the younger man.

"My brother, I want you to organise safe houses in the area for all our returning fighters. Make sure the area is well defended. Anyone who is suspected of being in contact with the government should be killed. Cleanse the area. I don't want any spies left who can inform on what we are doing." The younger man nodded and left.

Tariq sat back on the cushion. Whatever happened now, success had already been achieved. The Islamic Front was the biggest player in Iraq now. He had new recruits flocking to its banner and foreign governments would take them seriously. He already had overtures from high-ranking Iraqi officials about a ceasefire. His fighters had destroyed two oil refineries and the economy was collapsing. He would soon be in a position to demand concessions, and now that the attack in London had been so successful, he knew other foreign governments would be reluctant to become involved.

★★★

Rashid returned to the main chamber. He and three fighters had just walked around the corridors, checking there were no police or soldiers still in the building.

"We saw no one," he told Nathan. "However, at the other end of the building, the fire that Sohail started has taken hold, so we couldn't search down there. I doubt anyone would want to be near that fire, though."

"I will give our friend, the Prime Minister, a call to see how things are progressing," Nathan said. "Once I have spoken to him, we will start getting ready to move."

"You think he will follow our demands?" Samir asked, who was sitting next to Nathan.

"He is weak and he cares too much," Nathan said. "I can't see him trying to attack us."

"Nathan is right. He feels too much," Rashid said. "When Aashif had the rifle pointed at the Foreign Secretary's head, his face said it all. He won't want to risk any more lives."

"We better start planning our exit from the building," Nathan said, standing up.

★★★

"I just got a new report from the farm," Richards said, coming back into Sinclair's office. "The army bomb disposal boys have found a number of devices. They don't know how long it will take to disarm them, so we won't get any information from the farm for a while."

Sinclair nodded. "I don't know if they would have left anything incriminating, but anything we find might give us a handle on how they planned this thing. Have we managed to identify any of them yet?"

"We have." Richards passed over a number of pictures. "The first one, the man holding the Kalashnikov to the Foreign Secretary's head, is a man called Aashif Khan. He's from Birmingham. We are having his family home raided, but he left the country many years ago. He was spotted fighting in Iraq from time to time, according to the reports, but there hasn't been any news of him for a number of years. The second man is also British." Sinclair placed the first picture down so that they could look at the second. "His name is Abdul Baari and is from Leeds. We believe he was the driver of the coach that exploded at Westminster Abbey. His family homes are also being raided, but, like Khan, he has been out of the country for many years. His name also came up in reports of terrorist attacks in Iraq."

"And we have no idea how long they've been back in the country?" Sinclair asked.

"No, sir, but they may have been on the farm and it's in the middle of nowhere," Richards answered. "They could have been here for some time. The third man is interesting." Sinclair laid down Abdul's picture. "He is called Sohail Rind and the Americans have circulated reports on him for years. He is originally from Pakistan, went to university in Damascus and then travelled to Iraq to join the insurgency. The Americans have him down as a top bomb-maker, so I think the explosions were his handiwork."

"The thing I find so hard to take in," Sinclair said, as he put Sohail's picture down, "is that we haven't heard anything. Not a single report has mentioned any of these names or any rumours of a big attack."

"It looks like it was committed by people who have been out of this country for years or had no known ties to it," Richards said.

"But how have they managed to get into the country and amassed the amount of explosives and guns they've used?" Sinclair asked, looking up at Richards.

"I would imagine getting into the country was the easy bit," Richards replied. "Border checks are minimal if they used false passports, but they could also have come in illegally like thousands of others do every month. As for the explosives, people smuggle in tons of heroin, cocaine and marijuana every week. If you have a route set up and you do it over time, you can soon amass an awful lot. We don't know how long they have been planning it, but with the targets and the organisation involved, I would think it's been over a year – if not longer."

"What about the others?" Sinclair asked, looking at the

next picture. His phone rang just before Richards was able to speak. Sinclair picked it up and listened. When he put it down, he stood up and said, "We are to meet the Commissioner and go to Downing Street with him."

The time was 17.50.

★★★

"I would like to thank everyone for coming at such short notice," the Prime Minister began. "I want to hear what preparations have been made for the terrorists to leave Parliament. I will be making a broadcast to the country at 18.30, so I want to have the full facts as we know them. I want to be able to tell the public that this is coming to an end." The Prime Minister turned to the Commissioner. "Would you like to start?"

"Thank you, sir," the Commissioner said. "We have set out a route that the coach will take to RAF Northolt. We have been clearing a path through the traffic so there will be no hold-ups. It hasn't been easy as the traffic across London is grid-locked, but my officers are confident the route will be kept clear. However, Prime Minister, the coach will have to follow a marked car to ensure it stays on the route. If it deviates, we could run into trouble with the amount of traffic about."

"Thank you, Commissioner. What about the aircraft that will be used?" the Prime Minister asked.

The Head of MI5 spoke. "We have arranged with British Airways for a plane to be on the runway." She looked at her watch. "It should have landed and is probably being refuelled at this moment. The pilots are Arabs, as requested. They are British Airways staff, but are Jordanian nationals."

"What about the prisoners we are releasing?" the Prime Minister asked.

"We have already started transferring those that were in jails around London to Northolt," the Commissioner answered. "We will have those that were in jails around the country at the airbase by 19.00. They will be placed on coaches. When the terrorist coach arrives, we will form a convoy to make its way to the plane."

"Well, we seem to have everything under control," the Prime Minister said, looking around the table.

"Sir, if I may say something," the General spoke out, sitting forward. "I think we are making a grave mistake allowing them to go free and giving in to their demands to release hundreds of convicted prisoners. We are storing up trouble for the future."

"I understand your argument," the Prime Minister replied, looking down the table at the General, "but, in the circumstances, this is the best we can do. I do not want any more deaths. The country has suffered enough already. We will have time later to look at where we went wrong, and what could have been done better, but for now we will end this peacefully."

"I want to express my disagreement," the Head of MI6 said from the end of the table. "It's madness to let these people walk away. They will be heroes among their friends when they get back and every terrorist around the world will look at us as a soft touch. I fear we will see more of these attacks – and who's to say some of those you're freeing don't return to attack us again."

"It's something we have to do," the Prime Minister said. "If there was another way, I would take it."

"There is another way," the General said. "They will be on a coach, isolated. We can take them out in one go."

"No," the Prime Minister said, raising his voice. "They will still have hostages, including the Foreign Secretary, so no attempt to interfere with their journey will be made. Do

I make myself clear?" There was silence around the table. The Head of MI6 sat back, looked over at the General and shrugged. "Now, do we have the latest casualty figures?" the Prime Minister continued. Sinclair slid a sheet of paper to the Commissioner, who passed it to the Prime Minister. After looking at it for a moment, he asked, "Are these the complete numbers?"

"No, sir," Sinclair answered, "they don't include the casualties from the BBC, and the Shard and Westminster Abbey bombs are still being assessed. We, of course, expect the figures to rise as the rescue teams find more bodies. The figures for the attacks in Covent Garden and Oxford Street are, however, final numbers. The bombs from earlier today are close to their final numbers, but they may also go up a little."

The Prime Minister laid the sheet of paper down. He had looked at the figure three times and it still didn't seem real. "You say this figure is likely to rise?" he said.

"Yes, sir. As I said, the BBC, Shard and others have not been fully accounted for," Sinclair answered.

The Prime Minister looked up. "Thank you." He turned back to look down the table. "Now, everyone, when you leave, I want you to make sure that nothing stops us bringing this to a close with no further loss of life. Ensure we have covered everything and that all arrangements are checked. Nothing can go wrong." Around the table, heads nodded in response. He turned to look at the Commissioner and asked, "What time do you think the plane will take off?"

"We think about 20.00," the Commissioner replied.

"Thank you," the Prime Minister continued. "Well, once the plane is in the air, we will meet at 21.00." The Prime Minister's mobile went off before he could finish. He took it from his pocket and looked at the number. It was the Foreign Secretary's. He held his hand up and answered "Hello."

"Ah, Prime Minister," Nathan said, "so nice to hear your voice again. How are the preparations going?"

"Everything is being organised," the Prime Minister answered.

"Have you released all our jailed brothers and sisters?" Nathan asked.

"They will be at the airport. When you arrive, they will follow you to the plane," the Prime Minister replied.

"Very good," Nathan said. "What about our brothers and sisters held in other countries?"

"You know I have no way of forcing their release, but some governments have agreed that when the hostages are released they will free their prisoners," the Prime Minister replied.

"Very well. We will be leaving here at 19.00. Remember, no funny tricks or we will kill everyone," Nathan said.

The Commissioner held up his hand. "Tell him he must follow the marked police car to the airport and ask if we can send the fire brigade in to tackle the fire."

"Due to the problems with the traffic around London," the Prime Minister said, "it will be necessary for you to follow a marked police car. It will ensure you have a clear passage to the airport."

For a moment, there was silence. Then, Nathan answered, "Okay, we understand, but if anything tries to stop us once we are on the move, we will assume we are under attack and start shooting the hostages. The Foreign Secretary will be first."

"There will be no interference, but what about the fire in Parliament? Can we send in the fire brigade?" the Prime Minister asked.

"You will have time when we are gone to save your so-called Mother of Parliaments. I will call you again, Prime Minister. I so enjoy our chats." The line went dead.

The Prime Minister put the phone in his pocket and looked down the table. "The coach must not be held up once it has started its journey or they say they will start shooting the hostages. Commissioner, you will double-check the route. There must be no mistakes." The Commissioner nodded. "We can't send the fire brigade near the building, but as soon as the coach has left, get them in there. One last thing, the American Ambassador handed over a dossier on what they know of the leader of the terrorists." He pushed copies around for each of those present. "I daresay some of you might have seen this material already." He looked down the table to the Head of MI6. "It is the first I have heard of him. Okay, everyone, until later this evening." Everyone around the table rose and left the room, except for Sir David.

"What do you think" the Prime Minister asked.

"I think everyone will do what's asked of them. We can only hope it all goes to plan," Sir David said. "Now, Prime Minister, you have your broadcast to prepare for. I have had some of my office preparing your statement, so I will get them in and we can go over it." He looked at his watch. It was 18.20. "We only have ten minutes." He picked up the phone in the centre of the table, dialled a number and said, "You can come in now."

★★★

Outside Number 10, the others stood around waiting for their cars. "Commissioner, have you got things covered?" the General asked.

"We will double-check, but I'm comfortable that everything will go to plan," the Commissioner answered.

"It's just a thought," the General said, "but the coach that the SAS arrived in is sitting on Westminster Bridge. You can use it for the transfer to the airport."

"That would be handy," the Commissioner replied. "It will save us time getting another one through the traffic. Can I leave one of my officers to make the arrangements with your staff?"

"Of course," the General answered.

The Commissioner nodded. His car stopped and he got into it, followed by Sinclair. Richards climbed in the front. "You liaise with the General's staff about the coach," the Commissioner said to Richards, as the car pulled away.

"Yes, sir," Richards said.

The car left Downing Street, following a marked Range Rover with its emergency lights flashing. They headed down Whitehall towards Parliament Square.

"The fire is getting worse," Sinclair said.

They all looked ahead and could clearly see the flames coming through the roof. It was getting close to the Elizabeth Tower.

"The fire brigade are using their fire boats the best they can," the Commissioner said, "but the main fire is not on the river side of Parliament. The best they can do is hose water onto the roof, but they really need to get in close from the street side. As you know, the terrorists have denied us that."

The car turned right at Parliament Square, heading towards Victoria and New Scotland Yard. Sinclair turned in his seat to look back at Parliament. *I don't know how much of the old building will be left,* he thought, watching the flames jump out of the roof. As he turned away, he saw the destruction that had taken place at Westminster Abbey. The emergency services were still working hard. He could see several white sheets that were covering dead bodies in front of the abbey.

★★★

"It would seem they are going along with things," Nathan said, as he put the phone into his pocket. "We will be on our way home soon."

"Do you believe they have released the prisoners?" Samir asked.

"I think so," Nathan replied. "He said they would be on coaches at the airport, and would join us as we drove to the plane."

"I think we might just leave in time," Rashid said, pointing up. Smoke could clearly be seen drifting under the roof.

"That's your doing," he said, smiling at Sohail, who was lying back on the benches with a Kalashnikov cradled in his arms.

"I can only hope it burns the whole place down," Sohail replied, without moving. "Once we're out of here, of course."

"You better go and check," Nathan said. "We don't want the place burning down around our ears."

Rashid called two men to him and they left through the main doors.

Aashif walked over, He had been guarding the MPs on the floor. "Do you think we will pull it off?" he asked.

"It looks like it, brother," Nathan smiled. "They are so scared of any more deaths, they will do anything we ask. They would even let their Parliament burn down rather than upset us."

"What about them?" Aashif said, looking at the seated Jewish MPs.

"They will be joining us on a long holiday in Iraq. What happens then? Who knows?" Nathan said, smiling again. Aashif smiled back.

★★★

The Prime Minister was seated behind his desk, facing the camera. Sir David had just spoken to him and emphasised what he should say. He was now standing behind the camera. The statement in front of the Prime Minister had been hurriedly put together in the last ten minutes. It didn't seem complete, but Sir David had said not to deviate. There was so much that the public didn't need to know. Giving them what they needed to hear was enough. His last words had been: "Don't mention the number of dead."

He saw the director hold up his hand and then drop it.

"Good evening. It has been a sad day for our country," the Prime Minister began, "and since I last spoke to you, we have seen yet more of our citizens killed in terrorist attacks. My heart goes out to all the families of those who have lost loved ones or who have seen their relatives injured. Our emergency services have worked tirelessly to save, rescue and bring comfort to those who have been hurt. We thank them for their steadfast attitude in the face of the terrible things they've had to see.

"As a country, we have faced many dire situations and have grown stronger from our experiences. And, as a country, we must stand together and come through this dark episode. After much thought, I have decided to bring this to an end. I have instructed the police to provide safe passage for the terrorists to an airport, where they will be allowed to fly out of the country.

It is not a decision I wished to take, but, at this time, we have to take a pragmatic approach to the situation. I do not want to see anyone else lose their lives. I know that many of you will agree, but I also know that many of you will not. That is why it has been such a hard decision to make. I had to sit and watch as members of Parliament were murdered in front of my eyes, so choosing this course of action has not been easy. However, I feel it is the right one.

"We will have plenty of time to look back and question the decisions made during today's events, and also how we came to find our country in this situation, but my priority must be the safety of those still held by the terrorists. To that end, I want to bring things to a close in the most peaceful way possible. It might not be the way we want it, but it has to be done like this.

The director held up his hand, then dropped it again. Sir David came out from behind the camera. "Well done, Prime Minister, that was perfectly pitched."

The Prime Minister stood up and came round the table. "Come on, let's make sure this thing is brought to an end."

★★★

"What news?" the Head of MI6 asked.

The General was seated in the back of his car, which was parked at the bottom of Whitehall. He had the phone to his ear as he watched the flames dance along the roof of Parliament. "Things are go. They will use the SAS coach."

"Excellent," the Head of MI6 said, "I will have two of my men come over and set things up."

"We don't have long," the General replied.

"My men are experts. They have all the tools they need," the Head of MI6 said. "Just make sure there's not too many people around."

"We will move it somewhere discreet," the General said. "I am heading for Northolt, so I will leave one of my staff with the coach to meet your men."

"Okay, I will meet you at Northolt." The line went dead.

The General spoke to the officer sitting in the front passenger seat quietly. The man nodded and got out of the car, before turning the corner in the direction of Westminster Bridge.

"Driver, let's get to Northolt," the General said.

★★★

Nathan looked at his watch. It was 18.58. "Check to see if the coach is here," he said to Rashid, who nodded and walked to the door of the chamber.

Rashid and another fighter pulled the two doors open. A light haze of smoke hung in the air as they walked into the lobby and made their way to the main entrance. Rashid stood at the side of the door and took a quick look, then ducked back. The coach was there. He told the fighter to go back and inform Nathan.

When Nathan heard the news, he told Samir to join Rashid. He should go and check that no one was hiding on the coach and all was clear. Samir smiled and left. Nathan told the others to prepare to move. Aashif shouted to the sitting MPs to stand up. He and two of the fighters then went along the line, making sure that they had put their hands on their heads, Nathan walked to the front and looked up at the crowded MPs, who were still packed together on the green benches. "You have seen the destruction we have brought to your country today. It was your choice to back the Jewish murderers. It was your choice to bomb innocent women and children in Iraq. Next time you make decisions on the lands of my brothers and sisters, remember that those decisions you talk about in such casual terms will come back and haunt you. When you decide to bomb our lands, we will not stand idle. We will bring war to your streets as you bring it to ours. Stay out of our lands."

Nathan turned away. Sohail came to his side. "Get everyone out by the front door and ready to board the coach." Sohail moved away and waved his arm to Aashif, who pushed the Foreign Secretary in the back. The line of MPs made their way out of the chamber.

When the men had left, Nathan had a last look around and followed them out. He made his way to the front entrance where everyone was gathered.

"The coach is empty," Samir said.

"Good. Take four of the hostages at a time," Nathan said. "Sit them individually in the window seats and pull all the curtains closed."

Samir started to organise the boarding of the coach and Nathan walked out of Parliament into the warm summer evening. The sky was clear, except for the black smoke that was blowing across it from the fire. He looked around. The bodies of the five policemen that had been shot earlier were still lying where they fell. He couldn't see any other police or army, but he knew there were probably tens of rifles aimed at him from windows. He had no fear, though, as they wouldn't risk anything now. He walked towards the coach. Rashid was standing in the doorway.

It took about ten minutes to get everyone onboard. Rashid slipped into the driver's seat and started the engine. A police car about 100 yards ahead suddenly put its blue flashing lights on. It had a sign in its rear window that read: "Follow me".

"Do as the man asks," Nathan said.

Rashid laughed. "Your wish is my command, oh master," he said and pulled away, following the police car.

The time was 19.12.

★★★

"They've left Parliament," Sir David said. "We will have live pictures from the police helicopter in a moment."

The Prime minster was sitting in a high-backed armchair, with another glass of Scotch in his hand. Along with Sir David, there were ten other people comprising civil servant party advisors. "Has the Commissioner gone to the Northolt?" he asked.

"Yes, Prime Minister," Sir David said. "He wanted to make sure everything ran smoothly."

Suddenly, the picture on the television came on. The Prime Minister sat forward, took a drink from his glass and watched as the white coach made its way through the streets of London.

★★★

Nathan walked down the centre of the coach. Everything was quiet. He sat down next to the Foreign Secretary. "Well, my friend, it looks like we will be on our way home soon," he said.

The Foreign Secretary turned his head. "What has been the point of all this killing?"

"You ask me that question when you have sent your troops to my lands to kill us?" asked Nathan. "When we come to your land, you ask me what's the point of all this killing?"

"You can't believe you have achieved anything that will change the world?" the Foreign Secretary asked.

"Your country will think twice about becoming involved in wars in our lands again," Nathan said. "Your people have seen the cost with their own eyes, have seen the blood on their streets. It is something my brothers and sisters see every day. Don't you think that will change things?"

"The world is more complicated than that," the Foreign Secretary replied.

"You are a diplomat," Nathan said. "You don't see things like normal people. You spend too much time flying around the world feeling important – but away from your meetings, your grand dinners and your photo calls for the world's press, the real world suffers. You don't go hungry, see your land stolen, your children forced to grow up in a tent on some windswept hill and fight to feed them every day. That is the real world for my brothers and sisters."

"And this will change that?" the Foreign Secretary asked.

"Yes," Nathan said, "it will change things. Your country is just a mercenary for the Americans. They tell you which wars to fight and you do it. They tell you what way to vote at the United Nations and you do it. What has happened today will make your people think."

"Things are not that simple," the Foreign Secretary said.

"But that's where your wrong," Nathan said. "You like to complicate things to confuse people. You make up lies and threats that don't exist to justify your actions. You have to, because deep down, hidden inside you, you know that it's wrong."

"All decisions made by the British Government have always been to preserve peace," the Foreign Secretary replied.

Nathan laughed out loud and the others turned to see what he was laughing at. "You can't stop yourself, can you? Don't you realise what has happened today? Thousands of your countrymen and women have been killed and you still talk like some diplomat who is not affected by things."

"I am affected," the Foreign Secretary said, "but I don't think it will change how the world operates. The British Government will continue to make decisions that it believes are in the best interests not just of itself, but of the wider world. What has happened today won't change that."

"I disagree," Nathan said. "We have shown today what is possible. You were taken completely by surprise and it has cost you dearly"

"We learn by our mistakes," the Foreign Secretary said.

"I don't think you do," Nathan replied. "If you had, we would not be sitting here talking. You created all the problems that exist in the Middle East. For hundreds of years, you have treated it as a backyard. First, you drew lines on a map, dividing it up, not taking into account the people living there, then you created a country for the Jews. You turn a blind eye as they

242

ethnically cleanse the Palestinians from their land, attack the countries around them, steal more land and build houses for themselves and throw more Palestinians from theirs. You back dictators who suppress their people. You even sell them the weapons to do it – and now you sit there and tell me you learn from your mistakes."

The Foreign Secretary said nothing, then turned to look at Nathan. "If all you say is true – whether or not I agree – what has today proved?"

"You really don't understand, do you?" Nathan asked. "I think you have never lived in the real world. You travel in your car from place to place, visit the odd refugee camp, say the right thing in front of the cameras and you think you know the answers. Today has shown that you and your country don't know the answers."

Nathan leaned forward to look right into the Foreign Secretary's face. "Let me tell you something: I have lived in your country for years, along with my brothers here." Nathan waved his hand. "We have watched how you operate, how you suppress our Muslim brothers and sisters who live among you. We have watched everything. It took us years of planning. We walked the streets of London and stood among your people. We probably know more of what they think than you do." Nathan leaned in closer. "And another thing, do you really think we are the only ones you never knew were in your country?"

★★★

The Commissioner and Sinclair were standing in an operations room at RAF Northolt. Around them stood the Head of MI5, the General and a number of other army officers, the Head of MI6 with two other men, and some RAF personnel. The Base

Commander had just finished going over the route that the coaches would take to the plane, which was parked on the far side of the airfield – away from prying eyes.

The phone of the Head of MI6 rang. He spoke for a minute and then turned to the others. "We placed some listening devices on the coach and they're working well. Commander, could you get one of your men to patch through the audio?"

"My man will help." The Commander spoke to one of the RAF personnel, and he and the MI6 man went to a bank of computers. After a few moments, the voice of Nathan came out of the speakers. Everyone listened in on the conversation he was having with the Foreign Secretary.

When it was finished, the Commissioner was the first to speak. "Did you hear that? He implied there were other groups here."

"Well, you better start rounding them up," the General said.

The Commissioner ignored the remark. "Sinclair, when this is over you better start running background checks on all those who have taken part. Find all their known contacts. I'm sure MI5 will help." He turned to the Head of MI5

"We will give it all our resources," she said, "but we have to hope we get all the information that our friends who work abroad can give us." She looked at the Head of MI6.

He smiled. "We will, of course, supply you with anything we deem relevant to your investigation."

"You're too kind," the Head of MI5 answered.

"How long before the coach gets here?" the Commissioner asked, breaking the tension.

"Half an hour, sir," an RAF officer said.

CHAPTER NINETEEN

The phone on the Prime Minister's desk rang and one of the civil servants picked it up. He called Sir David over, who took the phone and had a short conversation. Once it was over, he passed it back to the civil servant and walked back to stand beside the Prime Minister.

"Prime Minister," Sir David said, "there have been five more explosions in shops in Covent Garden."

The Prime Minister looked away from the television. "Oh no," he said. His face looked tired and drawn. "Please tell me we aren't facing another attack."

"The police think that the devices were probably placed in the shops earlier," Sir David replied. "A few policemen have been slightly injured by the explosions, but luckily the area was still cordoned off to the public. They are checking all the shops in the area for other devices, but it may take days."

"You can let the police know that I don't want the area open until I have their assurance that there are no more bombs," the Prime Minister said.

Sir David nodded.

★★★

Aboard the coach, everyone was sitting quietly, but there was an air of tension. The hostages were all in seats closest to the windows. Nathan's men squatted in the aisle between the seats, occasionally getting up and walking up the coach to check on their prisoners. No one was allowed to speak.

"How much longer until we get to the airport?" Samir asked.

Rashid looked over his shoulder. "About twenty minutes, I think," he said, turning to watch the back of the police car that was leading them. Every street seemed to be deserted as they travelled unhindered through London.

***

Richards came and stood next to Sinclair, who had walked outside into the warm evening for some air. "Sir," he said, "there have been a few explosions in Covent Garden."

Sinclair turned. "Is it bad?"

"No, though some shops have been destroyed, and a couple of officers who were guarding the street have been slightly injured," Richards replied. "The Commander on the ground thinks they were planted earlier by the group who were intercepted there."

"The last thing we need is more deaths," Sinclair said. He watched as the General and one of his officers came out of the operations room. They had a conversation and the officer walked off. The General then made his way over to them.

"This is not a very good outcome," the General said, as he stopped in front of Sinclair.

"I don't think we had much choice," Sinclair replied.

"We had lots of choices," the General said, "but letting them leave is the wrong one." He turned and walked away.

"What do you make of him?" Richards asked.

"He is someone who is used to having his decisions obeyed and his ideas followed," Sinclair said.

"Well, he has lost out this time," Richards said.

They watched as the General crossed the road and stood on the grass opposite the main gate. As he did, two police cars, followed by three coaches – all with the curtains drawn – came through the gates. The vehicles drove for fifty yards and then stopped. Soldiers appeared and took up positions around them.

"I hate seeing that lot leave the country," Richards said. "You can be sure that most of them will try and come back to cause trouble."

Sinclair nodded. "It was the only way to end things without more bloodshed. None of us like what's happening, but the Prime Minister did the only thing he could in the circumstances."

"The coach will be here in ten minutes," the Commissioner said. He had walked up without Sinclair or Richards noticing. "I take it that that's the released prisoners."

"It would seem so, sir," Sinclair replied.

"The army aren't taking any chances," the Commissioner said, looking at the troops surrounding the coaches.

"I don't suppose they want them getting off and having a wander round," Richards said, regretting his flippancy as the Commissioner glowered at him.

"Do you think the hostages will be released?" Sinclair said, drawing the Commissioner's attention back to him.

"It's something we don't know," the Commissioner replied. "We can only hope the terrorists keep their side of the deal."

Sinclair had his doubts, but kept his thoughts to himself.

★★★

"Sir, we will have to think about doing another broadcast to the country tomorrow," Sir David said to the Prime Minister. "I think you should announce the official number killed then. It will help head off criticism for releasing the terrorists. It will allow you to point out that you didn't want any more people killed before a decision was made. You will be able to say that enough families had suffered already."

The Prime Minister looked away from the television, which was showing the coach's progress. "Do we have the total numbers killed yet?" he asked.

"Not yet, but by tomorrow I think we should have a figure close to it," Sir David said. "I have had news from the fire brigade. They said that the fire has caused severe damage to Parliament. They've stopped it getting to the Elizabeth Tower and Big Ben, but the Chamber of the House of Lords has been destroyed. They have prevented it from reaching the Commons Chamber, though. All the MPs who were held hostage have been safely brought out."

"How many were killed?" the Prime Minister asked.

"Including the Home Secretary, fourteen," Sir David answered.

The Prime Minister looked back at the television. "Fill my glass," he said, holding it up.

***

"We are nearly there," Rashid said.

Nathan got up and stood just behind him as the coach followed the police car, which had turned off the Western Avenue and was driving up the slip road that led to a roundabout. Rashid stayed 50 yards behind.

"Everyone be prepared," Nathan shouted.

All the fighters on the coach cocked their weapons.

Following the police car, they went round to their right and onto West End Road. There hadn't been any sign of traffic or people all the way, and this road was no different. Up ahead, they saw the police car indicating left and they saw the sign for RAF Northolt. Nathan patted Rashid on the back as he turned left onto the road that led to the main gates. The gates rose as the police car approached.

"There are the other coaches," Samir said, who had joined them at the front as they passed through the gates. The police car ahead pulled off and stopped.

"When you get level with the other coaches, stop," Nathan said.

"There are a lot of troops about," Rashid said.

"Stop now," Nathan said, and Rashid stood on the brakes, bringing the coach to a sudden halt. "I don't like it," Nathan said. He took the phone from his pocket.

★★★

The Prime Minister was watching the coach enter RAF Northolt when his phone rang. It was on the table next to his half-filled glass. He leant forward and picked it up.

"Hello," he said and instantly recognised the American accent on the other end.

"Prime Minister, I hope you're not planning anything silly," Nathan said. "We have soldiers everywhere. I want them away from the area now. You have two minutes or I will shoot the Foreign Secretary." The line went dead before the Prime Minister could reply.

The Prime Minister turned to Sir David. "Get hold of the Base Commander immediately. Tell him to pull all the troops in the area of the coaches back, and to hurry."

Sir David nodded and quickly picked up the office phone.

★★★

Sinclair and Richards, along with the Commissioner, had watched the coach come to a sudden halt. They could make out the driver and the two men who stood behind him, but couldn't see anything else of the inside.

"Why do you think they've stopped?" the Commissioner asked.

"I'm not sure," Sinclair said.

"Something's happening over there," Richards said. Sinclair and the Commissioner turned to see two officers running from the control room. One went to the General and the other towards the troops surrounding the other coaches. The General waved towards them and they heard him call them to join him. Taking another look at the coach, they crossed the road to join the General.

"We have to clear the area," the General said. "Let's go back inside."

"Has something happened?" the Commissioner asked.

"It seems a call came from Downing Street, which said that all troops must be withdrawn," the General replied, as they walked through the operations building door and into the main room. Sinclair and the others followed him. The General went and stood with the Head of MI6 and the two Army officers. Everyone resumed watching the CCTV screens.

★★★

"They are moving away," Rashid said, as they watched the troops disappearing from view.

"Okay, move forward slowly. When you get level with the lead coach, stop," Nathan said. Rashid put the coach into gear and inched forward. "Aashif!" Nathan called. Aashif came down the coach and stood next to Nathan. "When we stop, you and one of the others will get off and check that it is only our brothers and sisters on the other coaches. If it is, tell them to follow closely behind us when we move."

Aashif nodded and called another fighter to him. Rashid brought the coach to a halt next to the lead coach and pressed the button to open the doors. Aashif and the other fighter jumped off, scanned the area and then walked slowly around the front of the first coach. Aashif banged on the door and it opened. He stepped onboard. Suddenly Nathan and the others could clearly hear shouts of "Allahu Akbar" coming from inside the other coach. Aashif went and checked the other two coaches and then made his way back to Nathan. He climbed onboard the coach.

"They are full of our brothers and a few of our sisters, he said, a big smile on his face.

Nathan returned the smile. "Close the door, Rashid." When the door was closed, he turned to face all the others. "We are nearly there, brothers. When we get to the plane, Rashid and Samir will go onboard and check things out. Once they have given the all-clear, we will transfer the prisoners one by one. Aashif, you will make sure our brothers and sisters on the other coaches stay still until I give the signal for them to come aboard. We will be on our way home very soon." He turned back to look out of the front windscreen. "Okay, Rashid, let's go."

Rashid put the coach into gear and pulled forward. The other coaches followed him as he made his way towards the turning that led to the runway.

***

"It looks like everything has gone to plan," the Commissioner said.

"I won't feel happy until the plane has taken off," Sinclair replied.

"Why don't we go outside?" Sinclair heard the General say, and watched as he and the Head of MI6 walked towards the door, accompanied by an Army officer and another MI6 man who was dressed in a smart suit. He turned back to look at the CCTV screen. The coaches were just coming up to a turn that would take them towards the runway and the waiting plane.

"I think I will go and watch from outside," Sinclair said.

"I will join you," Richards replied.

"You two, go. I will stay in here," the Commissioner said.

Sinclair and Richards made their way out of the operations room and came out into the warm evening air. They saw the General and the others standing on the grass across the road and walked over to join them.

★★★

"There's the plane," Rashid said, with excitement in his voice. He turned the coach onto the runway. They were about 500 yards from it.

"Take it steady, brother," Nathan said. "Keep your eyes open for any surprises." Nathan turned to the others. "When we stop, you know what you have to do." He went and sat down with the Foreign Secretary. "It looks like the Prime Minister has been sensible."

The Foreign Secretary turned his head to look at Nathan. "What are your plans when we get to wherever it is you're taking us?"

Nathan smiled. "We have plans for you," he said, "but we can discuss them when we are in a more comfortable environment."

★★★

Sinclair watched the convoy of coaches turn onto the runway and head towards the plane, which was at the far end of the airfield.

"I think you can make that phone call now," he heard the General say to the Head of MI6. Sinclair saw him turn to the other MI6 man, who took a phone from his pocket. Sinclair watched as the man tapped in a number. He turned back to look at the coaches. They were only about 300 yards from the plane when suddenly the lead coach exploded. He and the others took a step back, ducking as they did. A fireball shot into the air and pieces of the coach flew towards them. The fragments bounced across the grass but landed short of where they stood. Sinclair watched as the second coach crashed into the first and exploded. Soldiers seemed to come from nowhere and were running from all directions across the airfield towards the coaches.

"What's happened?" Richards said.

"It appears their flight has been cancelled," the Head of MI6 said and chuckled to himself.

They heard gunfire as the soldiers approached the other coaches. The released prisoners were jumping from them and attempting to make a run for it, but were being shot before they could make twenty yards, Sinclair watched as the prisoners began to lie down on the floor and surrender. Two fire engines then appeared and sped past, heading for the burning wreckage.

Sinclair saw the Head of MI6 shake hands with the General, before he and the other MI6 man walked away towards their car, got in it and left.

"Well, we won't have to worry about them coming back to bother us," the General said to Sinclair and Richards, as he walked towards the operations room.

"Do you get a funny feeling about this?" Richards said.

"I think we should go back and see the Commissioner," Sinclair replied, "but let's not jump to any conclusions."

***

Tariq saw the news that the coach had exploded, with everyone onboard killed. He didn't believe the news reports that said the terrorists had blown themselves up by mistake while preparing more bombs. He knew that hadn't been part of the plan. He decided, then and there, that he would avenge their deaths – even if it took years.

***

"Do we have any idea what happened?" the Prime Minister asked those gathered around the table of the meeting room in Downing Street. It was 09.00 on the morning after the coach had exploded on the runway.

"All we can assume," the General said, "is that they were preparing more explosives to take on the plane or to leave on the coach as booby traps and something went wrong."

"Anyone else have any thoughts?" the Prime Minister asked.

"I would concur with the General," the Head of MI6 said. "There is no other explanation for it and we know they had a lot of explosives. It would seem that they wired something up wrong."

The Prime Minister looked around the rest of the table. A few other heads nodded in agreement.

"We are doing forensic tests on the wreckage, so that should give us some idea of what happened," the Commissioner said, "but that is going to take some time. I think the General is probably right in his conclusion."

"What of the convicted prisoners on the other coaches?" the Prime Minister asked.

"There were twelve killed on the second coach, when it

crashed into the terrorist's coach," the Commissioner replied, "and eighteen seriously injured. Another twenty were shot and killed trying to escape." He looked across at the General, who smiled at him. He turned back to the Prime Minister. "Fourteen others have gunshot wounds."

"Could we not have rounded them up without this loss of life?" the Prime Minister asked, looking at the General.

"Sir," the General replied, "they are hardened criminals who have been convicted of terrorist offences. They were determined to escape. My soldiers felt in danger and responded in the only way they could. If any of the terrorists had got their hands on a weapon, things could have been worse. My troops did everything to avoid bloodshed, and opened fire as a last resort."

"I didn't want things to end like this," the Prime Minister said.

"None of us did," the Head of MI6 said in agreement from the end of the table.

"How is the inquiry into the terrorist attacks progressing?" the Prime Minister asked.

"I think Sinclair can give you news on that," the Commissioner said, turning to Sinclair.

"We have forensic teams at the farm, which we believe was their base," Sinclair began. "It was booby-trapped, but luckily the army made the place safe. It should give us lots of forensic evidence in due course, but it's a big farm so that might take some time and we don't want to miss anything. We have discovered where some of the vehicles were bought and are looking into how they managed to get their hands on all of the explosives. We are using the names from the recordings to cross-reference them against databases to see if we can track where they came from and how they got into the country. We also have fingerprints from the terrorists killed in the Covent

Garden and Oxford Street attacks. We are liaising with police forces and security services abroad to put names to them. Also, the farm should give us a lot of prints –if that's where they all stayed."

"Thank you," the Prime Minister said. "When do you think we will have a report?"

"It could take some months," Sinclair replied.

"I would like an interim report in one month," the Prime Minister said. "I want to be able to tell the country that we are making progress and prove that we are getting to the bottom of things. I also want to be able to tell them that we have put in place measures that will ensure nothing like this happens again." He looked around the table "I would like reports from all of your departments, not just the police investigation. I want the country to know all our resources are working on this. The newspapers have been quite kind so far, but they will start asking awkward questions soon and I want to be able to give them answers." Everyone around the table nodded. "Thank you all for coming. Keep me informed of any developments."

"Prime Minister," Sir David said, when everyone else had left. "I think we should sit down and go over your broadcast to the nation."

CHAPTER TWENTY

S inclair, along with the Commissioner, stood outside the door to 10 Downing Street, waiting for it to open. It had been five months since the attacks that had devastated London. The bridge and tunnel at Dartford had still not been repaired and news was that it would be a year or more until they were in use again. The Blackwall tunnel was in the same state and word was that it was so badly damaged it may never come back into use. Another tunnel may have to be built. Heathrow was functioning, but still at only half capacity. It aimed to be fully up and running in the next couple of months. The Shard and the BBC building were being rebuilt, but would take years to complete.

The door to Number 10 opened and Sinclair followed the Commissioner inside. They were shown through to the meeting room, where they found the Prime Minister sitting and talking to the Head of MI6. The only other person present was Sir David.

"Commissioner," the Prime Minister said, as he stood and shook hands with him, "and Commander Sinclair, how nice to see you again." He shook Sinclair's hand. "Please take a seat, gentleman." Sinclair sat next to the Commissioner, with the Head of MI6 opposite him. "Now, I understand you have a full report on the attacks," the Prime Minister said, as he took the chair at the head of the table.

"Yes, sir," the Commissioner said. He pushed a large folder across to the Prime Minister. "There is a two-page briefing with major points at the front."

The Prime Minister opened the folder and took out the briefing notes. He read and everyone else remained quiet. When he had finished, he placed the paper back into the folder and closed it. "This is the final report?" he asked.

"It is, sir," the Commissioner said, "although our inquires are ongoing. That is a full report of all we know so far and all the forensic evidence currently gathered. You read in the briefing report that we were able to name twenty-three of the terrorists and that we traced the explosives used back to Iraq, where they had been looted from an Iraqi Army base. The explosives had been supplied to the Iraqi Army by the Americans."

"I read that," the Prime Minister said.

"If I may raise one thing that has worried us," the Commissioner said.

"What's that?" the Prime Minister asked.

"You tell the Prime Minister," the Commissioner said, turning to Sinclair.

"Sir," Sinclair began, "all the forensics we have on the explosives used, whether it was on the attacks at the bridge or tunnels, or the BBC building, Heathrow or any of the other attacks including Parliament, were from the explosives stolen from the Iraqi Army base. However, when forensics examined the coach that blew up on the runway, the explosives were different."

"What do you mean 'different'?" the Prime Minister asked.

"Well, sir," Sinclair continued, "they were British."

"British?" the Prime Minister asked. "I don't understand. What are you saying?"

"The coach carrying the terrorists and the hostages at Northolt was destroyed by explosives made in Britain," Sinclair said.

"And your point is?" the Head of MI6 asked from across the table.

Sinclair looked across at him, then back to the Prime

Minister. "Well, if the terrorists had been able to get their hands on explosives that were made in this country, how did they manage it? That not the only strange thing, though. According to forensics, the coach was blown up by at least 200 pounds of high explosives, and it would seem that the explosives were packed into the baggage area underneath the coach. Now, if they had British-made explosives, why didn't they use them before? Stranger still, from the time they left Parliament to arriving at Northolt, none of the terrorists were seen to go anywhere near the baggage holds."

No one said anything for a moment as they took in what Sinclair was saying. "Let me get this right," the Head of MI6 said, breaking the silence. "You're saying that the coach was destroyed by British-made explosives that were in the coach before the terrorists got on it."

Sinclair looked across the table. "I can see no other explanation for it," he said.

"And how did they get there?" the Head of MI6 asked

"I have no idea" Sinclair replied.

"Are you saying that you believe the explosives were planted in the coach by someone other than the terrorists?" the Prime Minister said.

"From all the evidence gathered, it would seem that they had no way of putting them there," Sinclair said. "And the explosives not being from the batch they used in all the other explosions does seem strange."

"Commander," the Prime Minister said, "would you please just spell out what you mean?"

"I think that someone planted the explosives on the coach and triggered an explosion," Sinclair said, "and I don't believe it was the terrorists."

"Do you realise what you're saying?" the Prime Minister said.

"I think from all the evidence the Commander has gathered, that is the only conclusion to come to," the Commissioner said.

"I find it ridiculous" the Head of MI6 said.

"I can assure you that we have looked at all other possibilities," Sinclair replied. "We know the terrorists had no way of getting to the baggage area of the coach, as they didn't load anything into it outside Parliament and did not stop on the journey."

"So, if you're right, how did the explosives get there?" the Head of MI6 man asked.

"We think they were already on the coach," Sinclair said.

"Where did the coach come from?" the Prime Minister asked.

"It was supplied by the army," the Commissioner said. "It was one of the ones used to bring the SAS to Parliament."

Sir David, who had sat quietly listening to everything, sat forward and looked at his pager. "Prime Minister, could I have a private word? Something very important has come up."

The Prime Minister looked at him. "Alright, gentleman, if you could just leave us for a moment," he said.

"If the Head of MI6 could stay, though, as this involves him," Sir David said, as he put his pager back into his pocket.

"Commissioner, Commander, if you would just wait outside for a few moments," the Prime Minister said. Sir David rose, walked to the door and opened it. The Commissioner and Sinclair went out.

"Now, David, what message did you get that's so important we had to stop the meeting?" the Prime Minister asked.

Sir David came and sat back at the table. "I got no message, just an old civil service trick to break up a meeting," he said. "I wanted to discuss something that I think we should consider before we go any further down the road that this report is leading us on."

★★★

Sinclair and the Commissioner were sat outside the office for ten minutes, when the door finally opened and Sir David came out. "Commissioner, if you would like to go back in now," he said. "Commander, the Prime Minister thanks you for the report and says you have done a great job. He will call you for further meetings as soon as he has read the whole thing."

"I will see you back at the office later," the Commissioner said, as he went back into the meeting room.

Sir David signalled to one of the staff who was standing by the main doors. "Please show the Commander out," he said. He held out his hand and shook Sinclair's. "I look forward to seeing you again." He turned and walked back into the meeting room, closing the door behind him.

Sinclair walked out of the front door and into Downing Street. He turned left and walked towards the big iron gates that barred the way for vehicles wanting to drive in. He passed through them, turned right and walked down Whitehall towards Parliament Square. In his own mind, he knew what had happened. He had explained it all to the Commissioner, who, after some scepticism, had thought it was the only logical explanation. The explosives had been planted by someone. They weren't sure if it had been the Army or the Secret Service, but they had definitely not been put there by the terrorists.

★★★

Sinclair walked out of his hotel into a biting northerly wind. Snow was falling, but lightly – although the forecast was that it would get heavier as the day went on. He walked across the pavement and climbed into the back of the waiting car.

Sitting back, he looked at the tall buildings that surrounded him. He had been in New York for two months now, having been offered the job of liaising with the Americans on anti-terrorism. It was a two-year posting.

Back in London, the Commissioner had called him in and said that he had the knowledge and the expertise needed to build a strong relationship with the FBI and other law enforcement agencies. He had been reluctant at first, as he had wanted to see the investigation into the attacks in Britain to their conclusion. However, the Commissioner had made it clear that changes were coming to the structure of the anti-terrorist team and it would do his career a lot of good if he took the posting – so he had.

He had stayed in touch with what was going on back home and had heard through the grapevine that his report and the recommendations in it were being considered, and might be implemented. The only thing he felt uneasy about was when he had watched the Prime Minister on television in his hotel room making a statement in Parliament on the final report.

He had stated that it was believed the terrorists had mistakenly triggered a bomb as they were driving towards the plane.